Night

of

Fire

Iain Cameron

For Evelyn, for your unstinting support and encouragement

ONE

He walked out of the building to his car, a smile on his face and no trademark scowl at the overflowing metal cigarette holder on the wall. Old man Quinlan, the MD of Quinlan Fine Foods, was as pleased as punch that he, Marc Emerson, had landed the Steels Supermarkets account when others had failed. Quinlan lauded him as the 'best salesman ever'. If Quinlan wasn't such an irascible sod, Emerson might have asked him to say it again. Compliments were as rare as a solar eclipse in this business and he basked in its warm glow; only last week Quinlan had called him a 'bleedin' moron' for losing a customer's order.

Emerson had come into the office at four and enjoyed a late lunch in the company canteen. There, he selected a salad and included a mini pork pie and a scotch egg from the Quinlan Fine Produce range, costing him nothing as the food was free, saving him making a meal that evening.

It didn't take long to drive from the company offices in Moulsecoomb Way in Brighton to the A27, and on reaching the junction, he headed east. The weak October sun of earlier was nowhere in sight, a thin mist and darkness making the sea in the distance look shadowy and indistinct. When he arrived in Lewes, he didn't take the first exit towards the town but carried on until the road crossed the River Ouse, before taking a left at the Southerham Roundabout and turning into the Cliffe Industrial Estate.

Emerson often visited similar estates and industrial complexes, but he had a special affection for this one, nestling as it did under the white chalk cliffs that characterised this part of southern England. He parked in front of a warehouse with no markings or insignia, nothing to suggest it was occupied by the Weald Bonfire Society. Not because anything illegal was going on inside, but he and other members of the Society wanted to keep their ideas secret.

November 5, Bonfire Night, is a time of great celebration in the UK, a night when the failure of Fawkes and his catholic confederates in 1605 to blow up King James was remembered. In nearly every village, town and city in the land, the event was marked by cheering crowds, bonfires and fireworks, although the reason why children held sparklers and whooped with delight at crackling Hell Raisers and exploding War Hawks was long forgotten by many.

A strong sense of history was still evident in Lewes, home to the largest and most famous Bonfire Night celebration of them all. At around eight o' clock in the evening, it kicked off with a parade by the six Lewes bonfire societies through the streets of the town. Their members wearing costumes, carrying lighted torches and banners and accompanied on their slow, dignified walk by a loud marching band.

The origin of Lewes Bonfire Societies dated from Victorian times, but despite the passing years, all six societies were fiercely protective of their identities and highly competitive in their attempt to put on the best display of the evening. The march culminated in a bonfire where the effigy, which had been tirelessly carried through crowded streets, was burned to the howls and jeers of a boisterous crowd.

Emerson opened the door and walked in. The air felt warm, his colleagues working here earlier in the evening had been using the heaters. The effigy being crafted by the Weald Society this year, a three-metre image of the prime minister, Ashley Stevens, was starting to take shape. The PM had been the first choice of nearly all society members, and no wonder. In the first three months of office, not only did he raise university tuition fees by five thousand pounds a year, but failed to take action in the summer when striking airport workers caused holiday chaos.

Emerson took a seat at a long table. Fire had always interested him, from accidentally burning down the garden shed, to developing explosives from fertilisers and weed killers and using them to fell trees. He loved the way it consumed everything in its path, the relentless energy with no concern for an item's utility or worth. His job was to harness this raw power and use it to excite and invigorate their viewing public. Knowing the capabilities of various commercial fireworks, a few months back he'd outlined the planned display on sheets and stuck them to the wall, partly to let him see how it would look and to give others the opportunity to comment.

He spent a couple of minutes looking to see if anyone had added any more comments, not that he could do much about it now, as a recent email informed him that the fireworks were arriving in two days time. After emailing members and asking for volunteers to help him unload and set up the firework delivery, he started work on his second task for the evening: incorporating a diversion into the procession route as a result of emergency road works.

He looked at his watch: ten past eleven. He continued to work for another fifteen minutes before deciding to call a halt. He closed the laptop, tidied his papers and headed for the door. Before stepping outside, he stopped, took a final look around the warehouse and reached for the light switch. A noise behind him caused him turn. A black figure and thousands of little bubbles came rushing towards him.

'Agh!' Emerson screamed. 'What the fuck is it? What did you spray in my eyes?'

He fell to his knees. His hands groped blindly for contact. He touched rough material, a leg. He tried to grip but a boot kicked his hand away.

'You bastard,' a voice hissed in his ear, 'you're gonna die.'

Emerson knew the voice but became distracted by a familiar smell: petrol.

'No! No!'

He heard a whoosh before a curtain of burning hot air swarmed over his face and the pain of a thousand wasps attacked exposed skin. He flapped at the flames with his hands but he couldn't see clearly and the heat made his skin sizzle. He fell to the ground, trying to roll, but something blocked his way.

He heard a voice; the last he would ever hear. 'Burn you bastard, burn.'

TWO

Detective Inspector Angus Henderson looked out to the back garden from his place at the kitchen table with envy. He hadn't thought he'd miss eating his breakfast out there when the arrival of the colder weather made it too uncomfortable to sit outside at six forty-five in the morning, but he did.

A few minutes later, he heard Rachel moving around upstairs and got up as he wanted to be out of the house before she came down. He drained his tea, walked into the hall and picked up his briefcase, quickly looking through it to ensure the report he had been reading the previous night was there before closing it.

Rachel had been out on the town last night with some of her colleagues from *The Argus*, the town's main local newspaper. They'd been celebrating the interview of a famous Hollywood actor by one of their fellow journalists, after the efforts of many of the nationals had failed.

While she was out enjoying herself, Henderson had been reading a forensic report. A pair of violent burglars were targeting the homes of housewives, arriving on their doorstep not long after they had dropped their kids off at school. They forced their way into the house, helped themselves to money, jewellery, phones, iPads, and didn't refrain from using violence if they met any resistance.

He reached for his jacket.

'Leaving early?' Rachel asked as she padded downstairs.

'Yep. I've a meeting first thing.'

'I'm sorry about last night, but let's face it, you were wrong.'

Henderson held up his hand. 'Look, I don't want to go over it all over again. You said your piece last night. I'll see you tonight. Bye.'

Henderson walked to the car, parked some way down College Place, his anger simmering. 'Never argue with a journalist, you'll never win,' an old desk sergeant in Glasgow once told him, after being doorstepped by a press cadre as he headed to his office in Pitt Street. He was right.

The day had started out grey with thick cloud cover, but with Brighton being so close to the sea, it could change to something different within the next hour. No matter, autumn had ended with warm temperatures and mild winds with none of the fierce storms of the previous year; with a bit of luck it would continue into winter.

He got into the car and drove towards Lewes, almost on autopilot. He had worked at Sussex House in Brighton for many years and wondered if one day his auto-driving would take him back there by mistake, now a forlorn sight of dirty windows and an empty car park. In common with all public bodies, the police had to bear their share of government cuts, and while he didn't mind working there, their new offices at Malling House in Lewes were so much better.

He turned on the radio, now tuned to Southern FM as DS Walters had taken charge yesterday afternoon on their way back from interviewing a witness. He retuned to Radio 4. Henderson liked to listen to music in the mornings, but for the last few weeks the Today programme's tenacious questioner had done some cracking interviews with the government ministers responsible for Brexit. Those bitter exchanges were a better way of blotting out last night's argument with Rachel than any record by Coldplay or Kanye West.

Malling House in Lewes was a large complex of buildings, some old, some new, located behind a stunning Grade 1 listed Queen Anne House. The site housed the headquarters of Sussex Police, the force responsible for policing a population of over half a million people in East Sussex and eight hundred thousand in West Sussex. The region included a few large conurbations: Brighton, Hastings, Newhaven, Eastbourne, Crawley and Worthing, all with typical inner-city problems of drugs, prostitution and guns, while other parts of the area were rural: small market towns and isolated communities, a mix Detective Inspector Henderson liked.

He walked to his office on the second floor but before he could take off his jacket, the phone rang.

'Henderson.'

'Morning sir. Lewes Control. I've received a report of a body at the Cliffe Industrial Estate, Lewes. Can you attend?'

'Will do. Any details?'

'Very sketchy at the moment. All I know is the

7

pathologist has been called.'

'Ok, I'm on my way.'

Henderson walked into the Detectives' Room, looking for Detective Sergeant Walters. He didn't really expect to see her this side of eight of clock, so any sensible detective, half conscious and without a major hangover, would do. But no, there she sat, staring intently at a report.

'Morning Carol.'

'Morning sir,' she said, looking up before placing the report on her desk.

'What's wrong? Insomnia? Or is the druggy upstairs in your building keeping you up all night with his Bhangra music?'

'What? No, it's not him. After my last hospital stay, a switch just flipped. After six or seven hours sleep, I'm wide awake and can't lie in bed. I have to get up. Gone are the days of lying there until the very last minute and a pile of broken alarm clocks in the corner.'

'I think it's called growing up. Your body no longer treats you as a teenager.'

'My body can't remember what a teenager feels like, it happened so long ago.'

'Grab your coat. We've got a fatality at a warehouse in Lewes.'

**

In the car on their way to the scene, Henderson's choice of listening was soon discarded and Southern FM reinstated, but he couldn't be bothered to argue.

Radio discussions and interviews were a delight that needed to be consumed alone, without Walters blethering about what she'd done last night or complaining about the boring radio programme if he left it on.

'So, what were you up to last night?'

'Rachel went out–'

'Poor you.'

'Yeah, poor me. I had some peace and quiet for a change so I read the forensics report of our violent burglars' encounter with the woman in Patcham.'

'Did you discover anything new? I hope you spotted something to help finger those nasty bastards.'

'No, I didn't but I'm confident we will. They might think they're clever wearing gloves and hats and say little while they're in the house, but if they ever cut themselves or spit on the floor, we'll get them.'

'They'll get cocky, they always do.'

'It's strange that none of our narks know anything about them.'

'Or say they don't which means they're a nasty bunch and not to be messed with, or an out of town mob nobody's heard anything about.'

'Which is why getting a fingerprint or a DNA sample is so important.'

'They must be doing some amount of research. How else would they know it's a woman alone and there isn't some big bruiser husband sitting upstairs because he's just lost his job or he's on the night shift?'

'I wish I knew.'

Henderson guided the pool car into the Cliffe Industrial Estate and easily spotted the warehouse in question, as pathologist Grafton Rawlings's car, a beautifully restored Austin Healey 3000, was parked outside. If the only police vehicle in attendance had been the dirty white Ford Transit van belonging to the Scenes of Crime Team, now sitting alongside the Healey, he wouldn't have a clue, as he could see any number of those dotted around the industrial estate.

From the boot of the car he removed and pulled over his suit protective clothing and shoes. Walters did the same. He pushed open the door of the warehouse and wished he hadn't, as his nostrils were filled with a putrid smell – a hideous mix of burnt ash and barbecued flesh. The corpse lay just inside the door. He could see the back of the pathologist leaning over and prodding what remained with his metal pointer while the SOCO photographer walked around the body taking pictures, the flash giving the little scene a ghostly Gothic quality.

Henderson reluctantly shut the door and bent down beside Rawlings, all the while holding a handkerchief to his nose.

'Good morning Grafton.'

'Morning Angus. Not a good start to a Tuesday morning, I'm afraid.'

'You're right there. He or she is still recognisable as a body. It's not the distorted, charred mess we often see in a house or car fire.'

'This is because there's so little combustible material around the victim, it didn't reach the high temperatures associated with house, car or factory fires. If it had happened over there,' he said nodding towards the far side of the warehouse where Henderson could see all manner of paper, wood and plastic, 'it would have left us something quite different.'

'And not much remaining of this warehouse either, I would bet. What are we looking at: suicide, or a tragic accident?'

'I can't say for sure until I can get the body back to the mortuary, but it's an odd place to commit suicide, don't you think? An accident was my first thought. Perhaps the victim tripped while holding an open canister of petrol or paraffin as they smoked a cigarette, for instance, but I don't see any evidence of a canister or a cigarette.'

Henderson had to agree it was an odd spot to choose as they were in an open area near the door, kept clear to allow deliveries and visitors, in what looked like a not very well-stocked warehouse.

'Any sign of other accelerants?'

'Not immediately apparent. Again, I will be looking for them when I get him back to the lab, because as we know, bodies do not spontaneously combust. What I can tell you is he's male, and at first glance I can't see any contusions or indentations, but as you can appreciate with everything blackened by fire it's hard to see anything at all.'

'So, at first pass, it doesn't look like either an accident or suicide. It could be murder if you find any evidence of an attack. The mystery hinges on the P-M.'

'You've just about summed it up.'

'Thanks Grafton,' Henderson said as he stood, thankful the pathologist would be doing the post-mortem and not him. 'See you later.'

Henderson looked around, keen to move away from the scene and find someone who could add some information to the scant amount of knowledge he'd unearthed so far. Close to a row of tables, a uniformed cop sat talking to a distraught-looking young man, shakily holding a mug of what looked like tea. Henderson nudged Walters and they both walked over.

'Morning sir,' PC Dave Peters said. 'This is Kevin McLaren, the gentlemen who found the body.'

'Thanks constable. We'll take it from here.'

Henderson sat beside McLaren. Walters wandered off in search of a chair.

'Hello Kevin. I'm Detective Inspector Angus Henderson, Surrey and Sussex Major Crime Team.'

'Hi.'

'What is this place?'

'Do you live local?'

'Brighton.'

'I guess you've heard of the Lewes Bonfire Night Celebrations?'

Henderson nodded. 'I've been to see it a couple of times.' Walters returned with a chair and placed it facing their witness.

'In which case you'll know there are six bonfire societies in the town. One of the six, the Weald Bonfire Society, uses this warehouse to build the effigy that we burn on the bonfire, store fireworks and outfits, plan the procession and the bonfire; it's our nerve centre, really.'

'I see. What's your role?'

'Me? I'm one of the helpers. I'm a self-employed computer programmer and every year around this time I take a few days off work and come down here. A few of us do the same.'

'Is this the reason why you came in here early this morning and opened up?'

McLaren nodded. He looked down at the mug and with an element of surprise on his face, as if remembering its presence, took a drink. Henderson liked his tea black; to him McLaren's brew looked sickly and smelled unpleasant, but for shock victims, and anyone finding a burnt-out body fell smack-bang into this category, milky sweetened tea hit the spot.

Kevin McLaren looked heavy in build, mid-twenties with light brown hair, combed to one side. It looked a conventional cut and nothing like the buzz cuts, size zero arches and hawks favoured by many young men of a similar age around Brighton. He at least tried to keep up with the trend for facial hair as the makings of a moustache and a few days' growth could be seen, but with the lad having such fair skin Henderson didn't think it would amount to much.

'What did you do when you first saw the body?'

McLaren had obviously shut the charred heap near the door out of his mind, as mention of it again made his hands start shaking, the surface of the tea rippling like the trailer for a trashy earthquake film.

'I...I had to take a closer look as I didn't know for sure what it was; an animal or a pile of rags or something else. When I did and saw it was...human, I ran over to the corner over there,' he said nodding to the left, 'and threw up my guts. I then called 999.'

'Do you know who it is?'

'How the hell could I? It's nothing but a...it's a black mess.'

'I'm sorry, I didn't phrase that right. What I mean is, do you know of anyone who might have come here this morning before you?'

McLaren shook his head. 'Whenever I take a day off and do this, I'm always in here first.'

'What about last night?' Walters said. 'Were you here?'

He nodded.

'Were you last to leave or do you know who was last to leave?'

'I wasn't the last one out as I usually don't stay long when I know I'm doing a full session the next day. Who was last to leave last night?' McLaren's face twisted in concentration as if he had been asked a difficult question.

'I dunno, Steve? No, maybe David. Oh, I remember now, Marc said he would come along later, probably after we'd all gone.'

'Marc who?' Walters asked.

'Marc Emerson.'

'Who's he?'

McLaren's face crumpled when he realised he might be talking about the charred corpse near the door.

'My best friend,' he said, tears dripping freely into his lap.

THREE

To Henderson's relief, they confirmed the fire victim's name shortly after the DI left the Cliffe Industrial Estate. Detectives had made a flurry of phone calls to track down other members of the Weald Bonfire Society, Marc Emerson's home address, his mother's, and that of his employer.

The photographer at the murder scene had taken a close-up picture of a distinctive ring worn by the victim. When shown to Francis Quinlan, the MD of Quinlan Fine Foods, where Emerson worked as a salesman, he recognised it immediately as Marc wore it all the time. Any lingering doubts evaporated like steam through an open kitchen window when they confirmed the BMW sitting outside the Weald Society warehouse also belonged to him.

Marc Emerson and his mother lived a few streets apart in Lewes, and after calling round at the victim's house and finding no one at home, officers went to see his mother. They said she took the news 'stoically,' and now Henderson wanted to see her to gather information about the dead man, and to update her on the developments from yesterday. They knew now her son had been murdered.

The post-mortem that morning at Brighton & Hove Mortuary confirmed a suspicion harboured by the pathologist. Traces of petrol were found on the victim's remains. There was no reason for Marc to be handling petrol, the warehouse didn't contain any and his car ran on diesel.

If Marc had accidentally set himself on fire, Henderson would expect to see evidence of his attempts at putting the fire out, such as moving away from the petrol source, discarding flaming garments and rolling on the ground. In such a situation, the DI would expect to see partial or serious burns, singed hair and damaged clothes, but not death.

If Marc had deliberately set himself on fire, the SOCOs would surely have discovered a container nearby. If made from plastic and engulfed by flames, traces of the material would still remain and would have been discovered by the pathologist. No, Marc Emerson didn't accidentally set himself on fire and nor did he do it deliberately; someone murdered him.

Henderson's boss, Chief Inspector Lisa Edwards grumped and groaned when he told her about this new development, as the violent house robberies were already causing her major grief. *The Argus* seemed to be on a crusade to make every instance of their villainy front-page news. He didn't need to point out to his boss the difference in seriousness of the offences, but promised there wouldn't be any let-up in the pursuit of the robbers. DS Gerry Hobbs would be put in charge of the robbery investigation while Henderson would investigate the murder.

Marc Emerson's mother had divorced Marc's biological father five years before, remarried, and was now known as Mrs Pickering. She was a chubby woman with dark brown hair in need of a wash, a freckled complexion and a slightly crooked nose. She smoked and, based on current evidence, did it regularly. However, the series of cigarettes she puffed in an almost continuous chain might also have had something to do with losing her only son.

The officers who came to the house last night also told him that Mr Pickering was not at home when they called round to deliver the bad news, and it required calls to several local hostelries before he could be located. Jeff Pickering returned to the house and made a token job of consoling his wife, and seemed more troubled about missing a drinking session with his mates than his step-son's untimely demise.

It was Henderson's turn to offer Marc Emerson's mother some bad news, but much to his surprise, Gillian Pickering didn't go to pieces on hearing the word 'murder'. Tears welled in her eyes; he and Walters sat quietly for a minute to let her recover. She dabbed her eyes with a handkerchief, lit a cigarette and turned to face them.

'He was clever at school, my Marc, and I couldn't have been more proud of him when he went to university. His dad was too, but it didn't stretch to paying the fees when the bastard fucked off with the woman across the road, did it?'

'How did Marc get into sales?' Henderson asked.

'He did the milk round thingy at university and everybody said he was a natural. He liked working at Quinlan's and they treated him well. Old man Quinlan is now on his third wife, would you believe. I can't see what they see in him myself. He's a fat, old Irish geezer with wandering hands and a dirty mind, but then he does drive a fancy motor and owns a six-bedroom mansion in Hurstpierpoint,' she said with a laugh.

'Did Marc get on well with everyone there?'

'Course he did, my Marc gets on with anybody. Mind you, he could be a bit of a charmer, takes after his mother he does. He dated a couple of women in the office. I told him not to as he had to work beside them, but he said he only needed to go into the office when he wanted summat, the rest of the time he was out in the car, talking to customers. One bird, I think she worked in the Accounts department or summat, wouldn't leave him alone after he split with her. She kept sending him texts and coming round to his house at all hours; the stupid cow.'

'What's her name?'

'Christine summat, I think.'

'Don't worry,' Henderson said. 'We'll get her name from Quinlan.'

'Did you see your son often, Mrs Pickering?' Walters asked.

'He lived here in this house until about six months ago. He's an easy going bloke my Marc, but he couldn't get along with Jeff, my new man. They went at it like a pair of alley cats whenever the two of them got together.'

'What did they argue about?'

'He didn't think Jeff treated me right, you know? It happens a lot in new marriages according to my friend Lena, and she should know with four kids all from different fathers. Collects them like cigarette cards, as my old mother used to say. In the end, Marc decided to buy his own place and move out. Best for everybody, I think.'

Henderson could see the look of pride on her face, her son defending her honour against the newcomer, not realising or caring if it drove Marc away.

'Did Marc's relationship with your new husband–'

'Jeff.'

'Did Marc's relationship with Jeff improve after he moved out?' Walters said.

Pickering looked to the ceiling but Henderson doubted she could see much of it for the cloud of cigarette smoke hovering over her head.

'Not really; just the same I suppose. He doesn't come around here much anymore. Why would he, just to get grief? I pop around to his house about once a week.'

'You said he could be a bit of a charmer, Mrs Pickering,' Henderson said. 'Do any other girlfriends stand out?'

'How do you mean, 'stand out' like?'

'You know, did any of them cause problems or harass him like the girl at Quinlan's, Christine did?'

'Not that I can remember. Most of them behaved as good as gold.'

'Did Marc ever marry?'

'Yeah, divorced about two years ago. She's called Juliet. Nice girl.'

'Do you still have her contact details?'

'Yeah, I think so. Wait and I'll take a look.' She rose from the chair and left the room.

'She talks about Marc as if he's still around,'

Walters said to Henderson in a hushed voice.

'News like this takes time to sink in. Everybody's different. I don't know about you, but I can see two suspects here.'

'I'm thinking Christine in Accounts is one. Who's the other?'

'The father in-law, Jeff Pickering. I don't like the sound of him. If Marc was so easy going, why were they always arguing?'

'Good point.'

Mrs Pickering came back into the room and handed the DI a piece of paper and a photograph. 'That's a picture of Juliet, and her address.' She resumed her position in the chair. 'Nice girl.'

Juliet had straight brown hair parted in the centre. The glasses made her look serious, but aside from them she was extremely good-looking with bright blue eyes and pearly white teeth. Perhaps she wore glasses to create a studious aura, inviting people to take her seriously and not be distracted by what lay underneath.

'Thank you,' Henderson said as he tucked the paper and photograph in his jacket pocket. 'Can I ask, what was Marc's involvement with the Weald Bonfire Society?'

'It was his dad's fault; his real dad, I mean. He'd been a member for years and one day decided to bring Marc along. Of course he was fascinated by fire, lighted torches and explosives. Show me a boy who isn't.'

'What did he do there?'

'Most of them do a bit of everything, but Marc's big

interest is fireworks. He tried to make the fireworks display, you know the one they let off at the bonfire after the procession, more professional. He wanted to tie it in more with the story behind the effigy.'

'This is when they take the effigy they've been carrying through the town and burn it on the bonfire?'

'That's right. It can be a politician responsible for introducing an unpopular policy or a footballer who's been screwing his wife's best friend; anything really.'

'Did he get on well with everyone at Weald?' Walters asked.

'I think he did,' she said, lighting up yet another cigarette. 'I've met a few of them over the years, some are good fun and others bloody bores, I can tell you. All they want to talk about is Bonfire Night.'

'How about other friends not from work or Weald?' Walters asked.

She thought for a moment as she continued billowing smoke at the yellowed ceiling.

'He's got a few close friends like Kevin McLaren, but I suppose the closest is, or was, Guy Barton.'

'We've met Kevin but not Guy Barton.'

'Guy Barton and his dad are cut from the same lump of wood: a couple of wheeler-dealers. The old man operated a market stall in Croydon before he opened a proper shop here in Lewes, but it closed when he retired. Guy and his dad will do anything to turn in a few quid. Of course, Guy and Marc fell out big time.'

'What did they argue about?'

'I can't really remember the details, but I do remember it came to blows.'

The detectives asked a couple more questions and a few minutes later, decided to call a halt. Walking down the steps outside the semi-detached house, Henderson gulped in lungfuls of fresh Lewes air, refreshing tainted body cells and improving the smell in his nostrils. Walters the ex-smoker didn't seem to mind.

'She didn't look very cut up about losing her son,' Walters said as they headed towards the car.

'She's had a day to get her head around it.'

'Yeah, but she didn't know yesterday that he'd been murdered.'

'I know,' he said, 'but maybe once she realised he was dead, she'd come to terms with losing him, or maybe it happened when she chose her husband's happiness over that of her son.'

'I think it turned out to be a fairly productive meeting, we've got three suspects.'

'I can only see two. There's a motive for Christine from Quinlan, and for Marc Emerson's step-father, Jeff Pickering, but I didn't hear enough to implicate his former friend, Guy Barton. We need to dig deeper.'

FOUR

Henderson walked into the Detectives' Room on the second floor of Malling House. He headed towards the area in the corner allocated to the team he put together for the investigation into Marc Emerson's murder. The team consisted of six detectives, all of whom were now sitting in front of him, and double this number of uniformed officers, currently engaged in carrying out door-to-door enquiries around the Cliffe Industrial Estate and undertaking many of the initial discussions with Marc Emerson's friends and associates.

Late Wednesday afternoon, the tops of desks strewn with papers, bins overflowing with plastic coffee cups and everyone itching to get home to crack open a bottle of beer or wine. If they didn't know it already, they were now working on a murder investigation and the tasks Henderson wanted them to do now would put the kibosh on leisure time and weekends for the foreseeable.

'On Monday night,' Henderson said, his finger tapping the victim's picture on the board, 'someone poured petrol over Marc Emerson and set him alight. The pathologist couldn't say for definite, due to the poor condition of the body, but he couldn't find any bruises or evidence to suggest he'd been drunk or high on drugs, but he's convinced the killer must have incapacitated him in some way first. Neither he nor I can see how someone could sneak up behind a victim and kill them by spraying them with petrol.'

'They might have used a stun-gun or some type of pepper spray,' DC Sally Graham said.

'You can buy these agricultural stun guns and some of them are strong enough to down a cow,' DS Harry Wallop, their resident country expert said.

There followed an animated discussion about stun-guns, anti-rape sprays, pepper sprays, CS gas and a whole range of equipment, much of which could be sourced from the police arsenal. Henderson soon brought it to a halt.

'The point I want you all to take is this killing has all the hallmarks of a deliberate act, our perpetrator must have come equipped with both items. However, I do think it's a bloody peculiar way to kill anyone.'

'Might be the killer improvised,' Sally Graham said, 'and picked up some material he or she found near the crime scene. There must have been plenty of combustible stuff lying around the warehouse.'

'There is, but crucially no petrol,' Henderson said.

'I think,' Phil Bentley said, 'they could be delivering some kind of message. Live by fire, die by fire.'

'You might have something there, Phil,' Henderson said, 'as our victim worked with fireworks. Although it would take us into the realm of rituals which I don't want to think about just yet.'

'It is peculiar,' Wallop said. 'I've heard of people dying in fires after their houses are deliberately set on fire, but never in a one-to-one.'

Henderson paused to take a drink of coffee. If bought from the staff restaurant or made in the little kitchen the detectives used, it was perfectly drinkable, but the stuff dispensed by the machines dotted around the building, like the one in his hand, was as bad as those left behind at Sussex House.

'The killer came up close and personal,' Henderson continued. 'It has to be someone who knew the victim well; knew his habits and movements. To find them, we need to take his working and private life apart. With the added complication of his membership of the Weald Bonfire Society, that gives three areas to concentrate on.'

He looked around at the faces. They were alert and listening. Not bad for the end of the day.

'Interviews will be conducted by two-person teams. Carol and Seb, you've been allocated Marc's employer, Quinlan Fine Foods. Talk to his close colleagues, the boss and anyone else who knew him. We know he dated a woman in Accounts and according to his mother, she wouldn't leave him alone after the split. Speak to her; find out if there are any others.'

'Ok,' Walters said.

'Harry, I want you and Deepak to investigate his personal life. He apparently was a bit of a ladies' man so there might be a long roll-call of ex-girlfriends to track down, and there's an ex-wife to consider. Are any of his girlfriends married and perhaps he incurred the wrath of a jealous husband or an ex-lover? Also, make sure you talk to Guy Barton. He and Marc used to be the best of friends but they fell out. Find out why and if there is any lingering resentment.'

He looked over at Harry Wallop and Deepak Sunderam who both nodded.

'Sally, you and Phil will take on the Weald Bonfire Society. Did the victim get on with everybody? Is there strong rivalry between the societies? Maybe someone from another team expressed jealousy at what Marc was doing?'

He let them absorb the tasks given to them while he drained his coffee cup.

'So far,' Henderson continued, 'we've identified three 'persons of interest'. I'm unwilling to call them 'suspects' at this stage, as we've got nothing to go on other than the opinion of a woman who has recently lost her son.'

He wrote the first name up on the board, no picture as yet. 'Jeff Pickering. The victim's step-father. He and Marc didn't get on, always arguing. Marc eventually moved out to get away from him. Does anyone know if we yet have access to Marc's house?'

'I tracked down a neighbour a few minutes before coming into this meeting,' DC Phil Bentley said. 'She says she's got a spare set of keys.'

'Good work Phil. To the team looking into his personal life, I'm talking about you, Harry and Deepak, I want his house given a thorough once-over. You're looking for a diary, laptop, bank statements, love letters; anything to help us identify a motive.'

'No problem,' Wallop said.

Henderson turned to the board and tapped the name written there. 'Harry, see what you can find out about this guy. We know he didn't like Marc, find out why and how the arguments panned out: are we talking handbags or did they get violent? When you're done, I'll interview him.'

Wallop nodded.

He turned to the board. 'Our second 'person of interest' is Guy Barton. Marc's mother, Mrs Pickering, says he works for the Council and he's not averse to accepting the odd backhander. Harry, this is also yours. We know the two men fell out big time. Find out as much as you can about him and his relationship with Marc Emerson.'

'Me and Sunderam will get to the bottom of it,' Harry Wallop said, 'don't you worry.'

'The third name to go on the board,' Henderson said as he wrote, 'is Christine, an ex of Marc's who works at Quinlan Foods.'

'Christine Sutherland,' Phil Bentley said.

'How do you know?' Henderson asked. 'Don't tell me you went out with her as well?'

'Me? No, I looked her up on Quinlan's website. She's the only Christine working in the Finance department. She's Finance Director.'

'Excellent. Now Ms Sutherland used to be in a relationship with Marc Emerson and after they broke up, she bombarded him with texts and repeatedly came around to his house.'

'I've known a few girlfriends like that,' Phil Bentley said.

'You've done it to a few ex-girlfriends, more like,' Walters countered.

'It might be something or nothing,' Henderson continued, 'but Carol and Seb, need to take a look. Also, get a sense of how the victim got on with other people in the business. It might not be an ex-girlfriend we should be looking at, but a co-worker, jealous of his success, or pissed off because he did something they didn't like.'

'I work beside a few people like that,' Bentley murmured, glancing at Walters.

'I hope I don't need to impress upon you the importance of these tasks,' Henderson said. 'In most murder cases, we depend on help from witnesses, CCTV and forensics, but with this one, there aren't any. We'll find this killer with a dose of good old-fashioned plod-work and a large measure of perseverance. Good luck.'

Henderson returned to his office. He sat down at his desk and picked up Marc Emerson's thin post-mortem report and flicked through it once again. Much of the victim's body was beyond analysis, or couldn't be dissected by the pathologist's scalpel as it would simply flake into pieces. If the killer had chosen this method with the intention of erasing all traces of forensic evidence, they'd done a bloody good job. They'd also done a good job disguising a motive, because as yet, Henderson didn't have a clue.

His thought processes came to a sudden halt when his boss, Chief Inspector Lisa Edwards, burst into his office. She threw a newspaper down on his desk and slumped into the visitor's seat. 'Look what the bloody *Argus* is printing now,' she barked.

He turned the paper around and there on the front page, the stark headline:

'House Robbers Strike Again – Police No Closer to Catching Vicious Attackers.'

'I heard about this one,' Henderson said. 'Gerry sent a forensics team over to the victim's house straight away, but I gather they didn't come back with anything.'

Edwards ranted and raved for a minute before she stopped, her anger vented but not sated.

'What do we do?' she asked. 'Every time they print this crap, the Chief gets a bollocking from some oik at the Home Office. He in turn calls in his ACC's and gives them all a rocket. ACC Youngman then collars me and I get hell and on it goes. It's my turn to shout at you, but I won't as we're wasting too much time with this as it is. We've got bigger and more important issues to worry about.'

'I agree. Maybe we're not looking at this problem from the right angle.'

'What do you mean?'

'We're doing all we can to catch these robbers. Can you remember the last time we sent a full forensic team into a house after a burglary? A quick dust of the broken window was all they got. Now, we've got them on standby and patrol cars are roaming the main housing estates ready to respond to a sighting, or God forbid, another robbery.'

'I know, I know, and so does the Chief Constable and all those above him.'

'What if we approach *The Argus* directly?'

'What, and try to appeal to their better nature? Some hope.'

'We could get the Press Office to talk to their contact at the paper and ask them to tone it down.'

'Tried it. They're not interested.'

'What if we target the journalist who wrote the story?'

'What, and throw the bugger in jail?' She smiled. 'Ah, now I see what you're getting at. You could ask your journalist girlfriend to talk to them, make them see sense. Who is it?' She picked up the newspaper from his desk and pulled it round to look at the front-page story. 'Rob Tremain. Do you know him?'

'Aye I do, our paths have crossed many times.'

'Does Rachel know him?'

'I wasn't thinking of involving Rachel.'

'No? Why not?'

'I could talk to Tremain. I could promise him some exclusive if he lays off the robberies.'

'Hang on a tick, are you sure? It's a dangerous game working with journalists, Angus. Before you know it, Professional Standards will be crawling all over you and this place, asking why *The Argus* has the inside track on your investigations. You could be suspended, dismissed even.'

'I know, but I would only pass on to him something about to be revealed or something not materially important to the investigation. It shouldn't raise too many eyebrows.'

She sighed. 'We need to do something, we can't just sit around here waiting for the next round of vindictive bile. You never know, another one like this,' she said pointing at the newspaper, 'and it could be the last straw for the Home Secretary. He may decide Sussex could do with a new Chief Constable.'

She paused, thinking. 'Right Angus, talk to this Tremain character, see if he'll take the bait, but listen, this can only be between you and me. I can't pass it up the food chain. If the shit hits the fan, you'll be on your own. I won't be able to help you.'

FIVE

Guy Barton walked into the kitchen, the smell of last night's empty Chinese takeaway cartons almost making him puke in the sink; difficult to do with it being full of dirty dishes. He groaned. He'd meant to deal with them last night but he'd been too pissed to think straight. Now the kitchen stank like the bins at the back of China Garden down on the High Street.

Despite the cold, bleak October day outside, he opened a window and let a blast of chilled air come into the room before slumping into a chair. He liked to rise early, even after a night on the tiles, getting up an hour before his wife, Lily, who commuted from their home in Lewes to London.

Lily worked for a major book publisher, in charge of one of its most profitable divisions. Some weeks she went into the company's offices near London Bridge, and at other times travelled to book fairs in Europe and the US, attended meetings with authors and was often interviewed by journalists and radio broadcasters. Today, he didn't know where she was going. She might have told him before she went out last night, but he couldn't remember.

He got up from his seat, filled the kettle, switched it on and stood near the open window, the chilled air cooling the hot flush breaking out all over his face, but not reducing the anguish he felt. His relationship with Lily was in a bad place, fights and silences, snippy comments and too many meals for one. She'd accused him of having a hang-up because she earned more than he did, but in response he would call her a highly-strung bitch who didn't know how to argue like a normal person.

In a way, they were both right. He did feel emasculated, a word his father used even to his face, at not being the principal bread winner in his own house. She, on the other hand, had grown up in the shittiest of households, much worse than his, with a domineering, bullying father and an alcoholic mother, and now Lily couldn't argue without losing her rag or bursting into tears.

His mate, Tony in the office reckoned it was something called the seven-year itch. Guy and Lily had been married only six years, but the symptoms were the same. He now found other women attractive, and this from a man who told everyone at his wedding that he had married the most amazing woman he had ever seen.

He failed to notice the kettle boiling, and in return for his inattention the bubbling, shaking machine gave his face a sauna-blast of hot air.

'Are you making tea or planning to stare at our untidy garden all day?'

'Morning love.' He turned to look at her. 'What time did you get in?'

'I'm surprised you're asking me. I came home long before you.'

'Did you? I don't remember.'

'Then you shouldn't drink so much, should you?'

She squeezed past and reached into the bread bin. The slim, curvy figure, ensconced today in a bright dress decorated in a floral print, an effective antidote to the cold, dull weather outside, tempted him to put his arms around her waist, but he thought better of it. She didn't do mornings, coming awake around eleven, and would use any excuse to wriggle free. Not that she needed an excuse today. Despite luxuriating in a long shower with copious amounts of Lynx soap, applying a large dose of antiperspirant and brushing his teeth for at least three minutes, he probably stank of booze, garlic and monosodium glutamate.

For breakfast, Guy would usually fill a bowl with cornflakes or Weetabix, but today he would make do with some toast after Lily left for work or maybe just a cup of tea. Lily would eat only toast in the morning with jam, butter or peanut butter. She told him she would buy something from the staff restaurant mid-morning, but he knew she often didn't.

Five minutes later, with her mug drained and a plate full of crumbs, she picked up her briefcase, rushed out of the door and embarked on the short walk to Lewes Station. Despite earning a high salary, she didn't own a car as she liked walking and they didn't live far from the station. In addition, their road, St John's Terrace, had permits, pay and display machines and parking restricted to one side of the road; not the strongest encouragement for multiple-car ownership.

At nine-thirty, he closed the front door and walked to his car. Guy Barton worked as a planning officer with Lewes District Council, responsible for approving building applications and making sure large developments were in line with the region's strategic plan. During this short walk, he was often accosted by neighbours concerned about their loft extensions or conservatory plans, but today the chilling wind kept them indoors and he reached his car unmolested.

He drove to the east of Lewes to inspect a large house being constructed there. In the Planning Office it was referred to as Pritchard's Folly, as the cost had exceeded the initial estimate by over one million pounds, the builders having to overcome several seemingly insurmountable obstacles along the way. Dale Pritchard made his money buying and selling oil on the Hong Kong Stock Exchange, a guy so rich he bought the site while the previous incumbent, a timber company, were still trading and relocated them to the north side of the town.

In common with many modern architects, the man Dale Pritchard employed conceived a building that eschewed the style of the traditional country house with its multiple floors, the use of local materials and traditional chimneys and fires. He instead had created a unique building with symmetrical lines, ten-metre long sheets of glass on every wall, flat roofs and tons of concrete, a material not seen in house construction since the 1960s. Locals called it 'the glass factory,' on account of the material's dominant presence in the house design and its factory-style shape, an unkind epithet which would wear off once they saw the completed structure.

He could see the site long before he got there, on

an elevated position, surrounded by flat land with no high buildings close by. Most of the work and expense had been invested in the foundations, inserting steel rods and encasing them in concrete, ensuring the chalky soil could support the heavy weight of the house and not tip the entire construction into a small lake nearby. With the ground work complete, the house rapidly took form and shape as most of the materials were prefabricated in factories in the UK, Holland and Germany.

There had been grumblings in the local press about the size of the house, occupying as it did a space of over five hundred square metres, and his boss regularly received letters from concerned residents. The 'lonely of Lewes' he called them, before throwing their missives in the bin, later to be retrieved and filed by his secretary. Often in large developments such as this, local residents overestimated the size and scale of the building, despite public access to plans and a model mock-up, causing much resentment and annoyance. It was Guy Barton's job to reassure them.

He bumped his car on to the building site and parked beside the project manager's car. Experience had taught him to avoid the space beside lorries and diggers if he didn't want his car covered in dust and mud, or to find out later it had a nasty scrape down one side.

He walked into the house and before seeing anyone, he heard someone shout, 'No, no, no!' in a voice that sounded like that of the project manager. 'You fucking idiots. The bloody thing's upside down!'

By the tone and volume of the shout, Guy reckoned

he wasn't referring to one of the four two-tonne windows, but something less important. A couple of months back the builders did fit one of the panoramic windows the wrong way round and his voice and anxiety levels had reached heights way above this.

Guy clambered over a small pile of rubble, the brick dust leaving a thin film on his clean shoes. He had wellingtons and a pair of steel toe-capped boots in the boot of the car, but the weather had been dry for the last few days and, as anticipated, the site didn't resemble the quagmire it had been on his last visit in early July.

'Ah, Mr Barton,' Rod Walker the project manager said, walking towards him, his Hi-Vis jacket and hard hat covered in mud and dust, making it difficult to determine their original colour.

'Those two fucking idiots,' Walker continued, jerking a thumb behind him, 'couldn't tell if a plant holder was upside down or not despite it saying 'top' on the top and 'bottom' on the fucking base. The bloody thing weighs ten kilos so we can't expect Mr Pritchard to turn it around himself when he moves in, can we? I ask you, do schools still teach people to read nowadays?'

'They do, but not everybody listens.'

He smiled, revealing a small gap in his front teeth. 'You're right there, mate. Listen, Mr Pritchard is running late. He said he'll be here in about fifteen minutes. Why don't you and I take a look round and I'll show you everything that's been done since your last visit?'

'Sure, go ahead.'

Walker was portly with a wild mop of white hair, looking every inch the eccentric architect, but he didn't make it after failing the exams and became a project manager instead. Guy once entertained dreams of becoming an architect, but football held more interest than university and, as a result, didn't do well in his 'A' levels. He had trialled for Chelsea and didn't make the grade, but he still played the 'beautiful game' every Sunday for a non-league club in Brighton.

'You can see we've finished the roof,' Walker said, 'and with it in place we're getting on with plastering and the electrics. Tomorrow we've got plumbers and fitters coming in to finish the bathrooms and kitchen. And over here–'

'Rod!' a voice behind him called. 'Come here, now!'

'Fuck. I do more hand-holding here than I ever did with my kids at home. Back in a minute Guy.'

He had seen enough of the house to know the layout and started work on the task he wanted to complete this morning: measuring up. Guy measured the dimensions of the bedrooms, the lounge and kitchen, before heading downstairs and doing the same in the cinema room, sauna and gym.

By the time Dale Pritchard's white Bentley convertible rolled up and parked beside Guy's old VW Polo, he had finished, but the measurements didn't agree with the plans in his hands.

'There you are Guy,' Pritchard said walking towards him. 'Sorry I'm late.'

'No problem. Rod's been showing me the progress you've made so far which is impressive, and I've just been measuring up.'

'Great. I take it everything's ok?'

Guy shook his head. 'Not everything.'

'No worries. Let's get ourselves a coffee and talk about it.'

They walked into the kitchen. It was a huge room, dominated by a large centre unit topped with a thick slab of glittering black granite which to Guy, looked like the runway for a fleet of drones. They still had plenty to do as the places where the fridge, freezer and cooker would go were marked by a succession of protruding grey wires, and the newly-plastered walls awaited tiling.

'Sorry, it's instant,' Pritchard said handing him a mug. 'It'll be another couple of weeks before they install the fancy Gaggia machine lying over there, and another two before I work out how to use the bloody thing.'

They sat on stools on either side of the drone runway, the glittering effect so effective it looked to be lit by LED lights underneath the surface.

'No bother, I'm not a coffee expert at the best of times and certainly not today. The house is really beginning to take shape.'

'If it wasn't for Rod we'd be months behind, especially with all the rain we had in July. I tell you, he's a great task-master.'

'I know, I've heard him shout. If we can talk about the measurements of some of the rooms,' Guy said, placing a folder on the worktop and opening it.

'I know what you're about to say.'

'What?'

'That we've been a bit cheeky with the dimensions of the cinema room. I'd always had it in my mind it would seat eight, but after seeing what a friend of mine did with his, I had to make it bigger.'

'I understand, but under current planning rules you are not allowed to materially alter the scale and size of this building.'

'Meaning?'

'I could raise an order and force you to reinstate the room back to its planned measurements. If you refuse to implement, it could mean a large fine and possibly a prison sentence.'

'To implement such an alteration will cost me anything between about thirty and fifty grand.'

'At least.'

'You said you 'could' raise an order. What would it take for you not to?'

SIX

The goalkeeper booted the ball out of his area. To the credit of the team's coaching staff, the boys didn't all chase after it like lemmings to a cliff. Instead, they allowed the lad on the left wing to collect and lead another attack for Falcon United, the under-14 side of Standen School.

DI Henderson was enjoying the game more than he had anticipated, perhaps something to do with the fine weather. It was a crisp, October morning, a bright blue sky with a weak sun moving leisurely towards its zenith and gradually burning off the cold mist that had hung over the grass in Preston Park when they first arrived.

Rachel had promised a colleague at *The Argus*, Sarah Pendleton, that she would come and watch her son captain the school football team for the first time. Not knowing much about football, Rachel asked him to come along and explain the rules and the nuances of the game, but in that role Henderson was superfluous as Rachel and Sarah had been gassing non-stop since they arrived.

He didn't mind as he could concentrate on the match, but he couldn't think what they found to talk about: the two of them were situated only a few desks apart in the offices where they both worked. Alas, despite standing beside two of *The Argus's* finest, neither could do anything about the problem he and his bosses were having over the reporting of the violent robberies. Sarah worked as a feature writer and the closest she ever got to crime was when faced by a woman wronged by an erring husband, and Rachel's focus was on the environment and rural affairs.

After talking to CI Edwards the previous afternoon, Henderson had called Gerry Hobbs into his office for an update. Hobbs was a seasoned Detective Sergeant and Henderson had every confidence he could manage such a high profile case, but he didn't look happy.

'Every robbery so far has happened between the hours of eight-thirty and nine-thirty in the morning,' Hobbs said. 'Typically, a woman comes back to the house after dropping her kids off at school, her mind on what somebody said at the school gate, or making a list of all the things she had to do that day, so she doesn't see the guy coming up behind her. Or they allow her to get inside the house and ring the bell before she's had a chance to settle.'

'What's so different about this one?' Henderson asked.

'A couple of days a week the woman, Mrs Loxley, who lives in Carden Hill, near Ditchling Road, stays on at school to have a coffee with the other people in the parents' friendship group.'

'So she doesn't come home at a regular time every day?'

'Nope,' Hobbs said.

'Ah, they're not depending on luck. They must be watching the house.'

'Could be, or it's someone they wouldn't notice tracking their behaviour, like a postman.'

'Yes, or a delivery driver or a street sweeper.'

'In which case, there's no point in asking householders to report people sitting in cars or strange people hanging around in the street.'

'Don't go there, we've been flooded with calls already.'

'I know it's not much,' Hobbs said, 'but it's a new bit of intel to add to the file.'

'Gerry, try and have a think if there's another way we can approach this. If you need more resources, I'm sure the CC will give them to you. He's under a lot of pressure over this.'

'I know. How about we comb the records and contact other forces and find out if robbers like this have been operating somewhere else? It's been going on here now for a couple of months, we've got a pretty clear MO.'

'It's worth a try. What do you need? People to man the phones?'

'I think so.'

'I'll talk to Edwards but I don't see it being a problem.'

The Falcon's number eight, a small, wiry lad with glue on his boots, danced his way through a posse of defenders, and as they all converged on him, he slipped the ball to the unmarked number nine. The big centre-forward couldn't miss and had the simplest of tap-ins. The whistle blew ten minutes later, the

Falcons trooping off the field 3-0 victors.

Henderson had earlier noticed the concentration on the face of a bald man in a blue quilted jacket, not a dad as he didn't shout and scream invectives at the referee for every overlooked foul; most likely a scout. A typical football vignette followed when the scout approached the number eight, not the big lad at number nine and the scorer of two goals, much to the chagrin of the centre-forward's father who strode up to the scout to remonstrate.

'Did you enjoy the game?' Rachel asked as they walked back to the car.

'I did. That little lad at number eight is a star in the making. Sarah's boy, Simon, played well too. Did you enjoy it?'

'Yes I did.'

'What was the score?'

'It was…2-1.'

'You didn't see half of it.'

'I've been rumbled, guilty as charged, but then Sarah can talk.'

'Whenever I looked over, it was you doing the talking. What do you find to talk about that you couldn't say in the office?'

'She's been telling me about her family, what a right bunch they are.'

Henderson received a potted version of Sarah's family history as they drove back home. When she accused him of not listening, he claimed with some justification that he was concentrating, the traffic much heavier now than it had been three hours earlier. In Brighton, cars poured into town in the morning and exited at night, not much different from many other towns in the UK. However, in summer, the influx of tourists could double the population, and at night the traffic jam would stretch for miles.

He drove Rachel's car into their one designated parking place in College Place, his own car several streets away, and got out. He picked up the post behind the door, and before the chirping got faster and faster and finally released the ear-splitting decibels of the big bell outside, silenced the alarm. He had grown up in a rural community in Fort William where alarms were fitted mainly to shops and cars, and if one went off, it didn't disturb the local residents half as much as it did in a tightly packed place like Brighton. Two false alarms would have the Neighbourhood Watch Coordinator at the door, and after three his colleagues in uniform would withdraw their support.

He made some coffee and sat at the kitchen table to read the Saturday papers. During the football season he would look at the sports section first, but at this time of year it was too early and the teams he followed had yet to create a decent run of winning results to break clear of the pack.

'What time are you going into the office?' Rachel asked.

'After lunch, but I'm not going into the office. I've got a team searching a house in Lewes. I'll go over there instead.'

'Is it connected to your burn victim?'

'It's his house.'

'Oh, is it? How creepy.'

'Not really. He didn't die there.'

'All the same, it must be weird looking through a dead man's things.'

'I suppose it is. I try not to think of it that way. I see it as trying to find out why he died.'

'Did you manage to arrange a meeting with Rob Tremain?'

'Why, did he talk to you about it?'

She nodded. 'He's wondering why the police are calling him and not the other way round.'

'He'll find out soon enough. I'm seeing him Tuesday night.'

**

At lunch Henderson devoured a large plate of tagliatelle. He didn't think himself capable of eating such a quantity of food, but the hours he'd spent that morning in the fresh air of Preston Park must have given him an appetite. Afterwards, he drove to Lewes. Not having had his fill of football news earlier, he tuned the radio to Five Live. As luck would have it, they were discussing Brighton's big clash with Portsmouth that afternoon and this kept him occupied until he reached his destination.

Marc Emerson lived in what looked like a recently built house in Spences Lane, his mother a few streets away in Hereward Way. Outside, a Vauxhall Vectra pool car, one Henderson had used before, and the white Transit van of the SOCO team, since cleaned after its outing to the Cliffe Industrial Estate on Tuesday. A couple of neighbours were out and doing what they could in their gardens in late October, but all the while keeping their eye on the strange goings-on in the trim semi-detached house nearby.

Henderson had called DS Harry Wallop while driving and he came out to meet Henderson as he approached. The DI was being cautious, just in case he blundered into the house and messed up a key piece of evidence.

'Afternoon Harry.'

'Afternoon, Angus.'

'How's it going?'

He led him inside and closed the door behind him.

'We've found a few items which could prove interesting. A laptop, a phone–'

'A phone? Grafton said at the P-M the victim had one in his pocket, but it was destroyed by the fire.'

'Maybe he had one for personal calls and another for business. I know some people do.'

'The only people I know with two phones are drug dealers. What else?'

'A mindfulness journal.'

'A mindfulness journal? What the hell is that?'

'I'm told it's a method for finding inner peace and calm.'

'I use a bottle of whisky for that.'

He laughed. 'What you do apparently is write down the things that make you happy, how you feel after certain events, ways to improve your life, that sort of thing.'

'You seem to know a lot about it. Are you into it?'

'No way. When I first spotted it, I phoned my missus; a friend of hers is.'

'Good work. Did you look through it?'

His face reddened. 'Just a little, to find out what it was about. Some of the things in there made me cringe.'

'It's that personal?'

He nodded. 'The bit I read, described how he felt about this woman; it's pretty detailed stuff.'

'In which case, I need to give some thought as to who I'll give the job to, but it sounds like it might tell us a lot about Marc. Anything else of interest?'

He shrugged. 'Not really, the usual collection of bank statements, photo albums, books and folders. Everything has been bagged and is ready to take away.'

'Good. Is there much left to do?'

'Maybe an hour or so. We've still got to finish a few things in the house and then it's out to the garden shed. The team are upstairs.'

'So I gather from all the stomping,' Henderson said glancing at the ceiling. 'Just be careful in the shed. Remember, Marc's speciality was fireworks and explosives. Who knows what he's rigged up.'

'I'll bear it in mind.'

'Thanks Harry. I won't keep you. I'll take a look around.'

'See you later, boss.'

Henderson walked into the lounge. He expected not much in the way of furniture as a prior check on house prices in the area revealed this to be an expensive place for a single guy, but to his surprise the room looked fully furnished. In fact, the polished wood flooring, large-screen television, leather settee with sumptuous armchair, and tasteful art on the walls made him think Marc had lived here for several years and not six months.

In the kitchen, the same story. The walls were lined with good quality units that might have been installed in the house before he bought it, but complemented by a dishwasher, fridge-freezer, coffee machine and juicer. Henderson tried but couldn't think of anything he could add to either room to make them more habitable. He moved into the hall and stood to one side as the SOCOs made their way downstairs, DC Deepak Sunderam at the rear.

'Afternoon sir,' they chorused.

'Afternoon guys. How have you found it?'

They stopped walking. If unused to it, the sight of three burly guys dressed in blue nylon oversuits and looking like extras from a Smurf movie could be disconcerting. 'It's the cleanest, tidiest gaff we've done in years,' Dave Severs, the team leader said.

'Yeah, clean as,' one of the other Smurfs said.

'You're off to do the shed now?' Henderson asked.

'Yep, and then I think we're finished.'

'Allow Harry to brief you before you go in there, as the owner knew all about fireworks and explosives and he may have left one or two surprises. Ok?'

'Sure thing.'

Henderson waited for them to file past before climbing the stairs. He counted three bedrooms and a bathroom, plus a hatch lying open to the loft. Bedroom one, a storage room for boxes and suitcases, and bedroom two, kitted out for guests with a crisp white duvet and more art on the walls.

Bedroom three, Marc's sleeping area. As such, it received the greatest focus of the team. It contained a bed, desk, wardrobe and tall drawer unit. He didn't see any point in rifling through drawers as the team had done this, and after taking a quick look at the contents, he bent down to examine the items bagged and boxed on the floor.

He donned plastic gloves and flicked through the mindfulness journal and instantly could see what Harry meant; comments about how he felt after a meal and about a recent meeting with his boss. He put it back and picked up a small black folder marked 'bank statements'.

Nothing caught his eye until he looked at the most recent statements. In June, the sum of ten thousand pounds had been credited to his account and a day or so later, out it went. The process was repeated over the next few months although with larger amounts. There was no way of knowing if Marc had moved this money from this account to another or used it to pay a large bill. It could also mean someone had paid Marc ten grand and he'd used the money to pay someone else.

The discovery raised more questions than it answered, but whatever the reason, it felt like their first real lead.

SEVEN

Lying half-in and half-out of the cupboard, Jeff Pickering reached under the kitchen sink with the long box spanner and tightened the nut under the tap. He normally employed a lad to do the donkey work, in this case to stand over the sink and make sure the tap was seated correctly, but the bugger had cried off this morning, migraine or something. If he did it again, son of a friend or not, the little toe-rag would get the heave-ho.

He didn't mind doing jobs like this, finishing off a new kitchen. It was much better than scrabbling around in mouse-infested lofts, trying his best not to fall through the ceiling. With the radio playing loud, his hand working on something he'd done a hundred times before and the numbing effects of alcohol still coursing through his brain from the previous night, his mind started to drift.

He couldn't claim by any definition to be a handsome man: a shock of blond hair that wouldn't lie flat no matter how wet, teeth too big for his mouth and a complexion that went florid after a few drinks, but he didn't go short of his share of the birds. When his second missus hightailed it after he hit her and the bottle once too often, he met a bird in the pub not long after and they'd shagged all night for the next two weeks. By the end of the third, she was in his house and cooking supper.

Last night, he'd proved that his marriage of nine months to Gillian Emerson hadn't blunted his edge. Everyone assumed him hitching his wagon to the homely Mrs E would calm him down, but did it hell. She was a good lady and looked after him, but she didn't like going out at night. He did, and if he ended up in bed with one of the birds from a group of five out celebrating their mate's forthcoming wedding, like he'd done last night, she had no way of finding out.

He couldn't fathom modern women. As a teenager, the man assumed control and women did what they were told, but fast forward twenty years and throw into the mix women's lib, high profile rape cases and a widespread knowledge of STDs and AIDS, and it was her way or the stairway. If he created a fuss, all it would take was a cry of 'rape' and he would see the inside of Lewes nick once again.

His phone rang. He cursed and lowered the spanner, but stayed put, upside down, facing the pipework as it would take too long to extricate himself. He rummaged for the little device among his many-pocketed overalls and got to it before the caller decided to ring off.

'Jeff Pickering Plumbing.'

'Jeff, thank goodness I caught you. It's Beth Atwood at Beechhurst Cottage. If you remember, you installed a new shower unit in one of our upstairs bathrooms about a year back.'

How could he forget? Early forties with a great figure and long legs. Always seemed to be walking past when he was lying on the floor. A cockteaser first class whose eyes seemed to suggest she would be partial to a bit of rough, but when he made his move, albeit a touch clumsily and smelling of Boss jointing compound, she rebuffed him and threatened to tell her husband if he didn't give her a discount.

'What's the problem?'

'There's a leak in one of the pipes in the boiler cupboard. It's made such a mess of the ceiling in the lounge that Eric thinks it will need re-plastering.'

'Is it bad? Are drips coming out of it or is it a continuous flow?'

'I can see a little valve thingy and water is coming out in a steady stream from the little screw in the front. I've got buckets and basins down but I'm not catching it all.'

'Hmm,' he said, as if thinking over a thorny problem. Isolating valves were a common failure point in boiler cupboards and under the sink, but cheap to fix: two pounds for a replacement valve and fifteen minutes' work to fit the little blighter.

'It sounds like a big job.'

'I don't care what it takes, I need it fixed today.'

'Tell you what, I'll come straight over there after I finish this job, but it means disappointing another customer.' He didn't have another customer until two-thirty. After this, he intended finding a pub and enjoying a long lunch with a couple of pints and a sandwich, but Mrs A didn't need to know.

'That's great Jeff, thanks. How much? You know I like to agree a price before a job starts.'

'Five hundred; four-fifty for cash.'

He went back to his work under the sink in sombre mood. It didn't stem from anything said by Mrs Atwood, or the fear of missing out on a wad of easy money, the lady in question was currently on her way to a cash machine, but thoughts of Marc Emerson crowded his brain.

His wife was cut-up about the death of the boy, and no bloody wonder, her only son? She did have a daughter but he'd only met her once and she never came back. Gillian asked if he'd killed Marc and he feigned surprise, but he did have a reputation for settling scores with his fists and on more than one occasion, he'd wanted to land a fist into Marc's Emerson's smug face.

It didn't help that he couldn't produce a solid alibi for the night in question. He'd been in the Dorset bar that night, as he had been the night before and the night before that, and for as many weeks as he wanted to count back. The problem with anyone asking, neither he nor his equally drunken mates could remember specific details of any one night, as they all seemed to blur into one. Gillian wouldn't let it rest and nagged him again and again, and in the end he needed to give her a smack to shut her up. It did the trick as she'd never raised the subject since.

He didn't like Marc Emerson from the first moment he'd laid his eyes on him. His mother looked out of shape and a bit on the lumpy side, and he expected her son to be the same. Instead, a smart salesman turned up in a nice BMW, wearing expensive casual gear, a handsome smile on his face and his hair styled and trim. In fact, he hated him; the boy was all the things he wasn't.

The little fucker had gone to university and while Pickering had been clever at school, his alcoholic father and doormat of a mother took no interest in his education. When he announced at the age of twelve that he wanted to be a doctor, they both laughed. To spite them, he fell in with a bad crowd and smoked dope and drank fortified wine in the woods at the back of the house. How he made it to the end of the school year and didn't get thrown out for falling asleep in class or selling drugs to the other boys, he would never know.

Not only did Gillian's son's degree get rammed down his gullet, but his activities at uni did too. The captain of the football team, treasurer of the Students' Union, President of the Film Society and popular with the birds. His anger became manifest and his solid grip of the spanner loosened. It fell, the heavy tool narrowly missing his face. The clang brought old Mrs Redfern into the kitchen.

'Are you all right Mr Pickering?'

'I'm fine, Mary. Accidents will happen.'

'You don't want anything happening to you, or your Gillian will be getting a complex; first her son and now you.'

'Have no fear. I'm tougher than I look.'

'It's such a shame about Marc. I always thought him such a nice boy. I bet you miss him.'

He nodded in agreement but under his breath he muttered, 'No fucking chance.'

**

Jeff Pickering pushed open the door of the Dorset bar and walked in. He had arrived earlier than usual as he had wolfed down his tea when Gillian disappeared into the lounge to watch Eastenders, a photo album of the times spent with her son on her knees. The atmosphere in the house felt morbid and he couldn't stay there any longer than he needed to. It was a crisp cold night with thick clouds obscuring his view of the stars, but not a hint of frost, which he welcomed as slippery pavements were the worst enemy of a man with too many beers in his belly.

He was enjoying some banter with Dave the barman, a spotty long-haired oik who invariably wore an old 'Alice in Chains' t-shirt regardless of the weather, when his best pal, Lou, came in. Feeling flush after pocketing four-fifty in cash from Mrs Atwood, he bought a round of lagers and large whiskies and carried them over to the table beside the fire.

'Cheers Jeff,' Lou said, before taking a big gulp from his pint of lager. He worked as the dispatch manager for a large logistics firm in Crawley and by his account, spent much of his day shouting at drivers and talking on the phone. No bloody wonder he had such a thirst.

'Did you see that bit in *The Argus* today about your Marc?'

'No.' Pickering didn't read much, he got all the news he needed from the radio which he listened to all day while working. Lou, on the other hand, looked through several local papers and two nationals to keep him up-to-date with the ever-changing world of road transport.

'The story was in the paper at the time it happened but sort of disappeared when everybody went gaga over the housewife robberies.'

'Does it say if anyone's been arrested for the robberies?'

'Nah. The cops are stupid. Give 'em a dead body, 'scuse my insensitivity, and they'll find the villains like that,' he said snapping his fingers together. 'Give 'em something tricky to solve like those robberies, and they can't find jack shit.'

He paused for a drink.

'As I said about your Marc—'

'I told you before, he wasn't my bloody son.'

'Keep your hair on, it's just a figure of speech.'

'There's nothing wrong with my hair.'

'Nothing that a gardener and a pair of shears couldn't fix, ha, ha. As I was saying, the story disappeared off the front pages these last few days but all of a sudden it's back. Have the police spoken to you?'

Pickering felt alarmed at the thought but feigned nonchalance and lifted his pint. 'Not since the night it happened. Nobody's said bugger-all to me and Gillian's never mentioned it.'

'Ah the same old story,' Lou said. 'The family are the last to know. Drink up mate and I'll get us another.'

The next hour or so passed pleasantly, the drink having a mellowing effect, ironing out the rough edges and pushing his problems into the distance. Lou was a season ticket holder at the Albion and could talk endlessly about league positions and transfer news. If Pickering nodded now and again or added a piece of controversy filched from Radio Five Live, Lou would fill in the rest for most of the evening.

On those nights, Pickering would say little, just sit there slowly getting pissed, his head filling with Lou's facts and statistics, details that would all be forgotten by morning. Other times, angry at a job gone wrong or the lack of work, he'd rant and rave while Lou feigned interest, his mind far away in the land of trucks, parcels and motorways.

He pushed back his chair and stood, a little unsteadily at first and announced he was going to the toilet. Early evening there could be a long gap between loo breaks of up to an hour, but after 9:30pm it shortened to about twenty minutes. At closing time, he often didn't make it home without pissing into somebody's garden hedge.

He stood back from the urinal making sure the splashes went down the drain and not on his trousers. He'd changed out of his working gear before coming out this evening, but the light-coloured chinos revealed every misdirected splash or drip.

The door opened and someone entered. He stopped his tuneless humming of an Ellie Goulding song, played almost every hour on the radio, or his toilet companion would think him potty. He liked toilets that provided a display of the front pages from today's newspaper in the eye line of the peeing patrons, as at times like this, he could be standing there for five minutes or more. He would mention his suggestion to 'Alice in Chains' Dave upon his return.

He finished, turned and was about to head out when he realised the man who'd come in earlier hadn't approached the spare urinal beside him or headed into a cubicle; he stood looking at him. He was about Marc's age, brown hair combed to one side and with a thin face. Pickering thought he recognised him, maybe from television or one of Marc's mates.

'Jeff Pickering?'

'Yeah, who wants to know? You a cop?'

'No, I'm no cop. I'm trying to find out who killed Marc.'

'What are you asking me for?' He leaned closer to the stranger. 'You think I did it, do you?'

'I don't know, did you?'

'I should give you a smack on the kisser for saying something like that, mate. 'Course I didn't, but if I did, I wouldn't tell the likes of you.'

'Yeah, but I know you and Marc had fights. He told me you smacked him around.'

'He deserved it, the cheeky bastard.'

'Where were you the night he died?'

'What's it to you?'

'It's a simple enough question, but if you don't answer it could make me suspicious.'

'I was in here, if you must know,' Pickering said, his anger rising. 'It's what I told the cops and anybody else who asks.' He pointed a finger at his accuser. 'What the fuck's it got to do with you anyway?'

'He was one of my best mates and he told me he watched out for you. You become an aggressive bastard with a drink inside your belly, he said.'

'Is that so? Well you should watch out for me too,' he said.

Pickering swung a fist but the stranger ducked out of the way and his trusty hammer blow landed on nothing but empty air. Before he could attempt another, Pickering doubled up in pain when a fist rammed into his gut.

'I'm not frightened of you mate, but I tell you, if I find out you killed Marc, I'm coming after you.'

From his low-down position Pickering saw the knee come up and before he could get out of the way, it smacked him straight on the nose. The stars he wanted to see earlier on his walk down to the pub were now in his head, the last thing he saw before he collapsed on the floor, blood oozing over the red, piss-stained tiles.

EIGHT

'I hear you've bought a place in Hove. How do you like it there?' DS Harry Wallop asked Deepak Sunderam, sitting beside him in the passenger seat of the pool car.

'It's a great place to live. I don't have any distance to walk to the supermarket or the seafront, but I would like it better if I had some more furniture.'

'I know what you mean, a detective constable's salary can only stretch so far. I remember my first place. I could afford a bed but no curtains or wardrobe. All my clothes were lying in suitcases for months.'

'It's not so much that I can't afford it. Most of the furniture has been ordered, but many of the stores in town are quoting six to eight weeks delivery.'

'Oh, I forgot. Your dad's helping you set up.'

'It's not the free lunch ticket it might sound. He'll want paid back when I get on my feet.'

'Yeah, but you should be fine, your lot...I mean, Muslims, don't charge any interest.'

He laughed. 'Muslims don't but Hindis do.'

They were driving into Lewes after a brief detour to the school of Harry Wallop's daughter, Daisy, in Shoreham. His wife often said the cherub-faced seven-year-old with a shock of blonde hair took after her father. She didn't mean in the hair stakes, although he and his daughter shared the same colour, his was short and receding at the temples. His wife was referring to their attitude, sense of humour and the way they both sucked on a pencil, but he could see another common trait in her forgetfulness. When he dropped her off at school first thing this morning, she had left her water bottle in the car and the trip to Shoreham was to stop her receiving a 'minus' from her teacher.

'It's a terrible way to die, in a fire, isn't it?' Sunderam said.

Wallop was about to say it was a common enough occurrence in parts of India, but fearful of getting the sect or region wrong, he curbed the thought. 'It sure is.'

'The day after I heard, I went out to the shops and bought four smoke alarms and put them in every room in the flat.'

'Really?' Wallop had done the same and replaced the batteries of those units already installed and added a few more.

They drove into Lewes, a familiar enough journey as both of them now worked there, but it never ceased to impress with grey, solid-looking houses, an austere prison, narrow streets and a thousand-year-old Norman castle. Wallop couldn't afford to live in Lewes even if he wanted to move there. He lived in Shoreham, not the prettiest of places, with a working dock and hundreds of light industrial companies, but they had a lovely house and he couldn't ask for better neighbours.

They located St John's Terrace without too much trouble but couldn't find anywhere to park. Ten minutes later, Wallop knocked on the door of the house belonging to Lily and Guy Barton.

When the door opened and Wallop saw the lady of the house standing there, he momentarily lost the power of speech. She had thick, shoulder-length hair, high cheekbones, deep blue eyes, and a beautiful, proportioned face undiminished by the addition of trendy specs.

'Are you the detectives from Lewes?'

'Yes,' Wallop replied, his voice magically restored. He pulled out his ID. 'I'm Detective Sergeant Wallop and this is Detective Constable Sunderam.'

'You better come in.'

They walked into a long room with a leather sofa and chair, huge LCD television, coffee table with books scattered on top and large windows at one end shuttered with wooden blinds. The absence of clutter such as toys, picture books and DVDs was a clear indication to Wallop that the Barton's didn't have kids.

'Can I get you anything, tea or coffee?'

He was about to say 'no' as earlier he had treated himself to a coffee and Deepak to a green tea, in appreciation of his tolerance at doing the errand for Wallop's daughter. Instead, he said 'yes' as he wanted to prolong the interview with this lovely lady.

He took out his notebook and made a few bland comments about his surroundings, trying to drive the face of Lily Barton out his head, swimming around in there like a large fish. He often made notes like this as he had a poor memory and by the time he returned to the office, he wouldn't be able to differentiate this house from one he'd visited a few days before.

The door opened but it didn't allow him another chance to gaze at Mrs Barton, it was a big man Wallop assumed to be her husband, Guy, from the photograph on the unit beside the television. He nodded acknowledgement and took a seat in the chair opposite.

He was tall with lightly tanned skin, short dark hair and three days' stubble on his face. Wallop's wife would probably say he looked 'dreamy' but he preferred 'good-looking' if somewhat rough. He looked muscular in a natural way, not like many of the guys who came out of the gym on Brighton seafront and couldn't walk properly because of their big thighs, or couldn't stretch in case they ripped their tight t-shirts.

'You're here about Marc's death, I assume?' Barton asked.

'Yes we are, sir,' Wallop said. 'Did you know him well?'

'Of course I bloody did. We were best mates.'

'How did you both meet?'

'We grew up together. Went to the same primary school and then the same secondary. I left at sixteen but Marc went on to sixth-form college and then university. Even though he moved away from home, we still kept in touch.'

Mrs Barton brought in a tray of cups and a teapot and set it down on the coffee table in the middle of the room. She poured and the detectives helped themselves to milk and sugar. Wallop took a drink, placed the cup on a coaster and lifted his notebook.

'What do you do, Mr Barton?'

'I'm a planning officer at Lewes District Council.'

'So you do what? Approve planning applications?'

'Yeah, among other things. I make site visits, study plans, talk to builders and do all the bloody paperwork the council asks me for.'

'And what about you, Mrs Barton?'

'I'm Managing Director of Merlin books, the romance division of Russell-Taylor publishers.'

'Do you have many books in the best seller lists?'

'We have two in the *Sunday Times* top twenty at the moment.'

'Yeah, but they're bloody pap,' her husband said, his mouth turned down in a sneer.

'Can you tell, detectives, that my husband doesn't like romance stories? In fact, as he rarely reads at all, it hardly makes him a good judge of any book, does it?'

'You don't like those kinds of books either,' Guy said. 'You only do it for the money.'

Not wishing to become involved in a domestic situation, God knows he'd seen enough of them in his first marriage, Wallop said quickly, 'Mr Barton, where were you on the night Marc Emerson died?'

'Which was when, exactly?'

'A week ago yesterday: Monday, the 24th October,' his wife said.

'A few mates of mine were working at the Weald Bonfire Society warehouse and after they finished their stint, about ten, we met up and went to the pub.'

'Can anyone verify this?'

'Talk to Tony Stevens or Tom Davidson at Weald, they'll tell you. When I say I went to the pub and drank only a couple of beers, I mean it. I had two pints and came straight home. Right love?' He looked over at his wife who nodded.

'Did you see Marc that night?'

'No, but someone said he was going along to the warehouse later.'

Lily turned to her husband. 'Why were you so interested in him, all of a sudden? You haven't spoken to him in months.'

'I thought you said earlier, sir,' Wallop said, 'that you and Marc were the best of friends? I don't think your wife agrees.'

'We had a fall out some time back.'

'A fall out?' she said, her expression aghast. 'The last time you both met he told you to go to hell and he never wanted to see or talk to you again.'

'He sure did, and his wish has been granted.'

Lily rose from her chair beside the window and left the room, but not before Wallop noticed tears streaming down her cheeks.

'Don't mind her. She gets like this at this time of the month.'

Wallop nodded as if he agreed, but knew if his wife heard him say something like that he would be eating Pot Noodles in the garage for a fortnight.

'Was your wife close to Marc?'

'Basically, everyone who works in the Bonfire Society socialises together. Lily's in it but I'm not, I sort of tag along. They go out for meals, go down the pub, a few go to the Amex to see the Albion, others to the rugby.'

'Sounds like a big happy family.'

'Yeah, something like that.'

'Did you ever think of joining Weald?' Sunderam asked.

'Nah, not me. I don't want to join a club that would have me as a member, to paraphrase Groucho Marx. I'm not interested in doing crappy jobs that other people don't want to do. I get enough of that at work.'

'Why did you and Marc fall out?' Wallop asked.

'What's that got to do with anything?'

'We are trying to find out as much as we can about Marc and the circumstances leading to his death. We will be the judge of what is relevant or not.'

Wallop had learned about the power of silence from DI Henderson. Too often in an interview, he would be tempted to say something to fill the awkward void, but the DI taught him to sit tight. As long as the interviewee knew they were expected to make the next statement, he would tough it out and wait for them to speak.

'I turned down his planning application.'

Wallop was watching his face as he spoke and noticed the faint trace of a smile; he didn't regret doing it one bit.

'Why did you do that?'

'He owns a semi in Spences Lane, yeah?'

Wallop nodded.

'He wanted to build up into the roof. His sister has a young kid and he wanted to put in a bedroom and bathroom for them to use when they visited.'

'Sounds straight-forward enough, to a layman like me.'

'Oh, you're not a layman, mate. You're a bloody expert. Everybody who sends in one of those fucking applications to me is a bloody expert. They know the subject better than me, they tell me often enough. I'm only the lowly council official whose only function is to give the bloody thing a rubber stamp.'

His face was red and his eyes intense; the question had clearly touched a raw nerve.

'Did Marc try to take advantage of his friendship with you and flout the rules?'

'Marc?' he said, a look of surprise on his face as if Wallop's words had brought him back to earth. 'Nah nothing like that. I turned down his application because I found out he was fucking my wife.'

NINE

DI Henderson pulled out his ID card and opened the double doors leading to the interview suite. He headed straight into Interview Room 3 and took a seat opposite Jeff Pickering.

'Thank you for coming to see me, Mr Pickering,' Henderson said.

Pickering nodded.

In reality, an interview room was the one neutral place left. Henderson did not want to see him at home with his wife there, and Pickering's suggestion of the Dorset bar did not merit consideration. The man in the 'person of interest' seat was not what Henderson would call handsome, not helped by the bruising on his face and tape over his nose, but no doubt acceptable to an overweight lady who didn't go out much and probably didn't ask what her spouse got up to.

He had a thick mop of untidy blonde hair, small piggy eyes, a weather-beaten face and a resting expression resembling a sneer. In Glasgow, where the DI worked before coming to Sussex, it would be enough for someone to confront him and demand to know who this insulting scowl was aimed at. Pickering had obviously come straight from work as he wore a boiler suit and badly stained boots.

Henderson explained it wasn't a formal interview under caution, but a simple fact-finding discussion and he could leave at any time. For the same reason, he did not utilise the recording equipment or have another officer with him.

'What happened to your face? Did you have a work-related accident?'

Pickering smiled then grimaced, the effort seemingly causing him pain.

'Nah, some disagreement down the pub.'

'Your role would've been what? As perpetrator or the victim?'

'Forget it; it's nothing.'

'Fair enough. I can see from your clothes you're some kind of tradesman,' the DI said.

'Yeah.' Pickering twisted his hefty bulk on the plastic chair, trying to get comfortable. 'I'm a self-employed plumber.'

'Have you always been self-employed?'

He shook his head. 'Started my apprenticeship with Booth & Son in Brighton and stayed there fifteen years. Ten, eleven years ago the papers were full of stories about plumbers making fortunes doing emergency work and such, so I jumped ship and set up on my own.'

'Any regrets?'

'Not doing it sooner. I mean, most trades go through feast and famine at various times of the year, but not me. I'm often so busy I have to turn work away.'

'How did you meet Gillian?'

'She was a friend of my first wife, Joanna. When

Gillian's husband left, she started coming on to me, you know? Some might say I should have been stronger, but she's a persuasive woman when she wants to be. In the end, my wife found out and she kicked me out. Soon after, me and Gillian got together.'

Henderson nodded but suspected Pickering had initiated the affair and not her.

'How did you get on with Gillian's children, Marc and Anita?'

'He didn't take to me right from the off. She was ok, I suppose. She lives in Colchester and doesn't come home often, but Marc lived under the same roof and the bugger gave me dog's abuse.'

'How do you mean?'

'Ach, you know what it's like when you don't get on with someone? Every little thing you do or say blows up in your face? Well, with him it was because I like drinking beer from a can and not using a glass, I leave milk out of the fridge and sniff too much at mealtimes, and me with a bloody sinus problem. It got to the stage we couldn't be in the same house together and I told Gillian straight: either he goes or I fuck off back where I came from.'

'What did she say?'

'I thought it might cause, you know, a crisis, but I didn't know he'd already been planning to move out. Like the good mother's boy he was, he'd only stayed put after the wedding to make sure his mother was all right with this new, strange man; the fucking tosspot.'

'Did you get on better with Marc after he moved out?'

He snorted. 'We got along fine then, as I didn't need to see him anymore. He'd only come to the house when I was out, and if I saw him in the street I would blank him and he would do the same to me. So I suppose you could say we got on a lot better after that, ha ha.'

'Do you regret it, now he's dead?'

'Regret what?'

'Not forging a more amicable relationship with your new step-son?'

He shook his head. 'Look, I don't know if you're divorced but when you meet another bird, it's like the first time all over again. You don't want to be lumbered with all the baggage that comes with her, like kids, you just want to go out and have a good time. You get me?'

'Sure.'

'Unfortunately,' he said, a small smile creasing his lips, 'it soon wears off and now all she wants to do is watch fucking *Eastenders* and *The Great British Bake-Off*. Whereas me,' he said pointing at his chest, 'I do hard, physical graft and after some grub all I want to do is go down the pub and get the smells and frustrations from work out of my system; you know what I mean?'

'Where were you the night Marc Emerson died, a week last Monday?'

'Listen mate, I don't want you to get the impression that just because I'm open about my dislike of the Emerson boy, means I would do something like what happened to him. Oh yeah, we had a few fights and he thumped me and I gave him as good as I got, but nothing more. I didn't fucking kill him; no way. Why would I bother when he'd already moved away? He was no longer in my face and as far as I was concerned, no longer in my life.'

'I understand, but I'd still like know where you were.'

He sighed. 'I was in the Dorset bar. I'm there most nights of the week and last Monday without doubt as I did two emergency call-out jobs in one day and I was in the money. Somebody must remember me buying a round, ha, ha.'

'Can anyone corroborate your story?'

He thought for a moment. 'Dave the barman, Lou my best mate, and old Joe and Harry, a couple of regulars.'

Henderson watched Jeff Pickering walk out the front door of the building before climbing the stairs to his office. It was late in the evening and most of the detectives had gone home, so he made a note to speak to them in the morning as he wanted Jeff Pickering's alibi to be thoroughly checked out. Henderson was aware that Pickering wouldn't be so open in his hostility to Marc if he did kill him, but he was such an angry and objectionable sod it was hard for the DI to see past it.

**

Henderson parked his car in the Churchill Square Car Park, but he had no intention of doing any late-night shopping. Instead, he made his way down Ship Street and into the Lanes, a pedestrianised area of narrow streets lined either side with jewellery and antique shops.

With most businesses in the town closed at this time of the evening, the groups of people he encountered were heading to or coming away from the numerous restaurants and bars tucked away in alleyways and side streets, some known only to locals or stumbled upon accidentally by tourists.

A few minutes later, he walked into the Bath Arms. With leather chesterfield sofas, a good selection of ales and an airy feel, on account of the door being left open in all weathers due the shelter it received from buildings in close proximity, he liked coming here.

He ordered a pint of Spitfire before taking a seat behind a small table to await his guest. He didn't have long to wait before he spotted Rob Tremain walking in. If he didn't know what he looked like and the only description he possessed was of a well-groomed individual, this guy fitted the bill.

Henderson got up and shook his hand, and walked over to the bar to buy him a drink.

'Cheers,' Tremain said lifting his pint of ice-cold lager. 'Here's to many more tête-à-têtes with the forces of law and order.'

Henderson said nothing but lifted his glass nevertheless.

'How's Rachel?'

Henderson laughed. 'You should know better than me, you probably see more of her than I do.'

'Yeah, but my job's like yours. You can be in the office for two days in a row and not again for the next three weeks. I haven't seen her for ages.'

'She's doing fine. Moving into her winter programme now with the country shows finished and the national gardens winding down.'

'I must admit, I like winter. You know where you are with cold weather, what to wear, what to expect. Most summers you don't know if it'll rain and be freezing cold or if the sun will come out and people in trousers will look overdressed. Of course,' he said, looking the DI in the eye, 'it's a bad time for policemen as dark nights mean more dark deeds.'

'Aye, you're right there, but more crime is also good for crime journalists.'

'Touché. How are you getting on with our Lewes burning man?'

Henderson had met Rob Tremain many times before, at major incidents, press conferences, or one of a crowd of reporters outside court or a police station after a high profile arrest. Unlike the scruffy individuals he often encountered, with unbrushed hair, three-days' stubble and crumpled coats, Tremain always appeared immaculately turned out, perhaps hoping to secure a spot on television news. His get-up tonight didn't include a suit, but jeans and a jumper, bought not from the high street but from expensive boutiques, giving him the appearance of an off-duty footballer.

'It's a difficult case as I'm sure you know. A fire destroys forensic evidence and with no support from CCTV or witnesses, we're forced to trawl through the victim's life.'

'As we've been doing. Are you targeting anyone in particular?'

'Not yet, but you could be the first to know.'

'Oh? What have I done to deserve this unusually favourable treatment from Sussex Police?'

'I could let you have the inside track on the burning man case, if you tone down your reporting of the housewife assaults.'

'The police trying to nobble the press? I'm not sure I like the sound of this.'

'I'm not asking you to stop writing the story. All I'm asking is you dampen down the sensationalist aspects of these attacks and say, move it to the inside pages. After all, we are talking about robberies here, violent and traumatic for the people involved, I know, but I'm investigating a murder.'

'Look at it from my point of view,' the reporter said. 'The housewife assaults are happening on at least a weekly basis and it seems to me you're no nearer catching them than when they started out.'

'I would dispute that.'

'Convince me.'

Henderson outlined the steps being taken, including: increasing the number of mobile patrols, shaking down known house thieves, reacting quicker to incidents and stepping-up the forensic analysis done at crime scenes.

'You're telling me nothing new, Inspector. I've heard it all before.'

'Listen Rob, there isn't much else we can do, short of throwing every officer at the problem, which would be a stupid thing to do. I'm confident there'll be a breakthrough soon.'

Tremain looked pensive for a moment. 'I take your

point, maybe I've been, let's say, too exuberant in my censure of Sussex's finest.'

'I'm glad you see sense.'

'If I did decide to do something, like shift the story to the inside of the paper and reduce the amount of police criticism, what can I expect from you in return?'

Henderson took a deep breath, choosing his words carefully. 'You will be the first to know about a breakthrough in the Lewes murder case, and I'm willing to meet you again like this to talk about progress.'

'Sounds good. Looking ahead to the future, what about other cases that turn up?'

'We'll talk about other cases when the time comes; this agreement applies only to the Lewes murder.'

'Fair enough, I had to ask.'

'Do we have a deal?'

They shook hands and drank to it.

Tremain put his glass down on the table. 'You know Inspector, my editor will be pleased to hear this. He's been telling me for days that the robbery story has run its course and coverage should be scaled back. I've resisted the pressure so far but now with your generous offer on the table, I think that time has come. A good result all round, yeah?'

TEN

'It feels like I've done a deal with the devil,' Henderson said.

'It's a difficult path to walk,' DS Edwards replied. 'Give Tremain too much and Professional Standards will be all over us like a bad smell, give him too little and he'll get pissed off and mess us around big time.'

Henderson was standing in the doorway of Edwards's office, leaning against the frame, a quick trip to see the boss and give her an update on his meeting with Rob Tremain. He turned to go. 'At least it should turn down the volume of criticism.'

'I hope you're right, but there's still a couple of robbers to catch.'

Henderson sighed. 'Don't remind me. See you later.'

He headed downstairs, his movement unhurried and his mind buzzing. He opened the double doors and walked through, heading for the morning briefing when DS Gerry Hobbs and DC Lisa Newman, rushing the other way, nearly bowled him over.

'Got a sighting boss,' a breathless Hobbs said. 'Two big guys matching the description of our robbers, sitting in a car in Woodingdean. Got to go.'

'Go get them!' Henderson called after them.

They careered down the staircase two at a time,

leaving an invigorated Henderson to enter the Detectives' Room to rally the Lewes murder team already gathered around the whiteboards in the corner.

'We'll kick off with Quinlan Foods. Carol, what did they have to say?'

'Seb and me talked to the Managing Director and owner, an Irish bloke called Francis Quinlan. If we didn't know he was rich from the smart suit and big Rolex, he told us often enough.'

'Is it a big place?' Henderson asked.

'It's a huge place divided into various sections dealing with different food types. Quinlan says the company trades on quality not quantity. He's got contracts with all the big supermarkets and only sells high end stuff. Seb liked the pork pie they gave him anyway.'

'What did you find out about Marc?'

'There's a team of four in the sales office, two guys who go out on sales calls and two who stay in the office doing admin and research. Marc, according to the MD is the best salesman he's ever had by a long chalk.'

'Is this him speaking well of the dead?'

'No, he showed us,' Seb Young said. 'We saw sales charts, profit figures, the bonuses paid to Marc compared to the other guy in the team, the whole nine yards. He really was head and shoulders above his colleague.'

'Did you meet him, the other guy?'

'No,' Walters said. 'He was out on a call.'

'What's his name?'

'Josh Gardner.'

'I can imagine if Quinlan is calling Marc the best salesman he's ever had and giving him big bonuses, the other guy might get a miffed.'

'It did put Gardner's nose out of joint,' Walters said, 'but Quinlan believes the competition made him a better salesman.'

'I don't know about that, but jealously is a strong emotion,' Henderson said, as he bent down to make a note on his pad. 'We need to speak to Josh Gardner.'

'We also spoke to Christine Sutherland,' Walters said. 'This is the woman Marc used to go out with. She works in the Accounts department as Finance Director.'

'What's she like?'

'She's very nice—'

'Nice?' Seb Young spluttered. 'She's a belter. Cracking figure, gorgeous face and she's got whacking big... a big salary.'

'As I said,' Walters continued, 'we talked to Ms Sutherland about her relationship with Marc and why they split. She said she felt really cut up at the time and only went round to the house to see if they could patch things up. She soon realised she was wasting her time and gave up.'

'Sounds rational when you say it like that, but Mrs Pickering made it sound more like stalking.'

'She did, but she's a mother defending her son against predatory women.'

'Maybe. How does Sutherland seem to you now?'

'Aside from DC Young's sexist comments, cool, logical and smart.'

'No simmering resentment over Marc?'

'None that I could detect.'

'Did she sound much like our killer?'

Walters shook her head. 'I don't think so.'

'Ok, Quinlan Foods seems to be a dead end, with the exception of one loose end, Josh Gardner. Harry, did you find out anything about the large deposits we saw in Marc's bank statement?'

'I'm still waiting for the bank to come back to me but I'm not hopeful. I think they'll say I need a court order.'

'If they do, I'll authorise it. I want to know.'

'Will do. The good news is we got to the bottom of Marc owning two phones. The one in his possession the night he died was his work phone, property of Quinlan Foods and destroyed in the fire. The one we found at his house is his personal phone, and as you would expect from a single man about town, full of texts from girlfriends, some of them explicit.'

'Anything threatening?'

'Not at all.'

'What about the laptop?'

'Much the same.'

'Get them both off to the high-tech unit. Have them look at deleted texts and emails.'

'Yes, sir.'

'How did you get on with Marc's mindfulness journal, DS Walters?'

'It's like looking through someone's underwear drawer. I'm halfway through but I can tell you it's a slog.'

'Anything pertinent to the investigation?'

'Nothing that will add to the knowledge we already have, but it reinforces his dislike of Jeff Pickering and how annoyed he was when Christine Sutherland wouldn't let go.'

'Interesting. Keep going with it.' He looked down at his notes then back at the team. 'Now, you've all heard Guy Barton's accusation that Marc and Lily Barton were having an affair. What can you add to this, Harry?'

'I took a look at the phone and laptop that I mentioned earlier were recovered from Marc's house; on there are messages from someone signing themselves as 'Tiger' in an email or 'T' in a text. It sounds like a bedroom reference but having kids who are into Peter Pan, I think it might be short for Tiger Lily. The texts came from a Pay As You Go phone and using a contact I've got at a phone company, they traced its most used geographical location to Lily Barton's house. The texts suggest Marc and Lily were having an affair right up until the day he died.'

**

Henderson returned to his office after the team briefing, his mind buzzing with the implications of what he'd just heard but still trying to get his hands on something more concrete than rumours and supposition. He began to write the names of the 'persons of interest' up on the whiteboard in his office, much like the three in the corner of the Detectives' Room, but with his personal take on the matter.

They were now at the frustrating stage of any

enquiry, trying to make sense of a large number of disparate pieces of information. If and when it settled into some semblance of order, it could take them in one direction, only to be diverted by better evidence at some later date. So far, only Guy Barton and Jeff Pickering, based on the team's investigations and his take on their personalities, looked worthy of further examination, although both men had reasonably sound alibis.

He couldn't rule out the involvement of Lily Barton, knowing she and Marc were having an affair right up until the end. A woman wronged at the termination of an affair was just as dangerous as the husband finding out. He would interview them both himself, but separately.

He needed to get over Jeff Pickering being such an odious character, too full of his own importance and too ready to use his fists to settle a disagreement. His latest disfigurement unsettled Henderson. It wasn't unusual in child abduction and child murder cases to find the step-father or uncle being attacked in the street by a neighbour or a stranger, but Marc Emerson didn't fall into this category. It could be something innocent like a football discussion gone wrong, but coincidences like this were hard to ignore.

He was adding notes and reminders to the whiteboard when Gerry Hobbs walked in and flopped into a seat.

'You look dead,' Henderson said. 'Did your suspects give you the run-around?'

'Running and wrestling.'

'Did you get them?'

He nodded.

'Was it the housewife robbers?'

'Yes,' he said, forcing a smile.

'Well done,' Henderson said, walking around the desk to shake his hand. 'What happened?'

'When we got there, they were inside the house robbing it. There was four of us: Lisa, me and two uniforms. We decided to wait for them to come out.'

'Wise move. If you'd gone into the house, you might have stopped the woman getting hurt, but in a confined space anything could happen. Every house has any number of weapons the robbers could have picked up and used against you.'

'Or it could have developed into a hostage situation. Any road, we waited outside and as soon as they closed the door behind them, we grabbed them, but one guy lashed out like a cornered cat and scarpered. I've been running over the back gardens of Woodingdean like a fell runner but he looked as unfit as me so I didn't lose sight of him.'

'How did you catch him?'

'Lisa followed in the car and when he came out of an alley to the road, she was out of the car in a flash and had him flat on the ground and cuffed before I got there.'

'Her first big nabbing, she'll be well chuffed.'

'She is. I'm just knackered.'

'You played your part too mate, don't you worry. Where are they?'

'Cooling off in the cells.'

Chief Inspector Edwards appeared at the door. 'I heard the great news,' she said. She walked in and grabbed Hobbs by the hand. 'Congratulations Gerry, at last we've nabbed that pair of bastards. The housewives of Brighton owe you big time.'

She turned to Henderson. 'Well done to you too, Angus.'

'*The Argus* will have no more excuses for jumping down our throats with sensational headlines and pictures of bruised women.'

'What about Tremain? You should back away from him now.'

Henderson shook his head. 'No, I can't do that just yet. I'll give him a call in a few minutes and tell him we've caught them, but I made a deal with him over the Lewes murder. If I don't see it through I'm sure he'll find something else to hang us with.'

ELEVEN

She looked around the room, lines of exasperation on her face. Lily Barton had worked with most of them for several years, and knew them to be a dedicated and focussed bunch, but for some reason, it wasn't gelling today. A meeting she believed to be straightforward and uncomplicated had been redirected down blind alleys, people taking sides and their discussions peppered with bitchy bickering.

The explanation for the acrimony quickly became apparent, and she chided herself for not spotting it earlier. Ashley, her genius graphic designer, had split up with Eve, one of her editors. Christ! The last time she inquired, they were still at the 'getting to know you' stage. With Marc's death still raw, she realised she'd taken her eye off the ball more than she thought those last few weeks.

'Hold it, hold it,' she said. 'We're not here to pull apart Ash's book designs, which I think look fantastic–'

'Yes, but–' Eve said.

'Eve, be quiet, you've said enough. I now want this meeting back on track. All of you, listen up. We're here to re-launch these terrific books by Marianne Lester. We've got a great new cover design which I'm sticking with, Sian has reworded the blurb and now all six books look fantastic. What I want from you guys is ideas on how we make the occasion of their launch, the book event of the year. So everyone, stop bitching about work already done and let's focus on what we need to do. Ok?'

Half an hour later Lily Barton returned to her office. She seldom looked at the view, rushing from one meeting to another, often clutching proofs or airline tickets in her hand. Since Marc's death, she noticed it more. Merlin Romance and its parent company, Russell-Taylor Publishing, were located in a glass and steel edifice at the side of London Bridge railway station. From her office on the eighth floor, looking east, she could see all the way to Canary Wharf, north to the arch of Wembley Stadium and close by, the Tower of London, St Paul's Cathedral and HMS Belfast.

She did wonder why smart offices with such spectacular views were given to senior executives as they spent so little time sitting in them. When they did, the blinds were often closed to aid concentration and, in the case of her Marketing Director, permanently, as he suffered from vertigo.

She supposed they did it so authors would be impressed when they came to discuss a new book, or in the case of her previous meeting, the re-vamp and re-launch of their back catalogue. Impress them it did, but at times it could backfire. Only last week she received a vitriolic email from one author, claiming the reason his royalties were so low had nothing to do with his poor sales record, but the 'upkeep of palatial offices in the centre of rip-off London'.

On her desk, the one photograph of Marc she could allow to be on display without inviting questions. It depicted happier days when she and Guy didn't argue, and he and Marc were still friends. Marc's then girlfriend took the picture of the three of them drinking Gluehwein in a mountain-top restaurant in Austria during a skiing holiday. Lily didn't know at the time, but this marked the stage when her love for Guy began to decline and her love for Marc increased.

Looking around at other parts of her office left a visitor in no doubt that she worked in the book business. The large bookcase facing her desk was crammed with books from some of Merlin's most celebrated and valued authors. Books lay on the meeting table ready to be discussed and finalised, and books sat on her desk, waiting for her to give them a green or red light.

In other divisions within the group, commissioning editors selected and prepared the books to be published, but in Merlin, the jewel in the Russell-Taylor crown, she did it. Merlin's success had been built on a knack she possessed for spotting authors who would become stars, and ruthlessly cutting out those that would not.

She picked up a manuscript from the pile, sent to her by a literary agent she respected and written by a mother of two from Newcastle. She slowly read the first chapter and speed-read the next two. The manuscript was placed on her green pile. She did the same with the next book but put it on the red pile. By six-thirty, two manuscripts lay in her green file and would be progressed while the six in her red file would not. She tidied her desk, located Karen King, her Senior Editor, and the two women left the building.

They arrived at Somerset House as the speeches were in progress. If Lily chose to do so, she could attend book launches two or three times a week, but rationed her time to a few of her favourite authors. Today saw the publication of a new thriller novel by the celebrated Dan Harland, a Taylor-Russell author but not one of hers.

After the speeches, she left Karen to socialise and indulge in her love of champagne, and located her friend, Donna Ester, a literary agent at the Grant-Dressler agency. They both recharged their glasses with fresh bubbly and took a seat on the balcony above the hubbub of clinking glass, loud laughter and hearty back-slaps.

For twenty minutes, the two women discussed several of the new authors Donna was championing, the missed deadlines of another and a potential television series for one of Merlin's most popular writers. The work completed and pushed to one side, Donna sat back cradling her glass.

'They still haven't identified Marc's murderer,' Lily said.

Donna leaned forward and grasped her hand. 'I feel for you, girl, I really do. I told you last time we met that I'd speak to a detective I know at the Met?'

Lily nodded.

'I did and he said much the same thing as has been in the papers. Cases like this can take a long time to solve as most of the forensic evidence is lost in the fire and they have little to go on.'

'I understand but I feel so vulnerable.'

'Are you still worried the killer will come after you?'

'No, it's not that. The threatening texts stopped a month ago and I haven't received one since.'

'I'm glad to hear it. I guess they must have come from an old girlfriend of his, like we thought.'

'I think so. Now he's dead, there wouldn't be much point.' Tears welled in her eyes but she wiped them away.

'Your stalker seems to be over you pinching her man,' Donna said, 'but you're not over him, are you?'

'No, and I don't think I ever will be. Do you think because the police don't seem to have a definite lead, the spotlight might fall on me and my relationship with Marc?'

'Yeah, it might, but so what? You didn't do it, did you? You've got nothing to worry about, girl.'

'I know, but you hear stories of people's names being dragged through the mud and losing their job and having to move house, bricks thrown through their windows and people calling you names in the street.'

'I think those things happen mainly in sex exploitation and child abduction cases.'

'Maybe I am being too melodramatic, but you've been in this business as long as me. Taylor-Russell might publish books with sex, violence, murder and rape between the covers, but as soon as one of their employees is involved in any sort of scandal, they drop them like a hot potato.'

'I must admit your lot are more conservative than

most, but it's double standards. I didn't see anybody wringing their hands in angst when they published *Siren*, the diary of the New Jersey serial killer. A best-seller is a best-seller at the end of the day.'

'True, but nobody said they couldn't be two-faced about it either.'

**

Lily Barton arrived home at eight-thirty, the two glasses of champagne she had at the book launch soothing the daily commute. She loaded the dishwasher and switched it on, did the same with the washing machine and turned on the oven for tonight's meal. She went upstairs to change out of her work clothes and had just come downstairs into the hall when the doorbell rang.

'Good evening Mrs Barton,' a tall good-looking guy at the door said, 'I'm Detective Inspector Angus Henderson, Surrey and Sussex Police.'

'And I thought my job title was a mouthful. Is this about Marc?'

'Yes it is.'

'Come on in.'

She walked into the lounge and turned to face the DI. 'Is there any news?'

'I'm afraid not. I would just like to ask you some questions.'

He spoke with a soft Scottish accent she couldn't quite place. A number of Scots worked in her company and she believed she could tell their accents apart, although on tonight's showing, it suggested her skill didn't work as well as she thought.

'Did you want to speak to me or Guy? He's out tonight; he goes out most nights if I'm honest. I don't know when he's coming in.'

'No, it's you I wanted to talk to.'

'Fine. Can I get you anything? Tea, coffee?'

'Coffee would great, thanks. White, no sugar.'

She walked into the kitchen and switched on the coffee machine and noticed her hands were trembling. He wanted to see her, not Guy. What did it mean; he thought her a suspect? She felt cross with herself for being so stupid. She knew she had nothing to fear and if something she couldn't explain turned up, she would hire a good lawyer.

She carried two mugs into the lounge and put them on the table as quick as she could before the detective could detect her tremulous shake.

'Thank you,' Henderson said.

Ah, now she could trace the accent. It sounded soft, with the occasional hardness of a city. He came from somewhere north like Inverness, or one of the rural communities out west.

'When Sergeant Wallop and Constable Sunderam talked to you and your husband on Tuesday, you left the room at one point. Your husband then told my officers that you and Marc were involved in an affair.'

'You don't beat about the bush do you? Straight for the jugular.'

'I'm sorry, Mrs Barton, but I don't want any ambiguity in our discussion. I'm sure you can appreciate how something like this might cause me to think it could have a material impact on this case.'

'Why? I didn't kill him.' She tried to sound calm and measured but it sounded strangled and pleading.

'I'm not suggesting you did. This is nice coffee by the way.'

Despite the circumstances and her own anxiety, she found herself warming to this guy, the composed and gentle way he spoke and his cool, unhurried manner.

'Thank you. Call me Lily. No one but delivery drivers call me Mrs Barton.'

'Lily it is. As I said, I'm not here to accuse you of anything. My main aim is to find out more about Marc. Can you tell me something about the affair?'

'Marc and Guy have known one another since schooldays. When I arrived on the scene, Marc always seemed to be around: meeting up with Guy to go off to football training, drinks down the pub, and latterly when Marc married, meals out with him and his wife. When they divorced, Marc had a succession of girlfriends and once or twice, they came on holiday with us.'

'When did you make the change from being Marc's friend to becoming his lover?'

She removed her glasses and polished the lenses, her way of introducing calm into a conversation and giving her time to think. She replaced them.

'It didn't happen in a drunken stupor, if that's what you're thinking, more of a gradual thing. One time skiing in Austria, I twisted my ankle. Guy didn't mince his words, he didn't want to miss any time in the snow and I'd find plenty to do mooching around the shops.'

'You make him sound harsh.'

'Do I? I don't mean to. I was angry with him at the time, being so selfish, but with us only being out there for a week, perhaps I would have done the same.'

'What happened then?'

'Marc decided to ski in the morning and spend the afternoons with me, helping me hobble around shops and sit with me in cafés drinking coffee. He took me swimming as he thought it would be good for my ankle. I can honestly say I was thoroughly enjoying myself for the first time on that holiday, and it seemed a natural progression when we kissed in the pool.'

This was the sanitised version for the police, but in the one told to Donna, she'd fancied him for ages and couldn't take her eyes off his great body. When he put his arms under her tummy to offer more support, she completely melted.

'The relationship carried on until the day he died?'

She nodded, not daring to speak in case the detective would see her tears welling up behind her eyes.

'Did you meet regularly?'

'Twice, sometimes three times a week.'

'When was the last time?'

'The Friday before.'

'In private, or when he came here to your house ostensibly to see Guy?'

'I would go over to his place, or we'd go out in the car. He never came here to see Guy. Marc and Guy don't talk anymore.'

'Is this because Guy found out about the affair?'

'Is this what Guy told your detectives?'

'More or less.'

'He did find out, but in a way he understood. Things between us haven't been great. If anyone asks, it's what he tells them.'

'Surely he didn't feel happy with an affair going on under his nose? I know I wouldn't.'

'That's just it. He didn't know it was still going on, he thought it had finished a few months back.' She bit her lip, not pleased with the deceitful words coming out of her mouth.

'Ah, I see.'

She looked down at her mug, the coffee slowly turning cold, but she didn't pick it up.

'So if they didn't fall out about the affair, what did they fall out about?'

'Guy works for the Council, in the Planning Department.'

She looked at Henderson who nodded.

'He hates being there.'

'Why?'

'Three words: money, money, money, or rather the lack of it. He enjoys the work but being a civil servant means low pay, low status and meagre pay rises.'

'Not a problem, I imagine for both of you. You're obviously in a good job.'

She sighed. 'My 'good' job causes more arguments than anything else. He feels impotent because I earn much more than he does. You see, his father used to be a market trader, everything in cash and giving nothing to the taxman. He can't understand why Guy still works for the Council; he regards any form of government as the enemy.'

'I see.'

'The great escape arrived when a friend offered him the chance of a half share in a sports shop franchise. Guy loves sport and all he needed was thirty grand. He wouldn't take any money from me, as he's too proud or stubborn to take money from his wife, so he asked Marc.'

'Did Marc have that kind of money?' Henderson asked, mindful of the large deposits he'd spotted in the victim's bank account.

'Probably not, especially after the expense of buying a new house, but Guy asked him anyway.'

'What happened?'

'Marc took a close look at the proposal, but told him no. He didn't like how the financials stacked up and couldn't see Guy being nice to customers and standing behind a till all day. The two of them had a big argument that ended in fisticuffs. Guy broke Marc's nose and Marc broke Guy's arm. In the end, it also broke up a fifteen-year friendship.'

TWELVE

In a corner of the Weald Bonfire Society warehouse, DC Sally Graham tried to get comfortable on the solid wooden chair. It wasn't the chair's fault that she felt edgy, but the witness sitting in front of them, Sam Healey, had just told her about all the explosives and combustible materials stockpiled inside the building behind them.

This was, of course, the place where Marc Emerson died over a week before. The police tape had been removed as the incident had been fully investigated, their analysis made easier as it happened in an open area with no place for a stray hair or cigarette butt to hide out. Just as well, with it being so close to bonfire night members of the Weald Society doubted they could find another place as big as this at such short notice.

All the same, the members didn't all come back to their 'home' without some reservations. Some of the younger ones, particularly those friendly with Marc, decided to stay away for a spell, but the majority came back and carried on with their work, confident that Marc would want them to do so. The main reason being Marc's stalwart belief in the Weald cause and his unstinting support for the ancient traditions of Lewes.

Nevertheless, Sam said the atmosphere in the

97

room was subdued, and the area near the door had become a shrine with dozens of bunches of flowers. Every night while society members worked, the door would open and someone would come in and place a bouquet or a toy on the growing pile. Some would stop and say a prayer, or simply bow their heads for a few seconds before departing.

'What do you do when you're not working here, Sam?' Graham asked.

'At this time of year, sometimes it feels that all I do is come here. No, I work for a credit card company in Brighton. I'm in the Marketing department and before you say it sounds glamorous going to all those sun-kissed beaches or sightseeing in a taxi around New York, just like the television ads, that stuff is all done by our American ad agency. Even so, I still get to work on some creative stuff. At the moment, I'm involved in designing posters for a campaign that's running on the London underground, and flyers which will be sent out to cardholders with their monthly bill.'

'Do you get to use your creative skills here at Weald?' DC Phil Bentley, sitting beside Sally Graham asked.

'I can draw, but at work we use systems like Photoshop.'

Bentley gave him a blank look.

'You know, photo manipulation software. We use it to take people out of photos, add items and people into scenes, enhance colour, remove blemishes; that sort of stuff. Make sense?'

'Yes.'

'Now, do you see the guy over there?'

The detectives followed his finger to a long table covered in papers and fabrics.

'Which one?' Graham asked.

'The guy with the loud shirt.'

A dapper looking gent with wispy grey hair, wearing a bright Hawaiian shirt and gold-framed specs was smiling and talking to the girls sitting beside him.

'Yep, I see him.'

'His name is John Greaves. He's a local artist with his paintings in a gallery in the Lanes in Brighton. Have you heard of him?'

'No, I haven't.'

'Me neither,' Bentley said.

'Believe me when I tell you, that man can draw. In about ten minutes, he drew a caricature of the prime minister and we used it to build the effigy which you can see being worked on behind the table.'

Graham could see it. It stood about three metres tall with the PM's face complete and recognisable, but the body, out of proportion with the head to emphasise the PM's small stature. The body was incomplete, a mass of curved wire and padding to which people were currently adding papier mâché.

'If you ask him nicely, he'll do one of you guys.'

'Thanks for the offer, but no thanks. I had one of them done a while back,' Bentley said, 'and my girlfriend at the time couldn't stop laughing. I swore I would never do it again.'

'If you don't do much drawing, Sam,' Graham asked, 'what else do you do?'

'I do everything, really. I help make torches, construct the float, help Marc out when he's setting up the fireworks.'

'I thought he worked for a food company?' Bentley asked. 'Don't you need to be trained to handle a big fireworks display?'

'I don't think you do, but I'm sure it helps. Marc took a couple of training courses to understand the chemistry and make sure he could deal with everything safely, like putting on a display during bad weather, or while being hassled by a bunch of drunks.'

'You're kidding?'

'No, it goes with the territory. A lot people see Bonfire Night as an excuse for a piss-up, and why not? By the time we light the bonfire around ten, I guarantee they'll be loads of drunken bums in the crowd. It makes for better banter when Jamie stands up to give his speech.'

Aged thirty-five, Sam Healey sported a thick crop of black hair, gelled and sticking up at random angles. Some would call it trendy, but to Graham it looked messy, although it was the only thing about Healy that could be called untidy. Even though he only came in this evening to 'muck in' as he put it, the jeans and jumper looked better than many people would wear for a night out.

With it being so close to the big day, many Weald members were in attendance and the detectives had their choice of interview subjects. Sam was their third of the night but it would be the last. It wasn't because of fatigue, but after two and a half hours of talking, they'd heard nothing new. No tales of dark pasts, drug, alcohol or gambling abuse, violent tendencies or hinting at something they would prefer to keep quiet. Perhaps they weren't hiding anything at all, maybe they had nothing to tell.

Graham now had a list of every Weald Bonfire Society member. It would be passed to one of the analysts on the team and checked against the Police

National Computer for criminal records, banning orders, unpaid bills or delinquent Child Support Agency payments. If any name raised a flag, it would give them grounds for further investigation but based on tonight's showing, she doubted if any would.

'There are quite a few people in the Society with useful skills,' Sam said, 'like sewing to patch up rips in banners, make-up to make us look like pirates, fundraising to pay for all this or sourcing wood for us to burn on the bonfire. We all do whatever it takes to put on a great show.'

'Do tensions exist between members?'

'Of course they do. Look around here. There's thirty, thirty-five people and no way do they all get on with one another. That would be unrealistic. When we get nearer the fifth, everyone's more tense so the volume gets louder and some ding-dong arguments go on, but they're soon forgotten when the procession starts.'

'Did Marc get involved in any these disagreements?'

He paused. 'I would need to go back to last year to think of a big one. It's so long ago, I guess it's not relevant anymore.' He leaned forward as if breaking confidences. 'I suppose you know Guy Barton and Marc didn't get along?'

'Yes, we do.'

'Guy helps out if we're short and socialises with a few of the guys so we often see him around, but I'd be mightily pissed off if I knew someone had been porking my wife.'

'Did it ever get violent?'

'Only once when they had a stand-up fight.' He looked at Graham who nodded.

'I don't think they've spoken to one another since. If we all go out for a drink and Guy turns up, Marc leaves.'

'What about the rivalry between bonfire societies?' Bentley asked. 'Is there much?'

Graham felt a bout of irritation at the sudden change of subject as she wanted to hear more about the altercation between former friends. The feeling disappeared in seconds when she realised the fight didn't interest her much, but the affair triggering it did, although she doubted if Sam could add anything new.

'Yeah, there's some. You see, there are six bonfire societies, all with their own dress codes, bonfires and history, and everyone wants their society to be the best on the night. So if one of the other societies happens to have a mishap on the big day or something doesn't go well with their preparations, we don't lose any sleep over it. In fact, we'd all give a mighty big cheer if something went wrong at Trafalgar.'

'The Trafalgar Bonfire Society?'

'Yeah.'

'Why do you view them differently?'

'I suppose it's like football teams. Most fans probably don't remember why Brighton and Pompey are such great rivals; they just are and everyone goes along with it. Well, Trafalgar and us have been at each other's throats for years. We drink in different pubs, we don't cooperate with them over anything and I don't think anyone has ever shifted their allegiance from one society to the other.'

'Does the rivalry ever spill over into violence?' Bentley asked.

'Violence? No, that's putting it a bit strong, but one

time, about a month ago, we caught one of the scum, that's what we call them, sneaking in here trying to take some pictures. Luckily one of our lads came in and confronted him. He gave him a pasting and 'accidentally' stood on his phone before sending him packing.'

Graham couldn't help but smile. Back at Malling House, she would be regarded by many as a stickler for procedure, someone who liked to do things 'by the book', but she'd been in the force long enough to realise some situations demanded summary justice. By calling the police, it would involve the combatants in a long list of questions, create a pile of paperwork for the officers involved and the perpetrator would most likely leave court with no more than a caution.

'Lucky for us he was spotted by someone who could look after himself and not little Lucy over there, or me who wouldn't say 'boo' to a goose. You see, the guy from Trafalgar had the reputation of being a bit of a tough nut.'

'Who beat him up? The big bloke over there carrying those boxes?' Graham asked.

'No, Kevin McLaren.'

THIRTEEN

'It's hardly worth getting the car out of the car park for such a short journey,' Walters said from the passenger seat of Henderson's Audi.

'I can see you walking down the hill in this drizzle,' the DI said, 'you'd be bitching all the way there. I'd never hear the end of it.'

'It's a woman's prerogative to change her mind, but I didn't mean walking, I meant taking the bus.'

He stifled a laugh. 'Is this the new you? More eco-friendly? Or a desire to walk everywhere to improve your... your fitness?'

'I'm pleading the fifth. Turn right here.'

Henderson turned into Sun Street, a tightly packed street of brick-fronted terraced houses, although parking was allowed only on one side of the road, just like the Barton's house in St John's Terrace, a couple of streets away. At this time of the morning, commuters had left for work and stay-at-home mums and dads must have been out shopping, as the detectives had no trouble finding a place to park.

When Henderson got out of the car he realised what at first sight looked like a continuous row of similar terraced houses was deceptive. Close up they were all different: some were large with rooms in the roof, others slim town houses. They walked to a house near the end of the road and knocked on the door. He waited a minute and reached for the door knocker again when it swung open. It was no surprise to find Kevin McLaren home at this time of the day as Henderson knew he worked from home as a self-employed computer programmer. A call ahead made sure he didn't have any plans to go out.

'Good morning, Mr McLaren,' Henderson said showing his ID card. 'DI Henderson and Sergeant Walters, Surrey and Sussex Police.'

'Ah, yes I remember you both from the warehouse. It's a good job you told me you were coming as I often work wearing headphones.'

'How do you manage with home deliveries?'

'If they're persistent and decide they don't want to leave a card, they bang on the door or rap on the window until I hear them. It often gives me a real fright, I can tell you. Come in.'

The hallway was tight, only allowing one body to pass at any one time, but tastefully decorated with pastel painted walls and light coloured wood flooring. He led them into the living room, more wood flooring and as to be expected from a young guy in a well-paid job, plenty of expensive hi-fi equipment and a large television. He offered coffee which they accepted, and both detectives sat down on the squishy settee.

'No computer gear,' Henderson said quietly, an unnecessary precaution due to the music playing in the kitchen and the rattle and grind of a fancy coffee machine.

'He must have an office somewhere else in the house if he's a self-employed computer programmer. Goes with the territory.'

'Probably in the basement. It's a nice place.'

'I think so too and it's giving me some ideas for

redecorating my flat.'

'You are joking? It's only been a couple of months since you did it last time.'

'Nine, to be exact, but I'm getting tired of it.'

McLaren came back into the room bearing mugs and biscuits.

'How's the investigation going?' he asked as he passed the mugs to the detectives.

'It was always going to be a slow process,' Henderson said. 'Fire destroys so much evidence, and being in a warehouse on an industrial estate, no witnesses. We're building our knowledge of Marc's life piece by piece.'

'You didn't find any forensic information you could use?' McLaren said, taking a seat opposite.

'No, I'm afraid not. We still don't know for certain if his assailant incapacitated him in some way with a drug or a spray, but we suspect this to be the case.'

'You're assuming they did, I suppose, because it wouldn't be easy to come up behind someone and cover them with petrol. Can I ask–'

'Hold on sir. This isn't a Q&A session or an update for interested parties. We're here to talk to you and it's for you to give us information, not the other way round.'

'I'm sorry, I'm so used to asking questions in my work, and I do find the investigation you're involved in interesting. Ask away.'

'Take us through the morning when you discovered Marc's body. I don't want you to start at the point you walked into the Weald warehouse but twenty minutes or so before.'

'Twenty minutes before? That would take me back here as I live only ten, fifteen minutes from the there.

I got up at the normal time, around seven, and about half-past, I drove over to the warehouse.'

'Try to visualise the industrial estate and the Weald warehouse as you approached. Did you notice any strange cars, people hanging about who didn't look like they should be there; anything unusual?'

'Ok. The first thing I noticed was Marc's car.'

'Why did you think he left it there?'

'I assumed he went out drinking with some of the team the night before. He did it now and again and would get a lift back to the estate in the morning from a neighbour who works there.'

'Were you working in the warehouse the previous night?'

'I was, but I left early knowing I'd be there for most of the next day.'

'Ok. Did you notice anything else?'

'The door of the warehouse was closed and locked, just as I expected. I opened the door and saw him lying there. I couldn't miss him as he was right in front of me. I can still see it when I close my eyes. It took me a minute or so to understand what I was looking at and when I did, I puked in the corner and then I called you.'

'Did Marc have any enemies?'

'I've thought about this and I've made a list. There's Guy Barton, Marc's step-father, Jeff Pickering, and the bloke Marc worked beside, Josh Gardner. Who's on yours?'

'I'm not at liberty to say. Why have you included Guy Barton?'

'Well, it's obvious, don't you think? He and Marc had a big fall out and ended up in a fight, and if he tells you that he doesn't want to join Weald, he's a liar.

He's desperate to get his feet in there but never would with Marc being a member.'

'You're not suggesting,' Walters said, 'that Guy killed Marc so he could join Weald?'

'I suppose it sounds like it,' he said looking less confident for the first time that day, 'but I didn't mean to. What I'm trying to say is, it's an accumulation of issues between the two of them.' He held up three fingers and counted them off: 'One, there's the fight. Two, Marc having an affair with Guy's wife, Lily. Three, Guy not being able to join Weald. I think it's enough to arrest him at least. What do you think?'

'Why did you put Josh Gardner on your list?'

'I suppose I've always found him creepy. Marc got on with him fine at work, he had to, but he didn't like him. He told me Gardner was secretly trying to steal his job and his girlfriend.'

'Which girlfriend are you referring to?'

'Christine Sutherland. Gardner might have fancied her, but the poor sap had no chance. She was besotted with Marc and would never leave him for a rat like Gardner.'

**

Henderson returned to his office after talking to Kevin McLaren. He dumped his folder of notes on the desk and walked over to the staff restaurant, a good opportunity to mull over some of the things discussed in the interview and buy a snack. He met DS Edwards coming the other way.

'Hi Angus, I was about to call you.'

'About anything in particular?'

'To tell you the ACC is cock-a-hoop about you guys

bagging the house robbers. He even dug out a bottle of 15-year-old scotch to celebrate. I don't make a habit of drinking at four o'clock in the afternoon, but as the man has been causing me so much grief lately, it would be churlish to refuse.'

'Aye, I would do the same, but I'd probably ask for a refill.'

'How are the interviews with house robbers going?'

'Slow at first, but once the SOCOs had a chance to go over the house where the two scroats live in Hove, they both caved in. They found jewellery, handbags and electrical equipment, much of which we can tie back to specific robberies. They're now at the deal stage. If they tell us about a dozen robberies they did in Surrey, will we go easy on the charges?'

'My advice is don't. I would rather sacrifice a few points on clean-up rates to see those two locked up for a long time. Their antics have increased my grey hair count no end.'

'I'll pass on your comments to Gerry, but I'm leaving the final decision to him.'

'Is that wise? It's such a high profile case.'

'I think it is. Gerry's more than capable. He's got his DI board coming up in a month, the more experience and responsibility he gets under his belt, the more he's likely to impress them.'

'Now I think about it, I can see how this could solve another problem.'

'Which is?'

'Danny Urquhart.'

'What's the latest? I haven't spoken to him in ages. He's been off work for months.'

'Four and a half to be precise. He's now developed some respiratory illness which is expected to keep him off for another three months. In my opinion, he's now forty-eight and I don't think he'll be coming back. I'm in the market for another DI.'

'So, you're thinking you might have an opening for a newly minted DI Hobbs?'

'Could be. Watch this space. How are you getting on with the Lewes Murder? Any good news to report?'

He summarised progress so far. It didn't amount to much after ten days of investigation, but he knew from the outset it wouldn't be a case that could be solved easily. Edwards departed a few minutes later, less jolly than before, but nevertheless still buoyed at having the house robbers in custody.

Henderson arrived back at his office, coffee in one hand, doughnut wrapped in a serviette in the other, and under his arm, *The Argus*. With no free hand, he didn't have a chance to glance at the paper on his walk back. Now, seated behind his desk with the coffee cup uncapped and the doughnut unwrapped, he eagerly laid the newspaper out in front of him.

In the last twenty-four hours, he'd passed on to Rob Tremain two stories. One, the capture of the housewife robbers, and the second, their progress or otherwise on the Lewes murder. Predictably, the robberies dominated pages one to three, page one with the sensational news, two and three with a timeline of the robber's crimes and an analysis of the police effort. Henderson felt annoyed that the house robberies appeared yet again on page one, but tempered by the belief it would be for the last time.

To his great relief, the comments supplied to Tremain were credited to, 'a spokesperson from Sussex Police,' as he did not want to alert the Assistant Chief Constable or Professional Standards as to his involvement with *The Argus's* quick release of the story. In the main, the articles were well-written and balanced, and when the police received a mention, it focussed on what had been achieved, not on how long it took.

On page five, he found the Lewes murder. He couldn't feed Tremain much as he didn't have much to give, but the journalist had done as Henderson suggested, and produced a profile of the murder victim and interviewed his mother and step-father. Despite the best efforts of the staff photographer, Jeff Pickering's picture had all the qualities of a police mug shot, or someone recently released from prison.

The tone of the article was good, praising the work of the police and including some quotes from the Senior Investigating Officer, Detective Inspector Angus Henderson. He couldn't detect any of the harpy cackling of previous reports about the housewife robberies, but was fearful that if he didn't get a result soon, it would start all over again.

FOURTEEN

She pressed the 'print' key and immediately, the machine in the corner began to pump out her report. Christine Sutherland smiled to herself, the satisfaction of another difficult job done well.

She walked over to the printer in slow, deliberate steps, causing Rashid, the twenty-two-year-old accounting trainee to look up from his work and take a long look. She liked men looking at her; and why wouldn't she? It took a lot of money to look like this: the smart clothes, nice make-up and styled hair, and it would be a shame if it was only appreciated by herself and the two lesbians who inhabited the Orders Office.

She collated the report, stapled it together and placed it into the in-tray of the company's Commercial Director, Brendan Flaherty. Christine did the work and Flaherty, the smoothly-dressed and cologne-doused assistant to the MD, got all the credit. Flaherty and the company's MD, Francis Quinlan, were cousins from the same village in County Mayo where they played football together, wandered in and out of each other's houses and often ate jam sandwiches together on the back step, like two characters from a turn of the century misery novel. Sutherland knew, no matter how well she performed, she could never get close to Quinlan all the while Flaherty still lived and breathed.

Now where did such a wicked thought spring from?

'Christine!'

She looked up to see Flaherty waving her into his office. Many girls in the building were wary of the man. As far as she knew, he hadn't done anything physical to alarm them, he valued his exalted position too much to make such a fundamental error. This included a fancy set of wheels, trips abroad and the money to dress like an investment banker with heavy pinstripes, white shirt and a handkerchief in his top pocket.

If not physical, it would be the hungry way he looked at them, in the queue for the canteen, as they bent over the photocopier or when he leaned in closer to look at the report they were writing. Sutherland didn't mind, as she could handle herself and didn't feel shy about using her not insubstantial assets for personal gain.

She walked into his large office and stood behind a pair of visitors' chairs, not giving him the satisfaction of sitting down and allowing him to ogle her legs.

'Yes, Brendan?'

'With Marc gone, Francis has asked me to take over some of his duties. One of the big things coming up is the opportunity to present a bid to Yate's Supermarkets next month. They're a big outfit in Northern Ireland and Francis has set his heart on getting in there. It's run by a family of prods, Orangemen by all accounts, but he's willing to overlook their misguided beliefs in the interest of commerce,' he said with a sneer.

'Why isn't Josh Gardner doing it? Aren't new

accounts his responsibility?'

'He's too busy, he's got a lot on his plate at the moment. Can you please sit down, you're making me nervous.'

Reluctantly she did as he asked. 'Maybe Francis is frightened that Josh might cock it up.'

Flaherty smiled but without humour. 'As I say, he's got plenty to do right now. Bottom line, Francis wants me to do it.'

'Ok.'

'I want you to be there with me.'

'I see.' Of course she could see, the man avoided doing presentations like a cat avoiding bath night. On the basis of past experience, she would not only be required to prepare the presentation, he would feign lack of knowledge or a sore throat and she would have to present the thing as well. Not to mention coming to her hotel room door to thank her for her efforts while holding a bottle of Bushmills or whatever they drank over there.

'It won't be an overnight stay, in case you're wondering. We'll catch a flight in the morning from Gatwick to Belfast and I'll have you back here by tea-time.'

He gave a quick synopsis of what he wanted her to do before saying, 'Speak to Vicky, she's got all the details.'

This was her signal to return to her rabbit hole. Flaherty was a man of few words, not for fear of revealing company secrets to gossip-hungry employees, but the idiot had nothing to say. He was an empty vessel, dependent on the skill of people like her to make him shine.

She walked away, annoyed that he didn't acknowledge Marc's passing in some way. The man was an Irish Catholic, for God's sake, honouring the dead went with all the sacraments he uttered in cold chapels under the stare of a pink-faced priests. It cost nothing to say: 'God rest his soul,' or 'May he rest in peace,' or some other fitting epitaph to tack on to the end of his bland, 'with Marc gone' comment. Instead, he behaved as if Marc's death had become nothing more than a minor inconvenience, something to be overcome with a slice of foresight and planning. Perhaps Flaherty's demise in a rather unfortunate accident would not be such a bad idea after all.

She ate lunch at her desk, a prepared salad of chicken and coleslaw, washed down with a bottle of mineral water. She was considered mad by many of the porky ladies who inhabited this building, for bringing in her own food when a range of Quinlan lasagne, quiche, chicken and all manner of savouries were available free of charge in the canteen.

These same ladies might feel able to let themselves go, enjoying as they did the security of a faithful husband and the love of dutiful children, but she couldn't. Her curvy figure was but one weapon in her armoury, and in her bid to become a millionaire before the age of thirty-five, she needed all the weapons she could muster.

At three, she walked over to the drinks machine and returned to her desk with a cup of coffee. On cue, Margaret Dee, the Accounts Payable Assistant who sat closest to Sutherland's desk, began packing up her things, her part-time day now at an end.

'Goodbye Margaret,' Sutherland said. 'I do hope your cat is feeling better by the time you get home.' If not, Sutherland would lose the assistance of the feline-besotted woman for weeks, as she tried to come to terms with her grief.

'Oh, I do hope so too. He's been so poorly lately, but the vet assures me these new pills will work.'

Margaret had the same organised and methodical approach to work as Sutherland, not surprising as she'd been the one who hired her. Margaret not only left her workspace tidy, but made out a list of all the jobs she intended doing the following day, and thanks to her meticulous attitude never came back unexpectedly to retrieve something forgotten.

Sutherland walked over to Margaret's desk and rummaged through her stacked in-tray, giving anyone who saw her the impression she was looking for an invoice. A minute or two later, she headed back to her desk holding a small pile of invoices and underneath, Margaret's little black diary.

Sutherland sat down and signed into the Accounts Payable system using Margaret's credentials. The smug little nerds who rarely ventured out from their IT lair believed themselves to be the cleverest cogs in the clock by changing everyone's passwords on a weekly basis, but this was before they faced Christine Sutherland.

With the Quinlan Accounts Payable System in front of her, she searched for two invoices, sent a few days ago to Quinlan by a company controlled by Sutherland. In a few clicks she found them. When she ran a scam like this in her previous company, she made the mistake of being too greedy by making the amounts too large, and, as a result, it was spotted quickly. The invoices in front of her were each less than ten thousand pounds, and without undertaking closer examination, had the appearance of being received from two of their largest suppliers.

She authorised the payment, conscious of the time as she wanted the date stamp on the transactions to be as close to 3pm as possible. If her little earner was ever discovered, Margaret would be their first suspect. Her claim that she always left work at 3pm on the dot wouldn't wash, as it would be a small stretch for her inquisitors, including herself, to believe she'd stayed an extra ten minutes to work her little scam. If by some miracle Margaret didn't take the fall, the time it took for them to arrive at this conclusion would provide enough warning for Sutherland to gather her things together and disappear.

She signed off the AP system and returned Margaret's little black diary to its rightful place. Christine wasn't so dumb she would now check her on-line bank account and find out how much this scam, now running for over six months, had made. No matter how little she thought of Quinlan's IT staff, such a move would leave a record for smarter people than the bozos who worked here to find. It could wait until she got home.

At six, Sutherland walked to her car, her face displaying the smile of another successful day. Unlike the senior management team and salesmen, who all drove BMWs, her company car was a VW Passat. The car suited her as it was comfortable and reliable, and with a fat bank account, she could buy any car in the BMW range she fancied.

The offices of Quinlan Fine Foods were located in the Fairway Business Park in Moulsecoomb, north-east of Brighton. This part of the city was suburban and dowdy with rows of semi-detached houses and ugly industrial units. When at last she approached Steyning Road, her route weaving through banks of trees with the rolling hills of the South Downs close by, she would often wind down the window just to breathe in the fresh, cold air.

She parked outside her rented three-bedroom house in the sprawling village of Steyning. The sad-looking man across the road would be peeping out, standing back so she wouldn't see him, but she knew he was there. If in a playful mood, she would give him a wave or a nod, but not today, she had other things on her mind.

She left her briefcase in the kitchen, poured a large glass of wine and climbed the stairs. When she first saw the house she loved it. It had been advertised as three bedrooms, when in reality it didn't offer more than two decent-sized bedrooms and a box room, but she didn't mind. It provided space with the freedom of the countryside nearby, not a semi in a busy street, packed with noisy neighbours and constant car movements.

She walked into the box room. She didn't fill it full of rubbish as in many houses, but left it clear, except for a small wall unit and a chair. Lying on one of the shelves of the wall unit were two boxes. She removed one, sat down and opened it.

Inside, copies of emails, photographs, locks of hair, theatre and concert ticket stubs; all memories of her time with Marc Emerson. She flicked through them, lifting a memory here and a celebration there, and as usual when she did this, tears fell on the box lid with a dull but satisfying *tap-tap*.

FIFTEEN

Rachel closed the dishwasher, the dinner dishes stacked neatly inside. Henderson enjoyed evenings like this, a meal at home, just the two of them. Of course, the peace could be instantly interrupted with a phone call from Lewes Control informing him of a major crime anywhere in Sussex, but times like those were mercifully infrequent.

'Fancy a coffee?' he asked.

'Yeah I do. But don't worry, I'll make it. You go through to the lounge and put your feet up. I'll join you in a few minutes.'

He walked into the lounge and sat on the settee facing the television, but didn't switch it on. He'd lit the gas fire before starting dinner and the room felt warm, maybe too warm, a hard thing to achieve with dropping night temperatures, but it wasn't a big space to heat. Thankfully, Sky wasn't broadcasting a football match tonight as the combination of his comfortable surroundings and the commentator's droning voice would put him out for the count before Rachel came in.

Not surprising for someone who worked for a newspaper, a copy of today's *Argus* lay on the coffee table. He picked it up. The wind had been knocked out of Rob Tremain's sails when Gerry Hobbs caught the violent house robbers, as another story occupied the front pages and he couldn't find anything about it in the other pages of the newspaper.

Of course, he had to make sure he didn't become Tremain's 'man on the inside,' assuming all he needed to do was write a critical article and the DI would come running. With the benefit of hindsight, he knew now they could have ignored Tremain's ranting last time and left him to eat his words when the robbers were brought into custody, but the force employed detectives not fortune tellers.

'Coffees,' Rachel said coming into the room. 'God, it's hot in here.' She placed the mugs on the coffee table and walked over to the fire.

'Only turn it down a little,' Henderson said. 'If you do it too much and the main burners go off, the temperature in here will drop like a stone in a couple of minutes.'

Rachel returned from the fire and plunked herself down beside him with a thump, almost spilling the coffee he held in his hand. For a slim, well-groomed woman who walked with elegance and style, she could be as noisy around the house as any teenager, clumping upstairs, her heels clanking across the floorboards and the radio blaring at top blast while taking a shower.

'Is there nothing on the box?' she asked.

'I'm sure there's plenty. With over two hundred channels, we're bound to find something we'd like see, but I don't fancy watching anything.'

'Why? Is this investigation bothering you?'

'Unfortunately for you as you have to live with me,

it is. Every case I work on bothers me all day and night until the time it's resolved. Sometimes, I'm just thinking about all the things that we should be doing, and other times, like now, re-examining what we've done and trying to determine if we're moving in the right direction.'

'I guess you need to look at everything as you didn't have much to work with in the first place.'

He sighed. 'True, but it's not as if we haven't met this scenario before.'

'You have? I've never heard of anyone being set on fire before like this.'

'Neither have I, but I've investigated plenty of cases where there's been scant evidence. Think of the body we pulled out of the Channel a few months back, and the stabbing in Hove three months ago of a banker by a complete stranger high on crack cocaine.'

'Yeah, I remember the drowning. You were just the same then.'

'There you go then. At least I'm consistent.'

'I could think of other more appropriate descriptions, but we'll park such a discussion for now. Tell me about this one.'

'Are you trying to humour me?'

'No, but I find talking to someone unconnected with the problem I'm struggling with often helps.'

'You're not going to blab about it in the office to your crime obsessed colleagues?'

'No. For God's sake H, I want to help, if I can.'

'Why not? I guess you're as good to talk to about this as anybody.'

'You're full of compliments tonight. Is it just you or

have I stumbled upon a trait affecting the average Scotsman?'

'I wouldn't say I was average.'

'I wouldn't say so either,' she said smiling. 'C'mon, stop stalling, talk to me.'

'Ok, ok. If we start by looking at the way Marc Emerson died, it's up there with stabbings and strangulations: the killer needed to be up close and personal. There is nothing accidental about his death; whoever set the victim on fire meant for him to die in what I imagine to be an excruciating, painful way.'

'But didn't you say early on in the investigation, he had to have been drugged or something in order for someone to douse him with petrol?'

'I did, but even though some drugs will incapacitate you and stop you fighting back, who knows how much pain the victim felt.'

She shivered despite the warmth in the room. 'Doesn't bear thinking about.'

'The process we go through in a situation like this is to interview everyone who knew him. In Marc's case, the people he worked beside, the guys he played football with, his close friends and girlfriends and, to add to the list, his membership of the Weald Bonfire Society.'

'It sounds like a lot of people to see.'

'It's plenty, but now having talked to many of them, we've come up with zilch. He was a nice guy who worked hard, made lots of money and drove a smart car. He had a number of girlfriends, but few enemies. The enemies we did find, his step-father and an old friend he fell out with a few months back, all have good alibis.'

'It looks like you've hit the proverbial brick wall.'

'That's how it feels.'

'What about ex-girlfriends? For some reason this killing makes me think it came from a woman's hand.'

'It does? Many of the officers in the murder team think the opposite.'

'You must have read stories about women slashing a businessman's suits or pouring paint over his car after an acrimonious split?'

He nodded.

'In any account I've read, they do it because the men they want to hurt seem to value the suits or the car more than them. Setting someone on fire is a league above this for sure, but it feels like the same distorted thinking: if he likes his suits or fireworks so much, he can have them back in spades. If it was a guy who attacked your victim, he would have hit him over the head with a baseball bat or stabbed him with a knife.'

'An interesting perspective.'

'With this in mind, have you talked to all the women in his life?'

'There are three who matter: his ex-wife, his ex-girlfriend and the married woman he was seeing. We haven't extended the net out to all his former girlfriends, but maybe we will if we get desperate. The ex-girlfriend is someone we became suspicious of early on as she'd stalked the victim for a few weeks after they split, but she's over it now.'

'That's what she's telling you, how can you be sure?'

'Carol interviewed her and I value her judgement.'

'I can't argue with you there. Carol would do a better job than some of your misogynistic colleagues who can't see past a pair of boobs or a short skirt.'

'I trust you're not classing all men in that category?'

'No, but you know what I mean. I see it all the time with journalists.'

'Funnily enough, Seb Young who partnered Carol for the interview did obsess about her figure.'

'There you go then.'

Henderson realised that dismissing Christine Sutherland or any other suspect so readily, could be fraught with dangers. Many murderers were often fine actors and consummate liars, psychopaths capable of fooling even their own doctors.

'Who else are you looking at?'

'His ex-wife'

'Oh, I can see a twisted divorcee in the frame. What's she like?'

'Did I give you the impression that the victim was a charmer and a hit with the women?'

'Yeah.'

'What sort of a woman do you think he would marry?'

'I don't know, good looking...'

'Check.'

'Nice dresser...'

'Check.'

'A woman who looks after herself and doesn't get fat and flabby...'

'Check.'

'Oh, I don't know. Intelligent, GSOH...'

'What's GSOH?'

'Good sense of humour.'

'She might have that. Think fashion model.'

'Oh.'

'She models for many of the big high street catalogues and was still keen and young enough to get back into it after the divorce. Domestic bliss didn't suit her, she said.'

'No hangover from the relationship?'

'None. She married too young and is glad to be out. She doesn't regret her decision and doesn't wish Marc any ill will.'

'I guess she's out of the frame. Who's left?'

'The married woman he was having an affair with.'

'I see a motive coming up.'

'You're right. She's married to a guy who would be my first suspect as he's big and brash and fell out with our victim big-time some months back. But, and it's a big but, he has a sound alibi.'

'You seem to have come full circle. What's the wife like?'

'She's thirty-three, older than Marc's ex-wife and six years older than Marc. She's as good-looking and curvaceous as his ex-wife, but also a smart lady. She runs a division of a major publishing house.'

'Not his normal choice of totty, using his ex as a guide?'

'Perhaps not.'

'Did you interview her?'

He nodded.

'What's she like?'

'Thoughtful and intelligent, and I suppose with working in the book business, she strikes me as studious.'

'If she reads a lot of crime novels, she'll be aware of plenty of ways to kill someone.'

He smiled. 'Too obvious. Her division publishes Romance and Fantasy books, and any case, she and Marc were having the affair right up until the day he died. We can't find any sign of rancour or disagreement. Quite the opposite in fact. I think she was intending to leave her husband for him eventually.'

She snuggled up beside him. 'How come you get to meet fashion models and good-looking literary women when the only people I interview are greasy old men with more hair coming out of their noses than they have on their head?'

'This investigation is not all about me, you know. We have to share around the pleasure of the interesting interviews.'

She leaned over and kissed him. 'All the pleasure you need is right here. Let's go to bed.'

SIXTEEN

DS Walters reached the edge of the Fairway Business Park in Moulsecoomb Way and slowed down. She ignored the index board as she knew where to go and Quinlan Foods was hard to miss. She turned into the entrance. The long grey building didn't have many windows and few vacant parking spaces so she parked in one marked 'Commercial Director'. She hoped if Brendan Flaherty came back while she was inside, he wouldn't mind.

Seb Young beside her was like a dog with two tails at the thought of coming back to this place. He loved food and she would have called him a glutton if he didn't look so thin. His thoughts would also be on Christine Sutherland and in this, the dog analogy was uncannily appropriate.

She pushed open the main door and both detectives signed in. A few minutes later, Maureen from the admin office approached and led them upstairs to the Sales Department before guiding them into a small meeting room.

Walters took a seat at the table, but Young continued to stand, peering through vertical blinds into the office beyond. 'Seb, what are you doing?'

'The Accounts Department is just over there. I'm trying to see if I can spot that gorgeous bird, Christine

Sutherland.'

'Sit down you clown, or you'll have us thrown out before we can ask a single question.'

He sat down and a few seconds later the door opened. Maureen entered bearing a tray of coffee and biscuits. When she left, Walters grabbed a biscuit before Seb scoffed them all. She had just popped it into her mouth when Josh Gardner came in, displaying the characteristics of a typical salesman, all vim and vigour.

'Good morning detectives, I'm Josh Gardner,' he said leaning over the table to shake their hands.

Walters didn't dare speak in case she fired biscuit crumbs at his nice clean white shirt.

'I trust Maureen has been looking after you?'

'Yes, she has, thank you,' Seb said, sensing her disquiet.

Gardner sat on the other side of the rectangular table which, judging by the number of chairs, could seat eight at a pinch. This room, like other parts of the building she'd seen, was bright and cheerful, the walls cool pastel colours and the furnishings light oak. This airiness created the impression that the company operated in a clean, modern environment and she hoped this continued into the food preparation areas on the ground floor, as she often bought their meals for one.

'We're here as we're conducting an investigation into the death of your colleague, Marc Emerson,' Walters said, her voice now operating normally.

'Tragic, it is,' Gardner said without too much conviction.

In the pictures Walters had seen of Marc Emerson, he looked expensively dressed, clean shaven, smart hairstyle, like any young businessman, out to make a good first impression. Gardner didn't come with Marc's good looks, but he exuded the air of a confident salesman, from the crispness of his clothes to the way he spoke and handled himself.

'Were you and Marc close?'

'I wouldn't say we were best buddies or anything, but we had a good working relationship. I mean when I first started here, he took me out on calls and I guess I looked up to him, but after a time when I'd learned the ropes I regarded him more as an equal.'

'But you weren't equal, were you?'

Walters let the comment hang without enhancement; Gardner's face betrayed a trace of anguish.

'How do you mean?'

'Mr Quinlan told us Marc dealt with all the large customers and was responsible for presenting the company's products to prospective clients.'

If Walters sounded blunt, it was her intention. Many of the salesmen she'd come across were windbags, and if they weren't careful they could spend half an hour with this guy and leave the building with nothing more than a ream of facts and figures taken from a company sales brochure.

'He started working here a couple of years before me and became old man Quinlan's, sorry, Mr Quinlan's blue-eyed boy, but,' he shrugged, 'it's all in the past now, isn't it? Mr Quinlan gave me Marc's accounts and Kelly out there will handle mine.'

'I understood this was temporary arrangement until someone else had been recruited.'

'It is,' he said shifting in his seat, 'but I'm confident Mr Quinlan will confirm me in the lead position and a new man or woman will take over my old accounts.'

With much of the wind sufficiently knocked out of his sails, Walters decided to move on to the reason for their visit today.

'Can you tell me your whereabouts on the night of Monday 24th October?'

He reached into a pocket and pulled out his phone, woke it up and tapped the screen a few times. 'Let me see. My last call was to Wilson's, a small chain of convenience stores in Eastbourne. After leaving there, I drove back to Brighton and got there around seven. I try to go into the office at least once a week, but not at that time of night, so I went straight home.'

'Where's home?'

'Wellbeck Avenue in Hove. Near Wish Park.'

Walters knew the area. Full of large semi and detached houses with gardens, garages and lofts.

'Are you married or single?'

'It's too big a house for a single guy,' he said with a self-satisfied smile. 'No, I live there with my partner Katy and son, Daniel.'

'We will need to talk to your partner.'

'You will? Of course you will. No problem.'

'How has it been in the office following Marc's death?'

'It hit the sales group the hardest, as not only did Marc work here, we operate as a team, much more than in the rest of the business.'

They left the meeting room and Josh Gardner a few minutes later and walked downstairs. 'You didn't say much,' she said to Seb as she pushed open the doors leading to the car park. 'Too busy looking at the biscuits probably.'

'I don't get a chance to say much with you there, Sarge. No disrespect but–'

'Excuse me.'

Walters stopped and turned.

The voice came from a young woman leaning against a wall, smoking. She put out the cigarette and walked towards them. 'Are you the detectives investigating Marc Emerson's killing?'

'Yes, we are,' Walters said. 'Who are you?'

'Cindy Summer, I work upstairs in Accounts.'

If Josh Gardner looked like a salesman, Cindy Summer didn't look like Walters's idea of an accountant. She was young, late twenties, diminutive in stature, with rod-straight black hair, a thin pale face and large staring eyes, looking more like an actor in a fantasy play than totting up columns of numbers.

'Have you found out who did it?'

'Not yet. Why are you interested, were you close to Marc?'

'Yeah, we all were; everybody liked him. Everybody's in shock and we're annoyed that Quinlan and his cronies in the management team don't show more respect.'

'In what way?'

'It's like he's forgotten. They're carrying on as if it never happened. The king is dead, long live the king. Do you have any suspects?'

Walters gave her the usual line about ongoing enquiries

'I suggest you take a good look at my boss, Christine Sutherland, and Josh Gardner.'

Walters was startled by the woman's fervour, not only the words and the rapid-fire way she said them, but her intensive stare, which she found unnerving.

'How do you mean?'

'Christine Sutherland had a three-month affair with Marc, but after they split, she wouldn't leave him alone. She went round to his house at all hours and badgered him to take her back whenever he came into the office. She wouldn't stop talking about him; still doesn't.'

'What about Josh Gardner?'

'He's a rat. He hated Marc. Always wanted to get shot of him. Now he's gone, he's trying to slip into his shoes. Didn't you notice? He styles his hair the way Marc did and he dresses the same, and if you don't think that's creepy, he's now driving Marc's old car.'

**

Henderson walked into the aptly coined 'Brew Room' and made himself a mug of coffee. It was often a foolish thing to do, coming here in the middle of reviewing a pile of interview notes and background research, as he often got waylaid. This time, he made it back to his office without being side-tracked and carried on where he left off.

The office he occupied was an improvement over the one at Sussex House; he now had a window, although with an uninspiring view over the roofs of other buildings, and the dimensions were larger. In comparison, it felt airier and a better place to work, it was just a shame the demands of the job didn't allow him to sit in there more often.

The team were in the process of researching the background of the three people now identified at the top of their suspects list: Guy Barton, Jeff Pickering, and one he'd added, Kevin McLaren the man who discovered the body.

In the case of Guy Barton, several questions remained. The obvious one, whether he knew about Marc Emerson's on-going affair with his wife, was there on the sheet in front of him. Did Guy believe they were no longer seeing one another, or did he know it had been going on until the day Marc died? The distinction mattered. In the first situation, a short-lived affair, many could forgive and forget, but the second, a full-blown relationship, would be much harder to forgive and impossible to forget.

This made Guy Barton his lead suspect. An affair of this nature could force the most mild-mannered individual into taking action, especially if some trigger had been pulled, for example, Lily packing her bags or asking for a divorce. Guy Barton did not come across as a mild-mannered individual; what would it take for him to snap?

He picked up Barton's alibi, a transcript taken from Harry Wallop's notebook: *At about five past ten, Guy went for a couple of beers with Tony Stevens and Tom Davidson. 'When I say a couple of beers it was only two and then I came straight home.' Guy looked over at his wife who nodded her agreement.*

His alibi had been followed up and the men he was with, Tony Stevens and Tom Davidson, corroborated the story, and the times quoted when he left the pub and returned home dovetailed into one another. With such a good alibi, he couldn't be the murderer, or could he? Both individuals, Tony and Tom, were close friends of Guy, Tony in particular might have been a member of Guy's fan club, according to Deepak Sunderam who had spoken to him.

The other corroborator was, of course, his wife. If neither of them were involved in killing Marc, she had no incentive to lie, but would she if Guy offered to take her back with no strings attached? Henderson also couldn't get over the antagonism evident between Guy and his wife when Harry Wallop interviewed them. It might have been due to Marc and Lily's affair, or the death of Marc, but Henderson believed the disparity between the two of them played a part.

Guy had left school with few qualifications, and after helping out in his dad's shop, started working for Brighton Council as a clerk. Lily, on the other hand, read English Literature at Durham University and began her career at a large publishing house in London. She joined Russell-Taylor, one of the 'Big Five' and quickly made her way up the ranks to divisional Managing Director. It perhaps didn't sound too grand a role to a layman like himself, but as Sally Graham pointed out, she'd spotted a similar position at a smaller publishing house being advertised in a magazine with a six-figure salary.

He knew many couples stayed happily married

despite one being smarter or higher paid than the other, but the Bartons didn't appear to be happy. Perhaps the dissatisfaction was Guy's, his inability to match his wife's earning power, or instead it was Lily's, imagining a new life with Marc but unable to leave Guy or make the leap. Henderson didn't know, but he couldn't ignore it.

He moved Barton to one side and picked up the profile of Jeff Pickering. On paper, an honest, hard-working plumber who walked away from a business that rewarded managers better than tradesmen to strike out on his own. In reality, their research revealed him to be a small-time crook and bully, sacked from his two previous employers for stealing copper, and earning jail time twice, once for the re-set of stolen electrical gear, and again for the assault of a boy of eighteen.

If anything, his alibi looked flakier than Barton's. Yet another man who spent his evenings in the pub, but unlike Barton who stopped drinking at two pints, most nights he stayed in the pub until closing time and drank a skinful. Pickering's corroborators, two guys he classed as friends, were themselves drunks with no idea if the obnoxious plumber slipped out for an hour to murder Marc, nor could they say with any certainty if he even came into the pub that night. At best, their recollection sounded hazy, their mastery over the dates and times involved worse than useless. As a result, Pickering still appeared on Henderson's list.

He picked up the final person on his list, Kevin McLaren. When interviewed, the DI and DS Walters came away with the impression McLaren took a greater interest in the police investigation than would be expected from someone who'd discovered the body of his friend. It could be considered evidence of guilt, the perpetrator trying to find out if the police were any closer in identifying him, but Henderson didn't think so. McLaren displayed no sign of nerves or remorse, quite the reverse in fact, a man confident and very sure of himself.

According to his LinkedIn entry he was a self-employed computer programmer. He'd attended Hurstpierpoint College in Sussex where he gained 3 'A' Levels and studied Chemical Engineering at Surrey University.

Henderson began to write down questions about Kevin McLaren which he believed remained unanswered, but his chain of thought was interrupted when his phone rang.

'Henderson.'

'Hello, gov.'

'Hello Carol. How was Quinlan Foods? Did Seb get any more freebies?'

'Of course, he can smell free food a mile away, but we found out something more interesting.'

'What? You saw how chicken pies are made and you've turned vegan?'

'Me? Never, I love bacon butties too much to do that. Put it this way, I think we've got two more names to add to our suspects list, and from what we heard today, we should move them to the top.'

SEVENTEEN

His hands flashed over the keyboard, a skill crafted over many years. Most of Kevin McLaren's clients had large and complicated websites, old legacy systems with miles and miles of code, and they frequently demanded new applications with plenty of bells and whistles. He didn't mind; the more code he wrote, the more money he made.

He set the program running and sat back, looking at the results while swigging a bottle of beer. He made it a rule never to drink while coding as a careless error could take weeks to locate and fix, but with the majority of the grunt work completed, tonight's task had been about adding some flash finishing touches.

Satisfied that the colour and tone of the screens looked right and the links worked, he uploaded it to his private server and sent his client an email inviting him to have a play with his revamped website. He pushed his seat away from the desk, put his feet up, closed his eyes and slowly sipped the beer, his way of shutting off one job in his mind, ready to start work on something else.

A few minutes later, he pulled the seat towards the desk and lifted up a nondescript blue file. In it, various press clippings, photographs and notes made by him about his murdered friend, Marc Emerson. He didn't go so far as to identify the culprit, but he reckoned he had gone further than the police as he could do something they couldn't: hack into computers.

He'd done this to the computers of each of his three suspects: Guy Barton, Josh Gardner and Jeff Pickering. While there, he'd looked at emails, Word documents, and for those computers that synchronised with their phone, text messages too. He quickly concluded that Jeff Pickering was barely literate and the only thing he used a computer for was to look at porn and send lewd messages to the woman he was seeing. He couldn't remember if he'd kicked Pickering in the balls when he'd bashed him about in the Dorset bar toilet, as it would have put the kibosh on his philandering for a spell; if not, he would do so next time.

Next on his list and a better bet than Pickering, Guy Barton. Marc made the mistake of screwing his missus, and who could blame him? McLaren thought her gorgeous, smart and well-paid, three great qualities in his book, but he believed it had cost Marc his life. If he could prove Barton killed his friend, he would make sure it would cost Barton his life too.

He turned to his computer and loaded a program called SkyBlu, and within minutes it activated on Guy Barton's laptop. The program, originally developed for the US Military, could interrogate a laptop and switch on the camera and microphone without the owner realising. He'd used it several times in the past without result, other than to enjoy a good look at Lily's ample boobs when she leaned over to look at something on the screen, and one joyous time when she walked into the kitchen naked.

He quickly scanned Barton's emails and texts but

found nothing from an accomplice congratulating him on another successful mission and no quips on social media about the loss of his worst enemy. He activated the camera and microphone. Even if Guy started using the computer, he wouldn't be aware of the camera or microphone's activation as nothing would light up to warn him. If Guy was more savvy with computers than McLaren believed, it wouldn't help as the program didn't leave any trace of its nefarious activities.

He could hear and see Guy and Lily talking in the kitchen, the laptop open on the kitchen table. It often took him a minute or two to become orientated, especially if people walked in and out of shot. Tonight, the Bartons were clearing up after a meal, Lily loading the dishwasher while Guy stood talking to her. McLaren pushed his seat back, picked up his beer and turned up the volume.

'Why are you going out again?' she said, as she slammed the dishwasher door closed creating a cacophony of high-pitched sound. 'It's been every night this week. I thought we'd sit in and watch a movie tonight. Is there something you should be telling me?' She paused, hands on hips. 'Are you seeing someone else?'

'You're one to talk.'

'How dare you.'

'You're right, I'm sorry I said that. I didn't mean it.'

'Why are you going out? Can't you see in the current situation it looks suspicious?'

'I know, but I can't help it. I promise, this is the last time I'll go out without you, ok? Saturday's Bonfire Night, right?'

She nodded.

'After then, when the fireworks and the parades are finished, I swear everything will be back to normal.'

'What do you mean, after the parades are finished? Are you planning something? Are you doing something with that degenerate, Ajay Singh?'

'What's it got to do with Ajay?'

'If you're not being so secretive about another woman then it has to be Ajay. You know I don't like him.'

'What makes you think I'm going to see him?'

'Somebody told me they saw you together. You're not denying it, are you?'

'I knock around with him now and again, if that's what you mean. It's not a crime is it?'

'No, it isn't a crime, but he'll lead you into it. He's been in bother all his life. You don't need to hang around with the likes of him.'

Guy walked away and said something like 'what the fuck do you care?' before disappearing from view. Seconds later, McLaren heard the front door slam.

What did Barton mean when he said it would come to a halt after Bonfire Night? It was clear, Lily didn't know, but he had some idea. A few days back, McLaren met a girl in a pub and being a true gentleman, offered to walk her home. On the way back to his place, he passed Stewards Inn Lane, a narrow road running parallel to the High Street, and spotted a figure entering a building. It had only been a glimpse, but enough to know it was Guy Barton. A sighting like this wouldn't ordinarily raise an eyebrow, but Barton was on his suspects list.

His first thoughts were of an affair, contrary to the reassurances given to his wife a few moments before, but those were soon dashed when McLaren moved closer. He realised Barton wasn't going into a house, but an empty building, owned and used at one time by the Weald Bonfire Society as a storage facility. A few years back, a leak from a burst pipe ruined five thousand pounds worth of fireworks and the society stopped using it. McLaren knew they still owned it, as he was the Society's treasurer.

Lily stood looking out of the window at the darkened garden for a minute or more before sitting down at the kitchen table. Facing the laptop, she buried her head in her hands and started to cry. McLaren didn't mind seeing Lily happy or angry but he hated seeing her sad. He shut down the spy program and put his computer into 'Sleep' mode.

He dashed into the hall, grabbed his jacket and ran out of the house, slamming the door behind him. He reached Stewards Inn Lane a few minutes later but could see no sign of Barton. This didn't come as a surprise as Barton would take the car as he hated walking anywhere, and by the time he found a place to park, it would take him another five or ten minutes to get here. McLaren took up the same position as he did the previous night, in the darkened doorway of a garage, with a good view over the storage room's entrance.

At times like this he wished he smoked or drank more than he did as he felt restless; a pack of cigarettes or a few cans of beer would while away the time. Private investigators, as portrayed in movies and books, just had to be dumb if they could stand and watch a house or a car for hours on end. To have such patience, their minds had to be empty, as his head buzzed like the inside of a wasps' nest: the search for Marc's killer, the activities of the police and how to get closer to the woman he desperately loved, Lily Barton.

His restlessness came to a halt when someone appeared at the top of the lane and walked towards him. It had to be someone who lived in the area as the lane didn't serve as a short-cut to anywhere. When the person moved nearer, he noticed they carried a holdall, and when the person stopped outside the old Weald storage facility, he could now see that under the hoodie disguise, the build was unmistakably that of Guy Barton.

McLaren waited, more patiently this time, as he knew something was about to happen. He did wonder how Guy Barton could simply walk up and open the building with a key. The keys for all the properties which the Society owned and had access to, were kept in a box at the main warehouse on the Cliffe Industrial Estate. The key for this storage facility wasn't missing as he could feel it now inside his jacket pocket. Barton must have made a copy, not a difficult job to do as the key box contained many keys and no one would notice if one key went AWOL for a spell. Intriguingly, Guy Barton wasn't a member of the society.

Less than five minutes later, Barton reappeared without the holdall. The way he stood in the shadows and looked up and down the lane several times spoke volumes to a man in such a suspicious state as Kevin McLaren. Barton wanted to ensure that no one had observed his nocturnal activities and looked pleased with himself to find it verified. He turned and locked the door and set off with the determination of a man who knew that in some pub on the High Street, a cool pint of lager had his name on it.

McLaren waited several minutes after seeing Barton disappear around the corner at the end of

Stewards Inn Lane before walking towards the door of the storage facility. He looked up and down the lane too, not because he didn't feel entitled to enter the place, but in case Barton returned. He turned the key, easier than he remembered, suggesting a recent oiling, and walked in. Half-expecting to find it full of illegal immigrants, drugs, or the banners and flags of a rival bonfire society, he felt disappointed to find it as dark, empty and damp as the last time he came here. He closed the door and locked it.

He reached for his torch and switched it on. It wasn't a big place, about six metres long by about four wide, and with his back to the door scanned the walls from left to right. His quick search revealed nothing and he now concentrated on the left side, going up and down and into corners. Coming up with nothing, he turned to the right. There on the far side, away from the damp wall, he spotted a tarpaulin and under it he felt sure, the things Guy Barton had brought here.

He put the torch on the floor and carefully folded back the tarpaulin. Just then he heard a noise at the door. He killed the torch, replaced the tarpaulin and moved to the opposite side of the room from the little heap of mysterious things. If the door opened and McLaren made a rush for the exit, Barton would suss his identity, despite the dark, as they knew one another well. He didn't want to confront him either, as even though McLaren could handle himself, he boxed and once did karate, Barton was a street fighter and if the things under the tarpaulin were illegal, he wouldn't be surprised to find him armed.

The door took longer to open than expected. He realised it wasn't Barton returning, but someone unfamiliar with the lock, or a burglar. He moved to a position closer to where the intruder could be intercepted, and waited. The door didn't provide a good seal and leaked light into the room. If he didn't fear it opening at any moment and smacking him in the head, he would have peered through a crack and taken a look at the visitor.

The door opened and a man entered, someone smaller and slimmer than Guy Barton, who immediately closed the door. Before he could turn, McLaren came up behind him, threw an arm around his neck, grabbed his arm and shoved it up his back. He pulled him backwards, knocking the intruder off-balance.

'What the fuck—'

'Shut your trap, mate. What are you doing here?'

'I'm a building inspector. Let me go or I'll call the cops.'

McLaren tightened his grip of the man's neck. 'Building inspector my arse. It's ten o'clock at night. You'll need to come up with something better than that.'

'Agh, let the fuck go, you're hurting me.'

'That's the idea, chum. What are you doing here?'

No response. He squeezed his neck and pushed the arm higher.

'Aghhh, right, you got me,' he said in strangled tones. 'I'm a fucking burglar, here to rob the place.'

McLaren laughed. 'Rob what? An empty space? You're some burglar, mate. You need to go back to thieving school.'

'I saw Guy Barton putting some stuff in here. I thought it might be worth a look.'

'You know Guy Barton? How?'

'Lemme go and I'll tell you.'

McLaren released his grip and stepped back.

The weasel sprang up and in a practiced move, pulled out a knife and waved it in front of him, emulating street punks in some movie he'd seen.

'Ha, you're not laughing now tough guy, are you?' Now it's m–'

Before he could complete the sentence, McLaren's boot smacked his knife hand, the blade sailing off into the gloom, and his fist flew into the burglar's face.

'Ah, you bastard,' the weasel said, doubling over in pain. 'You busted my nose and my finger's fucked.'

'You pull a stunt like that on me again, shit face, and I'll burst more than your nose.'

McLaren kicked the burglar's heels and dumped him on the floor, face up. He stood over him, pushing his boot against his neck. 'I want answers to my questions, now.'

'Arg...' he gargled as blood slipped down his throat. 'Can't... breath.' He eased the boot a touch.

'How do you know Guy Barton?'

'I've seen him before, in pubs. I know he works for the Council on the building side of things, and when I spotted him bringing stuff down here I thought it might be a store for tools and construction equipment.'

'Things you could nick and sell?'

'Yeah.'

It was a reasonable enough explanation and although he didn't fully buy it, he couldn't be bothered trying to extract something more plausible.

'What's your name?'

'Frank Skinner.'

'Aye right, and I'm David Baddiel. Now listen up

scum bag,' he said easing the door open with his hand. 'Get your arse out of here and if I see you down this way again, I'll go to town on your good looks. Understand?'

'Yeah, yeah.'

McLaren removed his boot and the weasel got up more gingerly than before, slinked out without another word, nursing his sore hand and holding his nose. McLaren watched him for thirty seconds before closing the door and walking back to examine Barton's stash.

He switched on the torch and lifted the tarpaulin. He sifted through a neat pile of dark clothing, wary of any mice or moths, and came across polo necks, balaclavas and cotton trousers. Close by, a couple of sets of bolt cutters, two sledgehammers, a range of smaller hammers and tools. He sat back. The weasel's information didn't look so far off. Barton was using this place to store equipment but it couldn't be for the Council as the warehouse didn't belong to them.

Perhaps this was yet another example of Guy Barton's greed and disregard for authority, a man not happy with a lovely house and wife, willing to risk it all for a few bits of stolen kit. McLaren didn't think so. He felt sure it was connected to the vow Guy made to his wife in the kitchen that 'everything will be back to normal' after Bonfire Night, but how?

EIGHTEEN

On November 5th, Bonfire Night, at seven in the evening, Henderson parked his car in the Malling House car park. Using the car park when not on duty could be regarded by an overbearing or officious boss as a breach of privilege. DS Edwards preferred to get annoyed about the more serious things in life like murder and armed robbery. Good job, as on Bonfire Night, town centre traffic in Lewes was banned and car parking spaces impossible to find.

'How long will it take us to walk there?' Rachel asked as she wrapped her scarf around her neck, before putting on a woolly hat and zipping her jacket up to its full extent.

'I don't know,' he said, 'twenty, twenty-five minutes? It depends on how soon we get caught up in the crowds. C'mon, let's go.'

It felt bitterly cold, the stars all visible, as if displayed on an HD television. If slippery downhill pavements glittering with an early frost didn't require such care, he would have taken a longer look at the celestial spectacle.

'Did I tell you where we're going for our Christmas party?' Rachel said. 'I got an email about it today.'

'No, where?'

'The Queen's Hotel.'

'Do they have a good reputation for hosting such events? And can they keep a bunch of drunk and rowdy reporters in some semblance of order?'

'I saw the menus and the food sounds excellent. Can they handle it? We'll have to wait on that score and see how it goes.'

'Based on last year, we should have a couple of squad cars and a meat waggon parked outside.'

'It wasn't so bad.'

'From memory, fights in reception, a dining area strewn with food and the fire alarm going off at various times of the night. I would say you lot need some kind of early police intervention.'

'I think the response we received from Sussex Police was a bit on the heavy-handed side myself.'

'This is because you left it until midnight before calling us. By then, the rowdy ones had started knocking lumps out of one another.'

'What about your lot? Where are you going?'

'I don't know. I suppose I should follow it up and make sure something happens. Now we're in Malling House with all the admin staff, everyone expects someone else will do it.'

'Knowing the police as I do, I expect it's written into someone's job description.'

'You could be right.'

The streets were busier now, a mass of people heading downhill towards the High Street. Henderson had been to the Lewes bonfire celebrations a couple of times before, once when he first moved down south and another when his daughter arrived for a visit. In a way, it was penance for not spending more time with her as he had been heavily involved in a big case.

The noise level increased too, not the sound of the parading Bonfire Societies, it was too early for them, but the squeal of excited children and the shrill voices of adults trying to make themselves heard above the background din.

They reached the High Street at six-fifteen, now dark and with nothing much happening in the street, but it did little to deter the crowds five deep on the pavement with expectant expressions on their faces. With some difficulty they made their way along the pavement to a place where the crowd numbers were thinner, and offering a decent view of the road. It didn't bother Henderson too much as he was taller than most of those around him, but he wanted to make sure Rachel could see the unfolding spectacle.

At about seven-thirty, it started. Not that they could see anything yet, but the noise of the now huge crowd rose to ear-piercing levels, anticipating the approach of the procession. From where they were standing on the pavement of Lewes High Street, to the left and right, and across to the pavement on the other side of the road, all he could see was thousands of people.

He almost forgot how narrow the High Street could be in places. Without such crowds, he could speak to someone on the other side of the road without shouting, but on evenings like this, the closeness of the buildings created a unique, claustrophobic atmosphere in which every sound and smell would be amplified.

Ten minutes later the first marchers approached. The big banner held up by a couple of guys amidst a large band of society marchers read, *The Trafalgar Society*, and bore the image of wooden warships in conflict. The society members were dressed as soldiers from the Napoleonic wars, carrying swords and rifles and most of them holding burning torches. With the blast of heat from their torches as they passed, it was difficult to believe winter still gripped surrounding streets and countryside.

In the middle of the procession, six members pushed a cart containing a giant effigy. The figure was perhaps three metres tall and broad with a fat frame, the stains on the shirt depicting his prodigious eating and drinking habits.

'Who's that?' Henderson asked Rachel.

'Where?'

'Who's the effigy meant to be?'

'Paul Ranier, The President of the European Union.'

'Ah, I see it now. I assume he's being pilloried for giving our car industry such a lousy trading arrangement with the EU.'

'Please don't talk about Brexit,' she said. 'It's all we hear in the office. What's going to happen to him?'

'He'll be put on the bonfire, someone will stand and denounce his crimes and then they'll burn him.'

'Best place for him and all his cronies.'

'Now, now, don't say such things,' Henderson said. 'Remember the case I'm involved in at the moment.'

'Sorry, just a figure of speech.'

Trafalgar took twenty minutes to pass and minutes

later, Weald followed. He didn't have to ask about their effigy as Harry Wallop had told him what they were creating, and even without his prompt he would have recognised the image as it looked a close likeness.

'It's the prime minister, Ashley Stevens, isn't it?' Rachel asked.

'The very man.'

'Won't the PM be annoyed about this? He seems to get annoyed about everything else.'

'It's only a bit of fun and even he should see it, although the lack of a sense of humour could be considered an essential job requirement for a prime minister nowadays.'

Weald told them their Society would appear in the parade out of respect for Marc, he wouldn't want to disappoint the crowds, but when they reached the bonfire a commemorative speech would be made. Henderson wished them luck, as the one time he'd made it as far as the bonfire a large crowd had gathered and many were drunk. Thankfully excess alcohol impaired their aim as some were trying to hit the poor speaker with bangers and rockets.

In the course of the next hour and a half, a tribe of North American Indians, pirates, a Scottish pipe band, smugglers, ghouls with white faces and many more, including Guy Fawkes, tied up and ready to be hanged, passed in front of them. Some time later, he realised many people were peeling off and following the marchers, indicating the tail-end of the procession. They joined them.

He took out his phone to take another picture of

Rachel and noticed a missed call from DS Edwards. There didn't seem much point in trying to call now, with a brass band in mid-tune in front of him and a drummer nearby, banging out a regular marching beat.

Before they reached the bonfire he ducked into a doorway and called his boss.

'Evening ma'am,' he said raising his voice above the general hubbub of the passing crowd.

'Evening Angus. God, is it still going on there? It's after ten.'

'It goes on until the middle of the night, I'm told.'

'There was a time when I had the energy for late-night festivities, but not now. I'm knackered if I don't get my seven hours.'

He laughed.

'The reason I called; have you passed Fenton's Jewellers?'

He thought for moment. 'I'm not sure as a lot of the shops have their grills down, and with all the smoke sometimes it's hard to see the other side of the street. Why? Did you forget to buy a last minute present?'

'No. There's been a break-in. It's not something we normally get involved in but uniform couldn't get a car down when the alarm went off, what with all the crowds and closed roads. The Commander asked around to find out if any of our people are down there.'

'What's wrong with uniform? I've seen plenty of them standing around.'

'The Commander's having trouble reaching them,

what with crowd control duties, the noise, and apparently one of the tar barrels upended and a few people got hurt.'

'Would you like me to go over there and take a look?'

'Yes. I expect uniform are there now but it would be good if you could make sure the site is secure until one of the burglary team can get there. I know burglary isn't part of our remit but we'd be doing Eddy a favour. He's a good man to have on our side.'

'I know. No problem.'

He returned the phone to his pocket and explained the conversation to Rachel.

'What, and miss the bonfire?' she said.

'Yes, but this might only take ten or fifteen minutes and the bonfire goes on for hours.'

She shrugged. 'I suppose so. I guess it gives me a chance to see a burglary at first hand. I'll get one over Rob Tremain for being first at a crime scene.'

They walked back the way they had come, not easy with a mass of people coming towards them. Fenton's the Jewellers wasn't hard to find, easily identified by the flashing blue light pulsing from their alarm box. However, getting in would present a problem with the door locked and the window protected by a metal grill.

They headed to the first turning off the High Street and after walking twenty-odd metres down St Martin's Lane, turned right again into Stewards Inn Lane. He soon located the back of the property, identified by the flickering light of torches and the voices and laughter of several men, not the behaviour of a gang of burglars.

The tall gate barring the entrance to the back of the jewellery shop had once been secured by a padlock and chain, but he found it lying on the path, the chain sliced in half. The door to the shop lay open, the lights inside now coming on. It felt a bit like coming late to a party, but the coppers in front couldn't have arrived at the scene more than a few minutes before them.

He stopped and turned to face Rachel. 'It's unusual for police officers to take their partners to a crime scene.'

'You do take me to all the best places.'

'This robbery isn't one of ours so I guess I can make an exception. A word of warning; on no account touch anything. If I see something dangerous or threatening inside, if I tell you to get out, I don't want a big discussion. Ok?'

'Yes, sir,' she said saluting. 'Don't worry H, I'll be on my best behaviour.'

Henderson, with Rachel behind, stepped over the threshold of the open door, taking note of the smashed door frame where the robbers had forced their way in using something heavy. They made their way through a storeroom and then into the shop.

A copper turned and spotted them.

'Hey! You can't come in here. This is a crime scene. No members of the public are allowed in here.'

Henderson pulled out his ID. 'DI Henderson, Major Crime Team.'

'Apologies sir, I didn't realise.'

'What's your name?'

'PC Bennett, Phil Bennett, sir.'

'How many of you guys are here?'

'There's only myself and PC Hodges.'

'Where's PC Hodges?'

He turned and called, 'Andy!'

Seconds later, a big guy appeared, at least six foot six or more.

'Andy,' Bennett said, 'this is DI Henderson from Serious Crimes.'

PC Hodges nodded.

'What have you guys noticed in the time you've been here?' Henderson asked.

'We only got here a few minutes before you.'

'Were you on crowd control, or did you come here by squad car?'

'Crowd control. We've been told no vehicles are getting through yet.'

'It should free up soon,' Henderson said, 'the parade is moving down the road towards the bonfires. So what can you tell me about what's happened here?'

'The chain on the gate out there's been cut by bolt cutters and they forced the door with, I guess, sledgehammers. They came into here and smashed the glass on just about every display and took everything in the cabinets except these big items like the plates and silver cups.'

'Yeah, cleaned them out,' Hodges said in a deep growl of a voice, 'hardly a bloody stick left.'

'PC Bennett, I'd like you to stand outside the gate and let no one in until the burglary team or owner gets here.'

He nodded. 'Yes sir.'

'And you, PC Hodges, I want you to go up to the High Street and nab at least two of your colleagues and start house-to-house in the lane and the streets at either end. Ask if they have seen anyone acting suspicious these last few days and if they've noticed anything unusual this evening. If the robbers banged in the door with sledgehammers they must have made some noise.'

'Not many of the houses face into the lane,' Hodges said, 'and it's getting late.'

'I know they don't, but we need to ask. Don't worry about waking them up, they've either been out watching the parade or can't sleep for all the racket.'

'Yes sir.'

'Off you go then Hodges, the quicker you start, the quicker it'll get done. You too, PC Bennett, and remember, let no one through except our people or the owner if he turns up.'

They disappeared out the door and down the path, Bennett's cocky walk suggesting a man happy with something to do, while Hodges walked with slouched shoulders, a man uncomfortable at using his own initiative.

Rachel came up behind him, put her arm through his and pulled him close. 'Oh, you're so masterful when you get going.'

'Get away, woman,' Henderson said extracting himself, 'or I'll give you something to do.'

He walked slowly around the display cabinets in the middle of the room, showcasing nothing more than broken glass, velvet ring holders and watch stands all carelessly discarded. It was the same for the glass-fronted units at the side of the room, the empty stands indicating they once held earrings, watches and necklaces; all of it gone.

He hadn't investigated a burglary since his days as a young DC in Glasgow, but this had to be one of the most comprehensive robberies he'd ever seen. It didn't look like a clumsy smash 'n grab with a quick getaway leaving jewellery scattered over the floor and cabinets untouched, but a systematic emptying of every piece of the jeweller's stock.

The gang knew they had time as the police couldn't respond to an alarm call with such large crowds outside, and they had no fear of being spotted as the metal shutters blocked all light from the street. Coupled with a deserted alley at the back, it would be a surprise if the shop hadn't been burgled before.

If this was his investigation, his first instinct would be to check the whole place for fingerprints and interrogate the CCTV cameras dotted all around the room. However, if the gang were smart enough to know the police response would be limited on Bonfire Night, they would also be smart enough to wear gloves and to cover their faces. No, he didn't look back on his early police career with rose-tinted nostalgia or hanker for a return to the Robbery Squad. The Marc Emerson murder enquiry had enough blind alleyways for anyone.

NINETEEN

Henderson filled his cup with coffee in the Brew Room, and walked over to join the Marc Emerson murder team in the corner, the windows partially blocked by three whiteboards covered in writing and photographs.

He moved to the front and took a seat on the edge of a desk. 'Before we start, did anyone attend the bonfire celebrations in Lewes last night?'

'Me,' DC Sally Graham said.

'Were you anywhere near Fenton's the Jewellers?'

'Not too far away. I heard they got burgled on the news this morning. As I was watching the parade, I noticed the alarm light flashing. I assumed it was a false alarm due to the noise of the procession or people leaning against the shutters. When the crowds thinned, I walked over and tried to look inside but I couldn't see a thing because of the shutters.'

Henderson went on to explain about the call from Edwards and how he and Rachel didn't get relieved for over an hour. When they did, they were met by an irascible prat from the Robbery Squad who didn't sound too pleased to be called out.

Henderson turned to the board where he'd written up the names of their five suspects in the Marc Emerson murder enquiry:

Guy Barton

Jeff Pickering

Josh Gardner

Christine Sutherland

Kevin McLaren

'This is the start of the third week of this investigation,' Henderson said, tapping the board with the marker pen for emphasis. 'Despite a load of legwork and dozens of interviews, why don't I feel able to name our prime suspect?'

'I think we've succeeded in eliminating a couple,' Harry Wallop said.

'Who?'

'I think we should take out Jeff Pickering and Kevin McLaren. We've analysed Pickering's alibi to death. Maybe a good lawyer could still pull it apart, but it convinces me. He's told us he didn't like Marc but I don't think he's got it in him to kill someone. He's all mouth and no trousers, in my opinion.'

'I think you're right, Harry,' Carol Walters said. 'He's loud and aggressive but too fond of the booze to step out on a cold night and murder Marc, and why go to all that trouble when he'd already left home? Quite frankly, I don't see a strong enough motive.'

Henderson thought about it. Pickering had done jail time and was a man hard to like, but he came clean about his antipathy for Marc. DS Walters was right, why would he bother killing his step-son even if at one time, he might have considered doing so?

'I agree,' he said putting a line through Pickering's name. 'He's not a pleasant man, but after Marc left the family home he wasn't in Pickering's face any more and therefore no longer an irritant. Also, I don't think setting a victim on fire is his style. If Marc had died from having his head bashed in with a brick or was stabbed with a kitchen knife, Pickering's name would still be there. One down. Why not Kevin McLaren?'

'When we first saw him at the crime scene,' Walters said, 'he was an emotional wreck. When we went to his house just over a week later, he looked a different person; all confidence and questions.'

'I've been thinking about his behaviour,' Henderson said, 'and you're right, it was quite the transformation. He also took a keen interest in the police investigation, too keen maybe.'

'Aye,' Harry Wallop said, 'but it might be because he felt vulnerable. Being a close friend of Marc maybe he's concerned that whoever killed Marc might be someone he knows or might come for him next.'

'Maybe, but there's something steely and resilient about him I can't put my finger on. I think he might be hiding something, or he's the vigilante type, hoping to identify the killer before we do. I want to leave him on.'

'Fair enough,' Harry Wallop said.

'Now to Christine Sutherland,' Henderson said. 'In my mind, she's less of a suspect than McLaren because we've got nothing on her other than she hassled Marc.'

'I interviewed her,' Walters said, 'and got the impression she is a normal, well-balanced lady. Sure, she went through a hard time when she split with Marc, but she's over it now and getting on with her life.'

'I agree with Sergeant Walters,' Seb Young said. 'I can't see her killing anyone, far less tipping petrol over them.'

'Did she seem sad or remorseful when talking about Marc?'

'Not at all. I think she's moved on.'

'It seems odd that at one time she couldn't leave Marc alone, and now she isn't bothered that he's dead.'

Walters shrugged. 'Time's a great healer. Some people, mentioning no names Phil Bentley, completely wipe their exes from their memory as if they didn't exist.'

Henderson was about to say, 'it was different in my day' but no, he knew plenty of people who behaved in this way, even with ex-wives.

'I'll take Christine off the list unless anybody else has got something to add?' He glanced around and, seeing nothing, drew a line through her name. 'This leaves three: Barton, Gardner and McLaren.'

'Barton's top of my list,' Phil Bentley said. 'I think he found out about Marc's on-going affair with his wife and snapped.'

'Yeah and there's been violence between those two in the past,' Walters said.

'Plus, his alibi's been corroborated by his wife,' Henderson said. 'He could have left the pub earlier than suggested, as not many people would have noted the exact time, and may have come home later than his wife said. Or she could be lying to protect him.'

'Why would she?' Walters said. 'If he killed her lover?'

'Perhaps she's involved in the plot too,' Harry Wallop said, 'and wanted to get shot of him.'

'Either way,' Henderson said, 'it wouldn't take long to motor over to the warehouse, sneak in at the time when Marc would be packing up and then attack him.'

He looked around and saw many nods of agreement.

'Right. Guy Barton is about to receive a royal shake-down. Sally, prepare a warrant for a search of the Barton household; we'll arrest him on suspicion of murder. Then, we'll leave him to stew in the cells for a spell while we wait for Pat Davidson and his SOCO boys to take his house and back garden apart and find some forensic evidence to link him to the murder.'

He looked at his watch. 'It's too late in the day for a search warrant and we don't want to bring Barton in without it. He would be sitting in the cells running down the clock on the limited time we can keep him in custody. First thing in the morning we pay him a visit. Ok?'

'Yes, sir,' Sally Graham said.

'What about the other two names on the list; Gardner and McLaren?' Walters asked.

'Neither of them sticks out as much as Barton. If we find nothing on him, then we'll go to town on the other two.'

**

Henderson walked downstairs and out of the building in confident mood. Guy Barton looked the part, sounded it and of all the suspects, had the best motive. The only difficulty was finding the evidence to prove it. Henderson knew with only supposition and suspicion there was a chance the investigation, despite expending much time and energy, could grind to a halt, and leave several people tainted with doubt and no conviction.

Their only hope would be if a house search found traces of the substance used to incapacitate the victim, a receptacle that once held petrol, or some items of clothing bearing relevant chemical residues. He didn't think a confession would do it. He believed the CPS would refuse to prosecute if Guy Barton professed remorse and blurted out a heart-wrenching story of hate and jealousy, no matter how complete and detailed. They would only proceed if they could produce the items he used in the murder. When the SOCOs entered the Barton household in St John's Terrace tomorrow, he would need all his fingers, and everything else, crossed.

He pushed open the door of a squat, three-storey building at the back of the Malling House complex and after showing his pass to the desk sergeant, climbed the stairs to the top floor. His contact in the Robbery Squad, Detective Sergeant Steven Rhodes, the grumpy git he'd met last night at Fenton's, was at the back of the room, surrounded by desks with various bits of stolen kit heaped upon them. To some people, it might look like a treasure grotto, but to Henderson it resembled the inside of a house clearing company's warehouse.

A smile crossed the lips of DS Rhodes as Henderson approached.

'Afternoon sir,' he said reaching out to shake his hand. 'Sorry about last night. My wife made such a fuss about me going out and then it took me over an hour to drive a couple of miles.'

'I can sympathise. It wasn't the best night to try and go anywhere in Lewes.'

Aged around mid-forties, Rhodes wore a scruffy jacket on an overweight frame. He had a youthful-looking face, but the receding hair didn't want to play ball. Rhodes did the only sensible thing he could in the circumstances, if he didn't want to be known as the guy with the comb-over, and kept it short.

'You can say that again. You're in charge of the Marc Emerson murder case, aren't you?'

Henderson nodded. 'Why do you ask?'

'I knew him, well not so much me, my son played football with him. They got on well together and a few times Marc came round to our house after a match.'

'What did you think of him?'

'A decent young man, polite and happy to help. A good centre-forward according to my lad, and a good-looking guy if you believe Maddy, my fourteen-year-old.'

'Did your son say anything about his state of mind close to when he died, you know, if he felt worried about anything?'

'He said Marc was being hassled by an ex-girlfriend, someone he worked beside, I understand, but I expect you know all about that.'

 Henderson nodded.

'He said he didn't get on with his step-father and had to move out otherwise one of them would have killed the other.'

'His step-father is a difficult man for anyone to get on with, even with the patience of Mother Teresa. Did he say anything more?'

'No, but I can ask him again if you like.'

'Yes, if you would. It might twig something lurking at the back of his memory.'

'So, I guess you're here to find out what we're doing about the robbery at Fenton's?'

'We didn't have much of a hand-over last night when you and your guys arrived. I can answer any questions that might have occurred to you since then and, more for interest than anything else, I'd like to know how the investigation's progressing.'

'Fair enough.'

Henderson went on to explain how he and Rachel had been walking with the procession towards the bonfire when DS Edwards called him. He went into some detail about what he found in the shop when he got there, and what he'd asked the two uniformed officers to do.

'They cleaned the place out, like you said,' Rhodes said. 'It suggests to me they had plenty of time to do it. I shouldn't let you see this but I will as you're more or less involved.'

He turned to his computer and tapped the keyboard with a dexterity surprising for a man with such chubby fingers. 'Take a look at this.'

Henderson wheeled his chair closer to the screen.

'This is the feed from the cameras inside Fenton's last night. There are four in the main part of the shop and one in the storeroom and any one of the shop cameras will show you what went on. For a change, we'll look at camera two.' He pressed a button and a colour image appeared. The picture wasn't bad, lit by the shop's security lights.

A clock on the corner of the screen read 21:40:50 and the seconds clicked by. The video had sound and Henderson could hear the noise of the procession outside, the dull thud of a bass drum and a tune being played by a brass band which he vaguely remembered.

'Any minute now,' Rhodes said.

On cue, the room filled with one, two, three individuals who began in an unhurried manner to smash the glass-covered cabinets with club hammers. It was like watching a group of mime artists, the thump of the hammer blows and the shattering of glass, drowned-out by the band as they walked past outside.

The robbers picked up rings, bracelets and necklace trays and unceremoniously dumped their haul into sport holdalls, before throwing the empty trays back into the cabinet. The three robbers wore black clothing, black balaclavas, and on their hands, surgical gloves.

'As an experienced robbery detective,' the DI said, 'what do you see?'

Rhodes scratched his chin. 'They came well prepared with the right tools, strong bags and dark clothing, suggesting a disciplined crew. They obviously knew about the Bonfire Night procession but then again, who didn't? Our guys are shaking down a list of known felons to find if there's any word on the street. Somebody should know them.'

'You would think so.'

'If you look at them closely, you can see differences. One is tall and skinny and as he comes near the camera, just about now, you can see his skin where the glove ends on his sleeve. He looks dark, maybe Asian.'

'Yes, I see it.'

'Of the other two, one is of average height but solidly built, while the third guy is smaller than him and slight in stature. The movements of the last guy suggest to me he's younger than the other two, maybe a teenager.'

Henderson watched the clock as they filled their bags methodically, without haste. A few minutes later when they all moved out of view, Rhodes said, 'It's all over, the robbers are gone.'

According to the clock on the computer screen, the robbers had been in the shop less than eight minutes and at no time could he hear any sound from inside the shop. Henderson knew exactly where he was at this point, as he could now hear the skirl of the pipes from a Scottish Pipe Band playing in the background.

Henderson sat back in his chair as Rhodes shut down the video. 'What was the haul worth?' Henderson asked.

'Fenton's say it's about eight million, but they're talking retail. Four at warehouse prices would be nearer the mark.'

'Whoa, not a bad reward for a few weeks' planning and less than ten minutes' work.'

'I should say so, but if they don't have contacts in the UK or overseas to get rid of the nicked gear quick, we'll have them. Stuff like this can be hard to sell, and some of the bracelets and rings are unique so they'll be easy to spot unless they're melted down. My advice is keep your eye on sites like eBay, Inspector, and see if you can identify anything. We certainly will.'

TWENTY

'What'll you have Gerry? Same again?'

Gerry Hobbs nodded as he finished the last of his pint. 'Aye I will, same again, Angus.'

He walked to the bar and ordered a pint for Hobbs and a half for himself. Not only did Henderson have the car with him but his name was also on the on-call list. If any major crime went down in the region tonight, he would be the first person Lewes Control would call.

They were in the Basketmakers pub in Gloucester Road, a street in the heart of the North Laines. This part of Brighton was famous for quirky, individual shops, a large comedy venue and a thriving street market every Saturday.

He carried a pint of Fuller ESB and a half of London Pride back to the table. Henderson tipped the half into his pint glass and raised it.

'Here's to the man who is the pin-up boy of all Brighton housewives for saving them from two violent toe-rags.'

'I don't know about pin-up but I'll drink to that,' Hobbs said lifting his glass and taking a gulp. 'Christ, this ESB is strong, either that or I'm out of practice.'

'The latter I suspect. I don't suppose you get out much with two little ones in tow.'

'Not as much as I used to, for sure, and when we do it's to one of these kiddy-friendly places with noisy ball parks and bars serving watery keg beer.'

'Been there and got a milk-stained t-shirt to prove it,' Henderson said with a smile.

'Don't look so smug, Angus, you could be heading there again.'

'How do you mean? Do you know something I don't?'

'Well, the first clue is you and Rachel moving in together.'

'We talked about it before and she said she wasn't ready to start a family. With Hannah and Lewis up in Glasgow, I think I'm done with changing nappies and walking the floor at two in the morning.'

'Women all say they don't want kids until they move in or get married, then it's non-stop hints at every opportunity. Take Catalina. Being Colombian and having a large dose of Latin temperament, I didn't get so much a big hint as an order to drop my kecks when it was the right time of the month.'

Henderson laughed. 'There's never a dull moment in your house.'

'You can say that again. This beer fair makes a job of sloshing through your system. I'm off for a Jimmy Riddle.'

Hobbs, somewhat unsteady on his feet, made his way out from behind the table and headed for the toilet.

Henderson looked around. The Basketmakers was a traditional pub, something of a rarity these days with the conversion of many Sussex pubs into restaurants with bars, and the growth of family friendly places like the ones Hobbs despised. Here, there was wood panelling on the walls, pictures pinned up all around and varnished tables with so many marks and stains, they looked to have been in place since the Queen's coronation in the fifties.

The toilet door swung open and Hobbs made his way towards the table. Seconds later, Henderson's phone rang. He sighed and pulled it out of his pocket.

'DI Henderson.'

'Good evening, sir. Lewes Control here. We've received reports of a firearms incident in Hanover Street, Brighton. One person is believed to have been shot but there is no sign of the gunman.'

Henderson slowly got to his feet.

'Do we know if the gunman is still at the scene?'

'I'm sorry sir, the report doesn't say.'

'Ok. If they haven't already been scrambled, I want an armed response unit, SOCOs and bodies to conduct searches and house-to-house. I want them over there as soon as possible.'

'Got it. Anything else?'

'No. I'm on my way.'

He walked towards Hobbs. 'Gerry there's been a shooting over at Hanover Street. I need to go. I know you're off-duty, but do you want to come with me?'

'You know I want to, but I think I've drunk too much to be much use. I feel quite pissed to tell you the truth.'

'No problem. Do you want a lift to the station?'

'Nah don't bother yourself, it's only up the road. I'll stick around here for another half hour, it's not often I get out for a few beers without the kids.'

'You can drink the rest of mine if you want.'

'Cheers mate, I might do that. Now get off and catch that bloody gunman!'

Henderson had left the car a few blocks away and felt annoyed at paying for three hours and only using one. The council got enough out of him already with a parking permit for the streets around College Place and the Community Charge, he sure didn't want to pay them any more.

Once in the car, he called Walters and told her to meet him there. Early evening traffic on the Steine was light. He joined the Lewes Road and passed St Peter's Church, a mighty grey and brown edifice, closed and dark at this time of night. The building was as large as a cathedral and the shadow and gloom it cast perfectly matched his foreboding mood.

Guns were a perennial problem for UK police forces although their use in crimes far less prominent than in many other industrialised countries. With the exception of some units within the Met and those guarding airports and other important installations, UK police officers did not routinely carry guns either as a sidearm or in their cars. Occasionally, there were calls in the media or by MP's demanding for this to change, most recently over the increased terrorist threat, and as an unarmed officer possibly about to face a gunman, he had to agree.

The response to a firearm incident fell on firearm-trained officers or a dedicated, standby team that responded to armed incidents, like the one he'd asked Lewes Control to scramble. On every call-out, every member of the team knew if they opened fire the incident would be investigated by the Independent Police Complaints Commission, and if the shots resulted in a death, an inquest and possibly a court case resulting in the officer's prosecution. Armed officers walked a very fine line between offering a deterrent and opening fire, one he faced himself a few years back in Glasgow. Then, he shot and killed a known drug dealer, Sean Fagin. He was suspended from duty for the duration of the inquiry and even when exonerated, he decided to move away from Scotland due to the amount of adverse publicity the case received.

He arrived at Hanover Street and despite taking no more than ten minutes to get there, a large crowd had gathered outside one of the houses. On the one hand, their presence could be a hindrance, but on the other, it felt reassuring. People would not be standing there if they knew a gunman was still on the loose. He parked the car some distance away and pushed his way through the crowd to the front. He spotted a uniformed officer stringing up incident tape. He made his way over and showed him his ID.

'DI Henderson, Major Crime Team.'

'Come through sir,' the PC said lifting the tape.

'Who was first on the scene?'

'That would be Constable Haslam. I think he's upstairs,' he said pointing at the house behind him.

He pulled the PC away from the crowd. 'I'm concerned about all these people if there's still a gunman in the vicinity.'

'Oh didn't Control tell you? We've got witnesses

who heard a shot and on looking out of the window, saw two people running out of the building carrying heavy holdalls. They got into a car and drove away.'

'Has anyone ID'd the car?'

'No sir, not yet.'

Hanover Street was long and narrow, the houses on either side of the road two storey terraces. A few had installed rooms in the roof making him think it would be an area where singles and young couples would live until kids came along, before making a move to somewhere bigger. The house he headed towards looked a dirty shade of white with small square windows and an untidy garden, similar in design to the houses on either side. There was enough light to see the wooden frames of the windows were rotted and in need of replacement, and the area of neglect extended to the inside of the house with a cheap, dirty carpet in the entrance hall.

'Constable Haslam!' Henderson shouted from the foot of the stairs.

'What are you playing at, Mackie, you Scottish twat? You know I'm up here. Come up and feast your peepers on what I've found.'

Henderson climbed the stairs and on reaching the top, came to a halt when he saw the body. Behind it, a constable sitting on the floor looking at something he held in his hand.

'It's not PC Mackie, Haslam, it's DI Henderson.' He then spotted what the constable had been looking at and raised his voice. 'What the hell are you doing handling what could turn out to be crucial evidence? Put it down!'

Haslam scrambled to his feet and dropped the offending article. 'Sir... sorry sir... I was only...'

'What happened here?'

Henderson walked up to the body and bent down and felt for a pulse. 'Have you checked this person for signs of life?'

PC Haslam pulled out his notebook, his hands shaking. 'We received a call of a shooting at 21:27. We approached the area carefully and talked to eyewitnesses. When they told us they saw the gunmen drive off, we entered the house and found the victim lying here. I checked for any signs of life but I couldn't find any. I believe he's dead. I was about to leave the scene for the SOCO boys when the item there,' he said nodding at what he dropped on the carpet, 'caught my eye.'

'What is it?'

He made to pick it up.

'Leave it,' Henderson said. 'Just tell me.'

'Sorry sir, I didn't mean...It's a woman's watch. Very expensive, it looks.'

'Haslam, go downstairs and help your colleagues set up a perimeter around this place and don't let me catch you touching vital evidence again.'

'Yes sir,' he said. Grateful for the dismissal, he rushed past and clumped his way downstairs.

Henderson attended to the body and felt for a pulse in his neck. He could see without further checks that he was dead: no movement, a pallid colour on the skin and a copious amount of blood pooled around him. Henderson eased the frame of the victim slightly to get a better view of the victim's face and almost fell backwards in surprise when he recognised him; Guy Barton.

'Bloody hell!' the DI hissed. On a list of people he expected to see in a situation like this, Guy Barton would be found near the bottom.

He had a bullet wound to the upper chest, which must have severed a main artery as he'd lost a lot of blood.

'Guv! Are you up there?' the voice of Carol Walters shouted.

'Yes, come on up!'

'Evening sir. How did your drink with the jubilant Gerry Hobbs go?'

'Cut short. I left Gerry in the pub, happy to be around grown-ups for a change.'

'Ha, ha. He should...my God, all this blood! What happened here?'

'Neighbours heard shots and saw a car driving away with two occupants inside.'

'Do we know anything about him?'

'You'll never believe who it is.'

'Who?'

'A man whose mug shot has been staring out from our whiteboard for the last few weeks: Guy Barton.'

She bent down for a closer look. 'Christ, so it is. I took him for a rough diamond, but not someone who hangs around with gun-toting scum-bags.'

'Are Grafton or the SOCOs here yet?'

'I didn't see the SOCOs but I saw Grafton's car pull up. He'll be here in a minute.'

'Good. Go and take a look in there,' Henderson said indicating the bedroom in front of him. 'The

177

copper who reached the scene first spotted a watch which he foolishly lifted.'

'Tut, tut. Knowing our luck, it will be the only one handled by the killer.'

Henderson snorted

She stepped over him and the inert form of Guy Barton in the hall and walked into the bedroom. She removed a pen from her pocket and used it to lift the watch dropped by the penitent copper.

'Looks expensive.' She moved closer to let Henderson see.

'It does. Bag it.'

She did so and looked around. 'There's some other stuff here.' She bagged two rings discovered on the floor and an earring in the cupboard. 'Is it too much of a coincidence that we had a jewel robbery in Lewes a couple of days ago and here we find a dead man with jewellery lying beside him?'

'I'm thinking the same thing,' Henderson said as he stood. 'When I first saw him, I thought 'drugs', but now I'm not so sure, although the gunshot wound doesn't square with the video I saw of our jewellery robbers.'

'Good evening Detective Inspector Henderson, Sergeant Walters.'

He turned to see the pathologist at one end of the small hallway. 'Good evening Grafton. You don't look too happy to be here tonight.'

'I'm not. It's been a hell of a week, what with a jumper in Hove and a body found in Churchill Square. I was looking forward to an early night and no additional bodies to clog up my mortuary.'

'This one shouldn't keep you long. We know the approximate time of death as neighbours heard a shot, and we know his identity.'

'Someone from your burning man case?'

'Good guess.'

'It comes with working with the police for so long.'

'Detective Inspector Henderson!' a voice called from downstairs.

'Excuse me Grafton,' Henderson said, squeezing past the pathologist in the narrow hallway.

Henderson made his way to the top of the stairs and looking down, saw the PC he had been talking to earlier stringing up crime tape. 'Yes, what is it, constable?'

'We've got a witness, sir. Someone's ID'd the gunmen's car.'

TWENTY-ONE

Henderson drove back to Lewes and parked a few streets away from St John's Terrace as he couldn't find a space close by. He'd left Walters at the crime scene to organise a fingertip search of the surrounding area and interview witnesses. With the help of Phil Bentley back at the office, a team had been set up to find the car used by the killers.

Their car witness was a lad called Daniel, the fifteen-year-old son of the neighbourhood nosey parker who was sitting close to the window when she noticed two men running towards a car and carrying heavy holdalls. Daniel was autistic with a great memory for remembering all sorts of stuff and they now knew the car to be a dark green or grey Vauxhall Vectra, with a registration number starting with BX57. Daniel apologised more than once for not providing the full reg, but the licence plate was dirty and the low wattage street lights used by the council to reduce costs made it hard for him to see it properly.

Henderson and DC Sally Graham got out of the car and walked towards St John's Terrace. He'd alerted the Family Liaison Unit and they were sending someone over, but if the FLO reached the Barton house before they did, they were instructed to wait for the detectives. In any event, he saw no one standing outside the house when they arrived so he climbed the steps and pressed the bell.

The door opened and no surprise, Lily Barton was standing there. What did come as a surprise was the effect she had on him. Even without make-up and wearing jogging pants and a sweatshirt, she looked beautiful. He chastised himself for having incongruous thoughts at such an inopportune moment.

'Oh, it's you, Detective Henderson,' she said. 'I thought it was Guy forgetting his keys again.'

'Sorry to disappoint.'

'I meant...It doesn't matter. You'd better come in.'

She led them into the lounge. 'Take a seat.'

'Thanks.'

'I've just been reading this new book by CJ Sansom,' Lily said holding it up. 'It's historical fiction, the kind of thing I read when I'm not working. Do you read much, Inspector?'

'No, I don't, not as much as I'd like. When I get wrapped up in a case like this, there isn't the time.'

'I understand. Can I get you both anything? Tea, coffee?'

'No thank you, Lily,' Henderson said. 'Could you please sit down? I'm sorry to say, I'm here with some bad news.'

'Don't you think I've heard enough for one year?' she said, as she took a seat in the chair opposite.

'Yes, I do, but earlier this evening your husband, Guy, was found at a house in Brighton with a fatal gunshot wound.'

Her face crumpled. 'I can't believe it; guns?

Where? When?'

'At a house in Hanover Street in Brighton, less than an hour ago.'

She started sobbing; deep chest-racking sobs, causing her upper body to shake violently. He couldn't stand to watch the poor woman fall apart in this way and he nudged Sally Graham. She walked over, sat on the edge of her chair and put her arm around her.

'I'll make us a cup of tea,' he said rising from the settee and leaving the room.

He leaned against the kitchen units while the kettle boiled. In the list of the many jobs he undertook, this one was at the shitty end of the stick and affected him more than seeing a dead body. Here were real people with busy lives, being forced to come to terms with a level of grief that often put the brakes on their world, while the rest of it continued to turn as if nothing had happened.

Since leaving Hanover Street, he'd been thinking hard about Guy's murder. He didn't intend saying much more to Lily tonight, but it looked to him like an argument gone wrong and not a drugs or stolen goods deal that had turned sour. His reasoning was based on the way Guy died.

The victim had been felled by a single shot. Not an assassin's double-tap to the skull or a drug-dealer's manic spray from an Uzi, but a single bullet to the chest. It was an area of the body not noted for instant death unless the heart or a main artery is pierced. In addition, they found the victim upstairs, near the door of a bedroom, giving the murder scene the aura of a domestic argument, and suggesting the shooter took a quick shot, or didn't intend to kill.

He returned to the lounge with three cups of tea, two sugarless and the other with four spoonfuls for Lily. Henderson had been so deep in thought, or the kettle so loud, he didn't hear the arrival of the FLO, Helen Vincent, now sitting on the arm of Lily's chair comforting her.

'Hello there, Helen. I didn't hear you come in.'

'Evening sir. I'm surprised as my husband says I walk with all the finesse of an elephant.'

He smiled. 'Would you like a cup of tea? There's more in the pot.'

'Oh yes, please.'

He handed out the cups and walked back into the kitchen to fetch another. When everyone was sorted and slurping tea self-consciously, he took a seat on the settee and looked at Lily, awaiting the inevitable questions, or perhaps being able to ask a few of his own.

'Who...do you know who shot him, Inspector?'

'I don't have a name yet, but two men were spotted fleeing the scene not long after the shooting. I'm confident we'll find out who they are soon. Where did Guy say he was going tonight?'

'He didn't. We haven't been talking much for the last few weeks; he often went out without telling me.'

She began sobbing again, quietly this time with Helen saying soothing words and gently rubbing her back.

A minute or so later Henderson tried again. 'Do you know if Guy hung around with criminals or unsavoury characters?'

'Other than the people he worked with at the council, you mean? He used to say they were all crooks,' she said with a wan smile. She paused for a moment, thinking. 'I suppose you could class his friend Ajay as an unsavoury character. I certainly don't like him.'

'Ajay?'

'Ajay Singh. He's a bloke Guy has known since his days at Varndean School. He's done time for thieving cars and such, hence the reason I didn't like Guy associating with him. Guy's moved on but Ajay hasn't.'

'Do you know where he lives?'

'This is the problem. He's never settled down. He lived with his mum somewhere in Patcham, but after being thrown out I think he's been staying with various brothers and cousins.'

'Is there anyone else you can think of? Someone who might wish your husband harm?'

'Apart from me, you mean, for letting himself become involved in something above his head.' She started to cry again.

Henderson looked at Graham who seemed to be in agreement with him. They both stood. 'We'll leave you in Helen's capable hands now, Mrs Barton. We'll see ourselves out.'

He turned and walked to the door.

'Wait a second,' Lily Barton said as she extricated herself with some difficulty from the seat. She came up to him, handkerchief in hand, her eyes red and raw.

'Thank you for coming here and telling me this so quickly,' she said. 'I know it can't be easy for you either.' She reached over and kissed him on the cheek. 'You're a good man, Inspector Henderson. Thank you.'

**

Henderson dropped Sally Graham off at her flat in Queen's Park and headed home. It was after midnight when he called DS Walters, still at the scene in Hanover Street, but beginning to pack up, and most of the forensics team were doing the same. Henderson didn't have a problem with them wrapping up only a few hours after arriving there, as given what they knew now, a fingertip search of surrounding areas was unlikely to reveal better clues than they found in the house. Door-to-door enquiries had done sterling work in finding their star witness, Daniel.

He was now in possession of fingerprint and DNA samples, the car registration plate and Ajay Singh's name. Unless the killer or killers were heading to the Continent or had good underworld contacts willing to hide them, he felt confident they would be in custody within the next few days.

In his head, he was clear about the way the murder investigation would progress, but utterly confused as to why anyone would target Guy Barton. With her lover burned to death and now her husband gunned down, a sane man would start to believe some kind of macabre vendetta was being targeted at Lily Barton. For the life of him, he couldn't imagine why, as he believed her to be one of the nicest and sweetest women he had ever met.

He arrived home and, as expected, Rachel was in bed. He didn't feel tired so he went into the cupboard under the stairs and pulled out a bottle of Adnams Ghost Ship, a beer recommended to him by Harry Wallop, their resident expert on all things East Anglian. He selected a glass from the draining board and walked into the lounge.

Rachel had obviously been using the fire earlier as the room still felt warm. He took a seat on the settee, poured the beer and picked up a pad and pen. There were several of each lying around the house, not surprising for a place inhabited by a journalist and a murder detective, both of whom liked to sketch out ideas, concepts or mind maps whenever the notion took them.

At first he outlined the steps necessary to catch Guy Barton's killers. The more he considered it, the more it reinforced his view the killing didn't bear the hallmarks of a deliberate hit, but a dispute gone wrong. The search would focus on finding two desperate criminals not two big-time shooters. He would fast-track the DNA samples discovered in the house tonight, research Ajay Singh and shake-down his known haunts, and be ready to respond to an ANPR, Automatic Number Plate Recognition system, sighting of the car once they discovered its full registration number.

He then wrote, 'Why?' He knew *how* Guy Barton died but didn't know *why*. Did the presence of the jewellery in the Hanover Street bedroom indicate his involvement in the robbery at Fenton's, and if so, did he fall out with his fellow robbers when it came to dividing the spoils? Or, maybe he knew the robbers and went to the house to blackmail them.

Many scenarios looked possible, but the DI couldn't see past the council planning official married to a woman who published romance novels. Guy Barton possessed a rough streak for sure, but it would be a huge leap to believing such an individual was capable of murdering Marc Emerson and then staging an audacious jewellery heist. If true, he was a serious criminal masquerading as a Local Government Official, and not the other way round.

The Emerson killing could be rationalised as a crime of passion, done in a fit of jealousy when Guy discovered Marc was still having an affair with his wife, even if his method of dispatch came from the pages of a horror novel. If true, Henderson had not only lost his prime suspect, but the Marc Emerson case was now closed. He should now feel the sweet taste of success, a bright light shining at the end of the tunnel, but he didn't.

Could this be because it was late at night, at the close of what had been a difficult and tiring day, or because he didn't believe Marc Emerson's killer was now lying in Brighton Mortuary?

TWENTY-TWO

Henderson yawned before pulling open one of the double doors leading to his floor. He'd got to bed at two last night, and in the past, the alarm going off at six rarely fazed him. Today it had, perhaps the first signs of getting old.

He entered his office and switched on the lights. He turned and headed for the Brew Room for a coffee, as tea at breakfast had done little to pep him up this morning, when DS Edwards appeared in the office doorway.

'Morning Angus.'

'Ah, morning, ma'am.'

'I heard the good news... well the good and the bad news, if you catch my drift.'

Henderson leaned on the edge of his desk. He didn't sit down; maybe his boss would take the hint and realise he wanted to be somewhere else.

'Yes, it's a two-edged sword,' he said. 'We've lost our main suspect so we don't have the luxury of re-interviewing him, but at the same time, the clues left behind at Hanover Street will go a long way in helping us solve the Fenton's jewellery robbery.'

'I didn't know this. I was talking about Guy Barton's murder and the loss of suspect number one in the Marc Emerson case. How does it impact the jewellery robbery?'

'Can we do this on our way to the coffee machine? I was heading there when you came in.'

'Sure, I could do with one myself.'

On the way, he explained about finding jewellery at the murder scene, close to Guy Barton's body. 'There's nothing to connect it to the Lewes jewellery robbery as yet, but we've put a request into the Robbery Squad for a list of all the items taken from Fenton's.'

'It sounds like a good lead,' she said, 'pieces of jewellery scattered over the bedroom floor and the killers seen fleeing with heavy holdalls.'

'I think so too. Milk no sugar?'

'Yes. I'm meeting the ACC this afternoon, I'll give him the good news.'

'I would temper the 'Marc Emerson's killer found dead' side of the story for the moment.'

'What do you mean? He is, isn't he?'

'We didn't take things that far. Guy Barton is, was, a strong suspect, for sure, but one with a good alibi that we've been trying to unpick ever since without much success.'

'Hang on a sec. I came down here thinking one murder had been solved, and now you're telling me it's not, and in fact we now have another one to add to it. It doesn't sound much like a good news story to me.'

'Put it this way, we've found more clues about the jewellery robbery in one night than a couple of weeks' work into Marc Emerson's murder.'

She placed her coffee down, untouched. 'I'll have to tell the ACC we're expecting a quick result on the jewellery robbery and Barton's murder, and see if it'll placate him, but if we don't nab them soon,' she said wagging a finger at him, 'there'll be hell to pay and no mistake.' She turned and walked out.

Henderson strolled back to his office, his mind more on the restorative effects of his beverage than Edwards' threats. He worked until eight-thirty before heading into the Detectives' Room for the morning team briefing. By the time everyone had assembled, he'd wiped one of the whiteboards clean and headed it up, 'Guy Barton.'

'Last night, for those who don't know,' Henderson said, 'Guy Barton, our prime suspect in the Marc Emerson murder enquiry, was found dead at a house in Hanover Street, Brighton. He died from a single bullet wound to the chest. Two people were spotted running from the house carrying sports holdalls and they are now our main suspects for his murder.'

'I got angry with a planning official once when he turned down the extension for my kitchen,' Harry Wallop said, 'but this takes the biscuit.'

'If everyone did that, they'd be dropping like flies in our street,' Phil Bentley said, 'my neighbours are always having work done.'

'We have two good leads,' Henderson said. 'As I go through them, Carol, please feel free to add any new information you might have.'

'Will do.'

Henderson paused to take a drink from his coffee mug, the second of the day. For some strange reason, it never tasted as good as the first. Perhaps some university don could conduct a research study and find out why, but knowing the amount of useless studies that came out of many universities, it wouldn't be a surprise to find that such a thing had already been done.

'The first lead we have is jewellery found in a bedroom at Hanover Street. A list of jewellery stolen from Fenton's on Saturday night has been requested from the Robbery Squad and I want you, Sally, to see if any item recovered from Hanover Street matches anything on that list.'

'Yes sir.'

'Also, have the larger items fingerprinted, but you'll need to eliminate the big mitts of a PC on the ladies watch as I saw the idiot handling it. Carol, did you take Haslam's prints last night?'

'Yep, I did.'

'Liaise with Carol after this meeting, Sally.'

'Will do.'

'Phil, how are you getting on with the hunt for their car?'

'The DVA came up with zilch when we gave them Ajay Singh's name so the car we're looking for doesn't belong to him. We then did a search of all the Vauxhall Vectras in the area with a prefix BX57. There are hundreds, but by eliminating all the light colours, we've cut it down substantially. We've split that list into two smaller lists, one dark green and the other the remaining dark colours. The dark green list is 55 cars and this has been sent to the DVLA to expand reg numbers and give us the addresses of the owners and then it's down to the door-to-door team.'

'And if you don't find a match,' Henderson said, 'I

assume you'll move on to your list of dark coloured cars?'

'Yes sir.'

'And if there's still no match, expand the geographic range?'

'Yep. The second strand of the investigation is to look through CCTV pictures on the night of the murder. Not knowing the suspects escape route is a big hindrance but we're slowly digging our way through them.'

'Keep on it Phil. We need that number.'

'Yes, sir.'

'Carol, did I miss anything?'

'You mentioned the jewellery. I spotted a few bits with a cursory search, but SOCOs found more in the house and some in the garden. Unless someone accidentally upended a woman's jewellery box, I wouldn't be surprised to find the pieces we have match the stuff taken from Fenton's.'

'Or another robbery,' Harry Wallop said.

'Could be,' Walters said. 'The door-to-door around Hanover Street didn't uncover much more than our car witness, but SOCOs discovered plenty of prints around the house and our analysts over there,' she said pointing across the office, 'are banging them into the system. I think everybody knows but I'll mention it anyway, we found Ajay Singh's prints all over the house. Last night, we only had Mrs Barton's suspicions that Guy was involved with Singh, we now know both men were in that house.'

'What do we know about Singh?'

'Petty criminal, small-time drug dealer. He's done

time for receiving stolen property and selling class C drugs. Not a hardened criminal by any stretch, but a persistent offender.'

'Dig out his last known address, his mother's address and any other addresses we can find for him and get uniform to start knocking on doors. At every address they visit, they are to ask for the addresses of his numerous relatives as he and his associate could be holed up in any one of them.'

'Yes, sir.'

'Anything else?' he asked.

'Nope.'

'Harry, call DS Steven Rhodes in the Robbery Squad and find out how they're getting on in their search for the robbers. Don't say anything yet to them about Guy Barton's murder, but if our investigations uncover some information about the robbery, such as Sally being able to match one of our pieces to Fenton's list, I want you to keep them informed. I don't want them thinking they've being side-lined and making a complaint to the ACC. Ok?'

'Right boss.'

'Anything else? No? We'll meet again at six this evening. Hopefully we'll have something more by then.'

Henderson returned to his office and picked up the phone. He dialled the number of Helen Vincent, the FLO assigned to Lily Barton.

'Hello Helen, how are you?'

'I'm a bit bored to tell you the truth. In cases where there's a house full of kids, I spend my time playing games with them or running round the garden, but of course here at the Barton's place there's only Lily.'

'How is she?'

'Morose, tearful, unable to concentrate; not an unexpected reaction after receiving a double-dose of bad news, in my view.'

'I understand. Where is she?'

'In the kitchen pottering. I'm out in the back garden having a cigarette so she can't hear me.'

'There's something I'd like you to do for me. I can't get over the odds against Lily losing a lover and a husband, the two people closest to her, in the space of a few weeks.'

'It does seem like awfully bad luck.'

'What if it has nothing to do with luck? What if it's deliberate?'

'Like a curse or someone who might be carrying out a vendetta against her?'

'Forget the curse. I don't believe in magic, but I'm considering the idea of a vendetta. I'm only flagging it as a possibility, a small one if I'm being honest, but I think we need to consider it.'

'I suppose you do, in the circumstances.'

'See if you can find any information lying around to support this theory. I'm thinking about death threats, stalking texts or emails, a hate campaign on social media, anything like that. Alternatively, you could ask Lily in some diplomatic way if someone or something is bothering her, that is if she's up for some gentle questioning.'

'I doubt it at the moment. She's taking this really hard.'

'How do you mean?'

'She spends long periods in bed or in her room, when she comes downstairs her eyes are red from crying and if I say something wrong, she runs off in floods of tears.'

'It can't be easy losing your husband in such a cruel fashion.'

'That's what I thought, but if I'm being honest, she talks more about Marc than Guy.'

'Really?'

'Yeah, just the odd slip, but it's my job to notice these things.'

'Is she planning to return to work soon?'

'She's not in a fit state, although getting back to some form of normality often helps people in this situation stay on the rails, if you know what I mean. I think she told her office she would be taking the rest of the week off.'

'Probably for the best. Thanks for all your help Helen. I know this is not one of your usual assignments but I'm sure you can see how this case is different.'

'You can say that again.'

'I'll call you in a day or so to see how you're getting on, but feel free to contact me anytime, ok?'

'Right sir, no problem. Thanks.'

TWENTY-THREE

'What do you fancy doing this morning, Lily?' Helen asked.

Lily put the mug in her hand down on the kitchen table. 'I think I'd like to go out, get away from the house for a while. I feel I've been cooped up here too long.'

'Sounds fine to me. What's your weakness, a touch of retail therapy or a stroll in the country?'

She thought for a moment. 'Let's go into Brighton. We can mooch around the shops for a time and then take a walk along the seafront. That should blow the cobwebs off.'

'No problem. If I let you have some time to yourself, say in about fifteen minutes? I need to make a few calls first.'

'Sure.'

Lily re-took her seat at the kitchen table with a refilled mug of tea while Helen busied herself doing what FLOs did: stacked the dishwasher, wiped the surfaces clean and went into the small study beside the loo, where she kept her stuff.

Lily didn't mind her presence. At first, on hearing about Guy's death, she wanted to be alone, but she realised she often spent time by herself: when reading book drafts, watching TV when Guy went out and when travelling to and from work on the train. It felt strange at first, having someone else in the house, but she soon got used to it, and brought back memories of her time at university when she shared a house with four other girls.

When DI Henderson first told her about Guy's death, she thought the detective was mistaken, he must have died in a car accident or something else. Guns and Guy didn't make sense in the same sentence. Guy's father had been a wide boy and was forever goading his son to do something adventurous, but she understood such comments to mean that he should start his own business, not get into gun fights with a bunch of criminals.

The newspapers were being cagey about the case and suggesting a drug deal gone wrong, but Henderson reassured her, through Helen, that no drugs were involved. The DI believed it to be connected to the jewellery robbery at Fenton's in Lewes on Bonfire Night.

Not only could she not get her head around Guy associating with criminals, but breaking into a jewellery shop did not compute. An off-license or a bank maybe, as he understood booze and money, not a jewellery shop as Guy knew nothing. He'd never bought her jewellery as a Christmas or birthday present, nor did she wear much beyond the basics; she didn't crave or ask him for a bigger engagement ring or a more expensive necklace. She had once seen a gorgeous bracelet in Fenton's but even though she could afford the ten grand price, when would she ever get the chance to wear it?

She looked up from the table to find Helen standing there, kitted out in a warm jacket, hat and gloves. She stood, a little confused as to where all the time had gone, and walked into the hall to do the same.

While driving into Brighton, Helen chatted about her family, talking mostly about her two children, Alice and Louise, and avoiding saying anything about her husband, Keith, for obvious reasons. If Lily was in work mode, which she wasn't, she might have inquired more about him to see how the FLO responded, but not today.

She did this frequently when reviewing early drafts of a book. She would stop reading and ask herself, what would the character do now? She would then continue reading and compare the two outcomes. It was the best way to determine if a scene was credible, otherwise it would pull a reader up short and spoil their enjoyment of the story.

They parked in the Churchill Square car park but Lily didn't last more than fifteen minutes in the shopping centre before the crowds, noise and the glittering shop windows overwhelmed her senses. They headed outside and walked down West Street, towards the seafront. A piercing, cold wind whipped up the street and to add to the winter gloom, the sea looked choppy and gun-metal grey.

They turned the corner into the Esplanade and both women were pushed backwards by the strength of the gust.

'Well, you wanted to blow the cobwebs away, Lily,' Helen said as they waited to cross the road at the pedestrian crossing, her hair moving around like a nest of snakes.

'I thought you meant something more sedate than this,' she said with a smile. It felt uncomfortable and chilled her to the bone but in a way, she enjoyed it.

On reaching the other side of the road, they walked to the railings overlooking the beach and stopped to look and see if anyone was stupid enough to be near the water on a day like this. To their surprise, an elderly couple were throwing a stick into the sea for their Red Setter to retrieve, and a windsurfer was doing something to his board before venturing out. Lily didn't know much about dogs, but going anywhere near the water at this time of year would give anyone a heart attack.

A few minutes later they walked in the direction of the Palace Pier.

'Can I ask you something, Lily?'

'Sounds ominous.'

'Not really. With the death of Guy and Marc, have you ever considered it might be someone targeting you?'

Lily stopped walking and stared at her, her mind confused.

'You can't be serious?'

'We're the police, Lily, we have to look at every angle.'

'I suppose you do but I'm nobody. I work for a book company. Words such as 'enemies' and 'revenge' don't go with the territory.'

'I understand, but I've read some horror and crime novels in my time and some of these guys have pretty warped imaginations.'

They resumed walking.

'They do, and some of my authors can be just as bad, but a woman plotting to steal another woman's man is as vicious as it gets.'

'So, you never had any trouble with authors when you turned down one of their books or you refused to go to their book launch or something?'

Lily thought for a moment.

'There was one guy, a big, hairy fellow who wrote historical romance fiction. I'll call him Alan. He'd been very successful over many years, won all sorts of awards and sold over half a million books. One day, he told us he wanted to write a science fiction book and naturally, we counselled him against it. He insisted and threatened never to write another romance novel if we didn't agree.'

'He sounds a nightmare.'

'He was, but we relented and he wrote the book. To no one's surprise, it tanked under a volley of critical reviews and sneering blog posts. Suitably chastised, he returned to the fold and began to write historical romance novels again, but the spark had gone. Two duds later, we cancelled his contract.'

'Not a happy bunny, I suspect.'

'No, and he came back the day after receiving the termination letter making threats to kill me and some of my staff, and shouting that he would burn the place down. Security threw him out and, last I heard, he'd started his own publishing company.'

'Did you receive other threats or hate mail?'

She shook her head. 'No, nothing. I think he'd been

drinking all morning to give him the courage to see me and the disappointment of being dropped overwhelmed him.'

'Did anyone else give you a hard time?'

'No. If think you'll find Marc or Guy's killer in the book business, in my opinion you're barking up the wrong tree.'

**

Lily and Helen returned to St John's Terrace late afternoon. Lily resumed her seat at the kitchen table, this time with a mug of coffee instead of tea, and a copy of today's *Argus* in front of her. Helen had disappeared into the study to write her report, or whatever work an FLO needed to do, leaving the house quiet, just the way Lily liked it.

She ignored the news articles on the front and inside pages and went in search of human interest stories. She began reading an article about a woman in Rusper whose car had been hit by a falling tree whilst driving, when the doorbell sounded.

She opened it and was surprised to find Kevin McLaren standing there.

'Hello Lily.'

'Hello Kevin. You better come in, it's freezing outside.'

She closed the door. 'Go into the kitchen. I'm in there reading the paper.'

She followed him in where he took the seat beside hers, marked out with a dirty mug and the spread-out newspaper.

'Would you like a coffee? I'm making another for myself.'

'Yes, I will thanks. If it's not too much bother.'

'It's no trouble. So what brings you here? I don't think I've seen you for a while.'

'Eh, no I haven't been around much what with the procession and all the clear-up afterwards. I came by to see how you're doing.'

She turned to the coffee machine. 'What do you fancy?'

'Same as you're having is fine for me.'

She didn't know Kevin well, but as a friend of Marc, she accepted him as such. He never seemed to have a girlfriend so they didn't go out on a foursome, but she often saw him when she went around to Marc's house. Occasionally, the three of them would go out, usually to something Marc and Kevin were interested in, but she didn't like him being there as the boys would hog the conversation, leaving her feeling isolated. Lately, she had become wary of him. Nothing serious, but looks from him that lingered too long and questions to Marc about her when she wasn't around.

'There you go,' she said a few minutes later. 'It might not be as good as Costa, but I won't charge you a penny, and think of all the calories you save by not having a rocky road or a chocolate muffin.' She tried to sound light and jolly, but it came out flat as if reading from a script.

'My arteries are grateful,' he said, raising the mug in salute. 'Thank you.'

He nodded at the newspaper. 'Is there anything in

there about Marc or Guy?'

She sighed as she sat down opposite. 'Nothing about Marc, and an article about Guy says the police are following up leads.'

'The usual.'

She leaned forward, keeping her voice low so Helen wouldn't hear. 'Yes, but I understand the police are now on to something. It sounds to me more than just a lead.'

'I hope so. It must be awful for you.'

'It is.' She couldn't help it; a wave of grief washed over her, crumbling all vestiges of normality and leaving her sobbing. She cried for Marc, for all the years they wouldn't share together, and for Guy, for not saying goodbye on more amicable terms.

She felt an arm around her shoulders, and thinking it was Helen, she didn't stir, wallowing in her own grief. When a face began to nuzzle into her neck, she opened her eyes in alarm and found Kevin there.

'Kevin!' she said pushing her chair back. 'What the hell do you think you're doing?'

'Don't be like that, Lily. I love you, I always have.'

She stood, her head in a spin. He took her in his arms but when she tried to pull away she couldn't, he was too strong.

'Kevin! Stop this at once.'

He bent down to kiss her but she moved her head to the side. 'Both Guy and Marc are gone Lily, let me look after you.'

'Let me go Kevin, at once!'

'I can't, Lily, I want you so much. Ever since that day at the races with you and Marc. I can't get you out of my head.'

'Let me go!'

He tried to kiss her again. This time with more success as her arms felt tired.

'What the hell's going on here?'

Lily and Kevin both turned to see Helen Vincent standing in the doorway. She had her hands on her hips and a look on her face that didn't suggest a sympathetic FLO, more a stern copper.

TWENTY-FOUR

On Tuesday morning, DI Henderson didn't go straight to the office but instead turned into Hanover Street. The street activity of the previous day had gone; no crowds of rubberneckers, TV cameras, reporters and only one police vehicle. It belonged to the SOCO team and after speaking to Pat Davidson, the Crime Scene manager, even they were pulling out mid-morning.

He got out of his car and looked around. It didn't look a bad place for a gang of jewellery robbers to hole up as much of the population in areas like this were transient, new entrants on the housing ladder only staying a few years, or houses let to students. The sight of guys carrying holdalls wouldn't be deemed unusual, nor their comings and goings at odd times of the day or night.

The house the SOCOs were examining belonged to Manish Johar, a cousin of Ajay Singh, but Johar didn't attract the DI's interest, he was on holiday in India where he'd been for the last few weeks. Analysing the fingerprints found all over the house, two people had been staying in the house, Ajay Singh and a man called Solomon Fletcher, both with criminal records. Less evident were the fingerprints of Guy Barton, suggesting he didn't stay there, corroborating what Lily had told them, but nevertheless an occasional visitor.

Henderson walked into the house, nodding at the constable on the door.

'Morning, sir,' voices chorused from the kitchen.

'Morning guys. Last day?'

'Yep,' Pat Davidson said. 'I'll be glad to get away from this place. What a shit hole. I don't think the house has ever been dusted or the bathrooms cleaned for months.'

'Bad as that?'

'Makes our job a nightmare. We have to dig through all the muck to get to what we need.'

Henderson carefully avoided all the packed cases in the hall, aluminium framed and containing all the team's detection instruments, chemicals, sprays and vials of collected material. They were solid to prevent the breakage of any materials inside but painful on the shins of the unwary. He climbed the stairs.

Pat could moan about the job like an old fishwife, as his mother used to say, but in only a couple of days since the murder, and with SOCOs help, they'd identified two suspects. Henderson felt confident they were on the right track as Singh's mother confirmed his friendship with Solomon Fletcher and Fletcher's mother did likewise. If the same progress could be made in the Marc Emerson case, his killer would now be awaiting trial. They also were convinced Singh, Solomon and Barton had robbed Fenton's. Jewellery found in the house matched items stolen from the shop and he'd viewed the robbery video again and felt sure he could see Barton's frame underneath the balaclava and dark clothing. Lily confirmed he had been out all night.

Henderson reached the top of the stairs. Guy's body had been removed but it didn't take a detective to understand what had happened here due to the large blood stain on the carpet. The P-M told them the victim didn't die straight away. The bullet, fired from a sitting position in an upward trajectory, pierced his lung, causing him to fall to the floor, where he slowly drowned in his own blood.

He'd come to the house this morning to try and understand more about the shooting. It would become an important point when Singh and Solomon were apprehended, as with two suspects in the house at the time of the murder, one might accuse the other of being the shooter. He planned to come to a definite conclusion today and when questioning both men, he would ask them to reveal their whereabouts at the fatal moment. From their answer, he would know who had fired the shot.

He remembered exactly where Guy fell, but if a reminder was needed, he had a photograph of the scene in his pocket. Due to the constraints of a small house, he was standing in a narrow hallway with a wall to his right and a closed bedroom door on the left, facing the bedroom where he believed the jewellery stolen from Fenton's had been stored. This offered two choices. The gunman had either been sitting inside the bedroom, or kneeling in the place where he was now stood in the hall.

The gun had been fired from a low position and from close range, a distance of no more than a metre and a half. He could see now the staircase was at least three metres from the body and his idea of someone firing as they stood on the second or third top step, leaning around the banister post to do so, didn't wash.

This left a couple of possibilities. The gunman might have been crouching in the hall, which seemed an odd thing to do, or his favoured option, sitting in the bedroom. He stepped into the bedroom and turned to face the position where Guy might have stood. From a sitting position, it all became clear in his mind. Singh or Solomon and Guy had taken the jewellery holdalls out of the cupboard and were looking through them. After a time, Guy got up to go, an altercation ensued and the person sitting in the position he was now, pulled out a gun and shot him.

All the pieces slotted together. Holding an imaginary gun, he gauged the distance between gun and victim, the trajectory of the shot, the positions of the fallen items of jewellery, Guy's body; it all matched up. He was convinced.

The question remained: why? What made Singh or Solomon take out a gun and kill their friend and one of their fellow robbers on the Fenton raid? Did he threaten to tell someone, or did he want to get out of the deal as it was becoming too dangerous?

Henderson said goodbye to the SOCO team and walked back to his car. He got in, closed the door and started the engine, trying to generate some heat. His deliberations this morning would help identify the shooter and ensure Guy Barton's killer went down for murder, a better result than never finding out who was responsible and both men being sentenced for murder under the laws of joint enterprise.

He called Walters and explained his findings.

'Excellent, all we need to do now is nab them.'

'How's the research going?'

'We've got the reg of the car.'

'Fantastic! How did you find it?'

'Phil Bentley picked the car up from a camera in the Steine. It is a green Vauxhall Vectra as our witness thought and it's registered to a cousin of Ajay Singh. We've put it up on ANPR.'

'Any response?'

'None yet.'

'With the car on the system and officers knocking on the doors of relatives and friends of Singh and Solomon, it's only a matter of time.'

**

The afternoon dragged by in a monotonous fug. It was the worst part of being a DI, waiting for a result to emerge, and not able to go out there and make things happen himself. Henderson ploughed through paperwork that relentlessly appeared in his in-tray with the alacrity of a virulent disease, regardless of his involvement in a big case or not. During a murder enquiry, it would be overtime sheets, claims for damaged clothes, car insurance claims and complaints from the public, and in the hiatus between cases, invites to seminars, committee reports, Home Office diktats and expense forms.

He had been about to append his signature to yet another form when his phone rang. He reached for it with undue haste, thankful for the interruption.

'Afternoon Angus, it's Steve Rhodes, Robbery Squad.'

'Afternoon Steve, how's it going with Fenton's? Anybody in the frame yet?'

'No, not a dicky. It doesn't help when CCTV shows bugger-all and the perps are all wearing gloves and balaclavas.'

'It's not what you call playing fair.'

'Why I called is I hear you think the victim of the murder from the other night is one of the robbery team from Fenton's.'

'Where did you hear this?'

'I can't remember.'

Henderson sighed. He'd wanted to keep this information back until the suspects were in custody. 'We found the murder victim in a house where we also discovered some items of jewellery. We requested the list of the items stolen from Fenton's from your team to check if any recovered from the house matched those on the list.'

'And do they?' Rhodes said, his voice failing to disguise his enthusiasm.

'They did—'

'What? Does that mean you know who the jewellery thieves are? When were you—'

'Hang on, Steve. I said we found jewellery in the house, I didn't say we know who the occupants are. Also, we don't know if our murder victim is part of the robbery team or went to talk to the robbers and things turned sour. He might be innocent for all we know, in the wrong place at the wrong time.'

'Oh.'

'At the moment, we're trying to locate two men that we know were in the house at the same time as our victim and I'm confident it'll happen soon. When we have one or both of them in custody, the story should become clearer.'

'Do you know their names?'

'No,' he lied. 'We only have a partial on the car registration number and even if I did know their names, I still wouldn't tell you as it would be idiotic for us to have two teams out there competing to find the same suspects.'

'Fair enough, but if you could tell me I could run their names against one of our in-house lists; see if they're on our radar.'

'If they've both got form, I'm not sure your analysis will tell us anything more than we can find out ourselves.'

'Yeah, but maybe we've got some proprietorial knowledge that might tell us where to find them. When something like this goes down, we hear rumours and stories all the time. A name helps the rumours make sense.'

Henderson had to admit it sounded sensible. 'If in a day or so my enquiries have drawn a blank, I'll give you a call.'

'Let's assume you do find them, when do I get a crack?'

'Steve, I'm investigating a murder. My first priority is to find out who killed the victim. My energies will then be focussed on obtaining as much evidence as we can to gain a conviction. I'm not interested in the robbery except if it provides motive.'

'I'm pleased to hear it. So, when will I get a crack at them?'

Henderson was getting tired of this. He imagined the words 'murder' and 'victim' would evoke some sympathy in Rhodes; they did not. The disappearance of a large cache of jewellery was evidently more important in his mind.

'When the murder case is done and dusted, not before.'

Henderson's mobile rang. He looked at the screen: DS Walters.

'If it's all right with—'

'Steve, I've got another call, I need to go.'

'But can I ask—'

'No. I have to go. Talk to you later.'

'Who are you being so rude to?' Walters asked. 'It's usually to me.'

'Steve Rhodes from Robbery. He's frightened we'll grab all the glory for the Fenton's robbery. He's trying to muscle his way in.'

'Well, this might be over before he realises. I know where our two suspects are hanging out.'

TWENTY-FIVE

Henderson approached a grubby Vauxhall Astra, parked in a busy Brighton street. He walked to the driver's door and bent down as the window slid open. Inside, DS Walters and DC Emma Jenkins looked over at him.

'Good afternoon ladies. Have you seen any movement?'

'Afternoon sir. No, not for a while. A young skinny guy who looked like the mug shot I have of Fletcher, walked down to that shop over there,' she said, nodding her head in the direction of a Mace mini-supermarket, 'about an hour ago. He bought a few things and headed straight back to the house.'

'Do we know if both our suspects are in there?'

'I think so. We noticed an Asian-looking guy coming to the window a few times and looking up and down the road as if trying to spot us or looking out for someone. From here, it's hard to tell for sure, but it looked like Singh.'

'That's good enough for me.'

Henderson glanced up and down Goldstone Road. They were in Hove but it could have been any number of streets in Brighton or Hove, cars parked on either side of long rows of terraced houses, as every resident owned one and often two. Even an anonymous police white van containing four firearm officers didn't look out of place among delivery vans and those belonging to firms of builders and carpenters doing some work further up the street.

'We go in five minutes,' Henderson said. 'Are you ready, Emma, your first armed raid?'

'I'm feeling a bit nervous, sir, but I'm sure I'll be ok.'

'Don't worry, it may be noisy but the guys with the guns and the bullet proof vests will be doing most of the work.'

'That's reassuring.'

'Given that one of our suspects is coming to the window at regular intervals,' Henderson said, 'don't run towards their building when you get the green light. Amble over as if you're looking for an address, in case they spot you. We don't want them legging it down the fire escape.'

'Will do,' Walters said. 'What if he isn't looking out for the police, but he's waiting for someone; another member of the gang or a fence to buy the jewellery. Shouldn't we wait and see who turns up?'

'No. Our priority is to nab Guy Barton's killer. I'm not willing to leave it any longer than necessary and run the risk of them getting away.'

'Yes, sir.'

'Good. I'll see you in five,' Henderson said. He looked over at the target house before standing, put his hands in his pockets and walked if heading for the small supermarket on the corner.

Uniform had been checking the addresses of Singh's numerous uncles and cousins. They walked away from this one believing it to be empty, when a neighbour told them about the recent arrival of two young men. The house belonged to an uncle who spent the British winter in India but fell out with his nephew over his criminal convictions and banned him from sight. Clearly, Singh had copied the key and stayed there while his uncle was away.

Henderson reached the van housing the Armed Response Unit and was about to climb in when he noticed two men crossing the road and walking as if looking for a specific house. The two men caught the DI's eye as they looked a mismatched pair. A small dapper man with gold spectacles, grey thinning hair and carrying an attaché case, beside him a man the size of a rugby front-row forward with a bashed-in face. His radio crackled. He touched the ear piece to activate.

'Are you seeing this?' Walters said.

'Yep,' Henderson replied. 'They look like a couple of villains to me.'

'The Little and Large Show more like.'

Henderson ducked behind the van as the door to the target house opened. A thin Asian guy stood there and invited the two men inside. They disappeared into the house and before the guy shut the door, he scanned up and down the road. Henderson got a good look at his face, it was Ajay Singh.

Henderson opened the back door of the van. Four faces, their bodies clad in black Kevlar vests and holding badly scratched Heckler and Koch short barrel MP5 carbines, turned to look at him. 'Change of plan gents, our suspects have just had a couple of visitors and I want to hit them before they get comfortable. Can you be ready to go in a minute?'

'We're ready to go now, sir, if you want,' Sergeant Billington replied.

'Excellent, let's move.'

He stood to one side and allowed the bulky individuals to pass, then using the radio, called Walters and told her about his revised plan. Henderson closed the van door and ran after them.

The white painted house consisted of a basement with a separate entrance, a reception room and kitchen on the ground floor and three bedrooms upstairs, all gleaned from estate agent details of similar houses nearby. To reach the door, they needed to climb a small flight of stone stairs, exposing the visitors to anyone inside who looked out of the front bay window. To minimise the chance of this, the door banger went up alone, while the other men crouched out of sight.

The door flew open after two bangs and they all piled in, Henderson at the rear. The armed response officers seemed to have achieved the element of surprise, perhaps the activities of the door banger being attributed to the noisy builders a few doors down. Whatever the reason, the four individuals kneeling on the floor looking at jewellery spilling out of two sports holdalls, looked up in disbelief.

'Who the fuck are you?' the uglier of the two earlier arrivals said, a much punched-in face shoehorned into a tight tweed suit, with a thick Brummie accent.

'Shut up, and don't move,' Sergeant Billington barked.

Using the cover of four carbines pointing at each of their heads, Henderson and Walters pulled out handcuffs. He hauled Fletcher to his feet, pushed him against a wall and patted him down. In his pockets he found a bag of pills and some cannabis. Officers from two patrol cars Henderson had waiting nearby were standing in the hall and after reading Fletcher his rights, Henderson passed him over to them.

Singh came next, and from his waistband, the DI pulled out a weapon: a Beretta 9mm. A 9mm slug had been extracted from Guy Barton's chest at the P-M and while he knew it was common enough ammunition, he would bet this was the gun that killed Guy Barton.

Holding it by the finger guard he handed it to a member of Billington's team. With the weapon's safety on, he ejected the ammunition magazine and pulled back the slide to eject any round still in the chamber. Then, flicking a switch, he separated the barrel from the body of the gun and held out the pieces. 'Clear,' he said.

Jenkins walked towards him with an open evidence bag and the Firearms Officer dropped the items inside.

'What's going on here?' Henderson asked Singh.

'What does it–'

'Shut the fuck up, Ajay, if you don't want your throat cut,' the Brummie in the tweed suit said.

'Speak when you're spoken to,' growled Billington from a position behind his trusty MP5.

Henderson handed Singh over to another copper and walked over to deal with the big man. The DI believed he was the minder and his smaller companion the buyer, therefore the black case beside the buyer would contain cash. He would take a look at it in a minute.

Henderson attached handcuffs and raised the big guy to his feet. He started to struggle and the DI avoided the backwards head-butt, a common tactic with aggressive suspects, but failed to anticipate the elbow to the gut and the heel to the shin. He yelped in pain as the big Brummie broke from his grasp and lurched forward. He barrelled into the two armed response officers but Billington was as big as his assailant and didn't flinch before dropping him with a practiced thump to the head from the butt of his carbine.

Henderson walked over, his leg throbbing, and pulled the big guy to his feet using the handcuffs.

'Hey, careful with my fucking wrist copper, that's a gold watch.'

'They're ten a penny around here, mate,' Henderson said. 'Did you nick one while your mates weren't looking?'

'Fuck off.'

Henderson patted him down and found a gun in an inside pocket. It was a scratched and marked Remington, perhaps a weapon he'd owned for years or one handled by many others. 'Where did you get this?' Henderson asked. He handed it to Jenkins, who passed it over to one of Billington's team to make safe. 'Is it rented?'

'Fuck off.'

'You're a man of few words and not all of them

pleasant.'

In various cities across the UK, guns could be hired for short periods, used for their intended purpose and then passed back to their owner. By doing a test firing and comparing the ridges and marks on the bullet with bullets recovered from other firearm incidents, they might be able to tell if this one had been involved in the furtherance of other crimes.

Henderson handed him over to a cop. He was young, but looked as though he could handle himself. 'Be careful with this one,' he said, 'he tried to escape.'

'He'd look a right sight running down the road with his hands 'cuffed behind his back. C'mon mate, let's go.'

Henderson turned to deal with the last man sitting, the jeweller, when he heard a scuffle outside. He walked back into the hall to see two coppers dragging the big man to the car, his body inert between the two officers as if he'd just been punched in the gut.

Henderson went back into the lounge and reached for the other guy. Slightly built with silver spectacles and grey receding hair, he had the look of hard steel in his eyes. The man made a move to grab the handle of the small case but Henderson pushed his arm away.

'It's mine.'

'It was,' the DI said, 'but it's mine now.'

As expected, his pockets contained nothing incriminating and he offered no resistance.

'What's going on here?' Henderson asked before he handed him over to another constable. 'You came here to buy jewellery stolen from Fenton's in Lewes, didn't you?'

'I don't know what you're talking about. I'm saying nothing until I talk to my lawyer.'

Henderson smiled. It didn't happen often that such a comment would make him happy and he wanted to savour it. 'Fat lot of good it's going to do you, mate. Everything I need to send you and your gorilla to jail for a very long time is sitting here in this room.'

'We'll see about that.'

'Take him away,' Henderson said.

With the last of the suspects out of the room he thanked the armed response officers. They trooped back to their van while he walked into the lounge to await the arrival of the SOCO team. Walters began to sift through the evidence on the floor while Jenkins looked around the room.

'How's your leg?' Walters asked.

'Throbbing like a Fat Boy Slim soundtrack, but if it solves a murder and a robbery, it's a small price to pay. How much is in the case?'

'It's all fifties bundled into thousands. A hundred grand I would say.'

'What did the Robbery Squad say this stuff was worth, about four million?'

'Fenton's said eight which Steve Rhodes said would be retail prices, but at wholesale prices it would be around four.'

'In which case, a hundred grand or even two hundred grand, doesn't come close.'

'You're right. Do you think our two Brummie boys were trying to pull a fast-one?'

'What, strong-arm Fletcher and Singh into accepting their first offer?'

'Yeah.'

'Not with so little cash and not with Singh armed with a shooter. Maybe they wanted to take a look at them first, see what kind of people they were dealing with. Mind you, if they did decide to roll them over, the big Brummie bloke is about the size of Fletcher and Singh combined.'

'Why do I have the feeling you're thinking about something else?'

'What if the hundred grand is a down payment, a gesture of goodwill perhaps, with the rest of the money to come after seeing and verifying the merchandise?'

'Sounds more like it.'

'Which means what, Detective?'

'It means they must have a stash of money nearby, being looked after by an associate or lying in the boot of their car.'

Henderson reached into his pocket and held up two sets of car keys: one on a Vauxhall key ring, the other, Mercedes.

'Where did you get those?'

TWENTY-SIX

DI Henderson walked into the interview room with DS Walters. On the other side of the table, Solomon Fletcher. They had already interviewed Ajay Singh with DS Hobbs handling the unenviable task of interviewing the two Birmingham boys, otherwise known as Gerald Rattigan and his gorilla, Barry Forshaw.

Armed with both of the Brummies' names they interrogated the PNC with predictable results. Rattigan had been a fence for over thirty years, buying stolen goods from all over Europe and selling them to a network of corrupt jewellery shops. It was a fantastically lucrative business, jewellers were happy to take the goods from Rattigan not only because they would pay less than the wholesale price, they also received exquisite pieces of jewellery they couldn't buy anywhere else.

Barry Forshaw was a stereotypical thug, depressing in his similarity with every similarly employed individual who walked the streets of any British city. He started off in approved school for glassing a classmate and graduated to prison after a steady stream of assaults, some serious, and a large dose of drug trafficking. No offences had been committed for the last five years, no doubt the influence of his association with Rattigan and adoption of his subterfuge methods, and maybe an element of an old con 'wising up'.

They said little since being arrested and were no more loquacious when paired up with their legal team who came down from Birmingham to represent them. Henderson wished Hobbs good luck before the interview and meant it, as it was likely to be a very tedious process. In Hobbs's favour, the fingerprints of Rattigan and Forshaw were discovered on the hundred grand and jewellery found in the house in Goldstone Road, and on the sum of one and a half million from the boot of a large Mercedes saloon parked nearby. Even without a confession, the CPS would be biting their hands off to have a chance of prosecuting those two.

Walters manned the technology as Henderson shuffled his papers purposefully while watching the suspect. Solomon Fletcher looked young for a twenty-two-year-old, with trendy floppy hair and clothes that might have suited an older brother if he had one. He looked nervous, rubbing his hands together and refusing to look at the two detectives.

His brief didn't come from the well-heeled Birmingham legal practice that were representing Rattigan and Forshaw and some would regard this as an error of judgement. Fletcher looked like the weak link in the chain, but perhaps the threat of having his throat cut if he talked was sufficient incentive for him to keep his mouth shut. The man here to represent him was a duty solicitor, one he'd encountered before, Tom Nelson.

'Mr Fletcher,' Henderson said after the preliminaries were completed, 'you are charged with the murder of Guy Barton.'

'What...what the hell's this?' Fletcher screeched. 'I thought you wanted to talk about the thieving of some jewellery.'

'I must object,' Fletcher's brief said. 'You are trying to provoke my client.'

Good, Henderson thought; the more rattled he became, the better he liked it. 'Surely this hasn't come as a surprise to you? It's there on the charge sheet.'

'I know but I thought Ajay would–' He stopped, wanting to say more but unable to continue.

'Ajay would do what? Take the rap for it? No, he denies it. He blames you.'

In fact Ajay Singh said nothing, no doubt mindful of the threat from the Brummie pair hanging over his head. Henderson was mindful of the threat too and started Ajay's interview and now Fletcher's with the Barton murder, which, as far as he believed, did not concern the two from Birmingham.

Tears came now, trickling down the face of a young man caught between two stools. He rocked the seat back and forth and ran a hand through his hair, and any moment Henderson expected him to take handfuls of it and pull. In the past, similar behaviour would be taken as a sign of mental disturbance, but nowadays was more often associated with persistent drug use.

'I didn't do it, I didn't fucking do it,' he repeated.

Henderson gave him a few moments to vent his anxiety before he said, 'We'll come back to it later. Tell me about the robbery.'

'Eh? What?'

'Tell me about the robbery at Fenton's. The one you did with Guy Barton and Ajay Singh.'

'How do you know about it?'

'Ajay told me.'

'Did he?'

'Don't look so surprised. I know all about it, but I want to hear it from you.'

'Oh, I dunno.'

'Listen Sol. You denied murder and I more or less believe you, but nothing will convince me that you weren't part of the team robbing Fenton's.'

He stared at the desk for a long spell, leading Henderson to think he wouldn't get much more out of him today.

'It was Guy's idea,' Fletcher blurted out.

'What was?'

'It was Guy Barton's idea to rob Fenton's. He's a building control officer for the Council, right?'

'Yes, he was.'

'Ok, he *was* a building control officer for the Council. Well, he did some work at Fenton's, checking their renovations were in keeping with building guidelines or something. He came to Ajay and me and said he knew how to get in there. He said we should do it during the Bonfire Night parade as it would be noisy and no one would notice the alarm going off, and even if they did, the cops wouldn't be able to get there in time for the crowds.'

'Right on all counts. How well do you know Ajay and Guy?'

'Ajay and Guy went to school together so they've known each other for years. My mother lives beside Ajay's mum and the two of us would hang out and smoke some dope. Guy joined us now and again.'

'So, you three pals, smashed the back door into Fenton's and filled a couple of sports holdalls full of jewellery.'

He nodded.

'Speak up for the recording, Sol,' Walters said.

'Sorry. Yeah, the three of us filled up a couple of holdalls with the stuff from Fenton's.'

'What happened then? What did you do with the loot?'

'We took it to the flat Ajay and me were staying in Hanover Street.'

'To await the arrival of your buyer, Gerald Rattigan?'

'What d'ya think we were doing? Fuck, I mean no, I'm not saying nothing about them.'

'It doesn't matter if you do or you don't. The four of you were caught looking at jewellery in the Goldstone Street house. We know that and we can prove it. Seven police officers at the scene will swear to it and I'm confident with the fingerprints of you, Ajay and your buyers all over the stolen jewellery, it will be enough for any jury to convict you all. Rattigan and his Rottweiler are going down, don't you worry about them.'

Fletcher put his head in his hands; he was cornered.

'You are bullying my client, Inspector. I really must ask you to bring this interview to a close.'

'If I do that, Mr Nelson, I'll just go through the same questions, tomorrow, the next day and the day after that. Let's get it done today.'

He looked over at Fletcher who didn't object. Henderson took this as acquiescence.

'You admit you stole the stuff, Sol. How did you find a buyer?'

He looked up. 'Ajay knew them.'

'Where did he find them? You can't just look them up on Checkatrade.'

He smiled. 'Don't be soft. Ajay met a mate of Rattigan's when he was inside. When Guy came up with the idea, Ajay called him.'

'What happened with Guy at Hanover Street?'

'After the robbery, Guy came round and after a few beers, we were celebrating, like, he said he wanted to take a look at the stuff. Him and Ajay went upstairs.'

'Where did you keep it?'

'In a cupboard in the back bedroom.'

Henderson mentally put a tick against his hypothesis.

'Where were you while they were upstairs?'

'Watching telly in the living-room.'

'What happened then?'

'I got told most of the story by Ajay, as I wasn't there at the time, right? I only came in at the tail-end, ok?'

'I see.'

'They were looking at the stuff when Guy picked up a bracelet. He said it was the only reason he planned the robbery. He'd always wanted to buy it for his wife as she loved it, but he couldn't afford the ten grand it cost. He said they were going through a bad patch and maybe it would, you know, help improve things between him and his missus.'

'Ok.'

'The two of them started arguing; Guy said he was taking the bracelet away and Ajay said no. We agreed when we started planning this, none of us was to take anything; that was the deal. Guy got up and made to walk away when Ajay pulled out a gun.'

'Where was Ajay?'

'Sitting in the bedroom beside the bags of rings and stuff.'

Henderson put another tick against his hypothesis.

'Ajay threatened to shoot him if he didn't give it back. They stood facing one another in a big stand-off; Guy adamant he was taking it, Ajay saying he couldn't. I came up the stairs and I couldn't help it, but when I saw the gun and the look on Ajay's face, I panicked. I shouted, 'Ajay!' and then he fired.'

It was a gut-wrenching story and Henderson hid his feelings behind a cup of cold coffee, but in Walters's eyes he could see tears. He remembered the bracelet in question, recovered from Guy Barton's jacket pocket at the post mortem.

'Ajay had the gun in his waistband?'

'Yep.'

'Why did he have it?'

'He said the buyer was a heavy dude and if things went pear-shaped he would use it to threaten them.'

'Did he often carry a gun?'

'I never saw it before, even when we did other jobs like boosting cars or buying dope from dealers.'

'What happened then?'

'Ajay panicked. Told me we had to get out of there fast. We threw all the stuff back into a couple of holdalls and hightailed it to Goldstone Road.'

Henderson wrapped the interview up ten minutes later and walked back to his office with Walters.

'I should feel good, elated even,' Henderson said. 'We've cracked Guy Barton's murder and solved the Fenton's jewellery heist, but in talking to Fletcher and Singh, neither made any reference to Marc Emerson.'

'You're right. Ajay knew Guy well, and he'd only heard of Marc's name, nothing more.'

'What does it tell us?' he said as he walked into his office and slumped into the chair while Walters took the visitor's seat.

'It tells us,' she said, 'either they're lying about Marc Emerson, but I don't think so as it came out in naturally in conversation, or Guy kept Singh and the criminal side of his life separate.'

'The latter I think. Singh is the more accomplished liar but Fletcher is an open book. I was looking at his face when I mentioned Marc's name, no nervous twitch, no guilty look; same with Singh.'

DS Hobbs walked into the office and took a chair beside Walters.

He sighed. 'God, what a painful experience.'

'That bad?'

'Whatever your record is for 'no comments' it's been broken by a mile.'

'What? Even when you placed the evidence in front of them? Their fingerprints are all over the stolen gear and we found a million quid in their car.'

'I know, I know, and why do you think they were in a house in Hove with a couple of jewellery robbers? They called round to see Ajay, an old friend of Rattigan's, of course. His friend just happened to be in possession of all those nice pieces of jewellery and being in the business, he thought there would be no harm in taking a look.'

'The bare-faced cheek. What about the money?'

'That was to buy a house he fancied the look of.'

Henderson smiled. 'Funny, we didn't find any estate agent details in their pockets or when searched their car.'

'They're in Micky Mouse land, boss,' Hobbs said, his voice filled with exasperation. 'Any jury will convict them for handling stolen goods, and in addition, we've got Forshaw for being in possession of a firearm.'

'I'm concerned about Rattigan,' Henderson said. 'He'll get a couple years from a lenient judge and be out in six months for being a model prisoner.'

'He's a leech. It's people like him that make people like Singh and Fletcher rob jewellery shops.'

'I've just had a thought. In fact I don't know why I didn't think of it sooner. Where did Rattigan get over a million quid in cash?'

'Good point,' Walters said. 'Nobody carries that amount of money around nowadays.'

'We know drug dealers can generate large sums of cash but Rattigan isn't into drugs, as far as we know.' He thought for a moment. 'Call Birmingham, Gerry and see what they can tell us. They might know about another big jewellery heist that went down in their patch. In which case, they might be pleased to hear we've got one of their compatriots in custody. With a bit of luck, we might be able to hang a money laundering charge around his neck.'

TWENTY-SEVEN

Henderson arrived at the office at seven-thirty on Wednesday morning, his usual start time, but with an extra spring in his step. The team went out last night to celebrate their success in arresting the killer of Guy Barton and the robbers of Fenton's. For him, a little black cloud hung over the frivolity as he didn't yet know the identity of Marc Emerson's killer, but as some of the team believed it to be Guy Barton, it would have been churlish to say otherwise.

He didn't go on to a nightclub after the pub as he couldn't dance and wouldn't know many, if any of the songs being played. While in the pub, he didn't mix his drinks and stuck to beer which went some way to explaining why he didn't feel so bad this morning, but his good mood had nothing to do with alcohol.

He was keen to investigate the gun taken from Rattigan's bodyguard, Barry Forshaw. Early indications were it had been used in other crimes and he would be interested to see what further research could uncover. He would take great pleasure in sending a number of emails to other forces which might help them clear up some of their unsolved cases.

He first dealt with a rash of emails that had come into his mailbox since last night, from the Robbery

Squad wanting to know when they could see his suspects, a congratulatory note from his boss, one from the Assistant Chief Constable, and from a couple of officers he knew in the Met. At nine he wandered into the detectives' room to look for a willing gun researcher but one look told him all he needed to know. Faces looked gaunt, loads of empty coffee cups filled bins even at this time of the morning, and one or two looked to be asleep.

Realising nothing much would be completed this morning, he returned to his office. He had only resumed his seat for about two minutes when DS Edwards came in. She slumped into the visitor's chair as listlessly as Hobbs had done the day before after his encounter with the 'no comment' Brummies.

'That was some night of celebration last night, Angus. What was in those cocktails?'

'I don't know as I didn't drink them. I spent the evening drinking beer.'

'I can't drink beer either. It must be my age or something.' She leaned over his desk. 'I didn't say anything I shouldn't have, did I?'

'No, I think twenty per cent pay rises for everyone is a generous action in the circumstances.'

'What? I didn't say that, did I?'

He smiled. 'No, but you should have.'

'Thank the Lord. I'm not prone to shooting my mouth off when drunk, but there's always a first time. Nowadays, one word or a hand in the wrong place and it's curtains. One career down the toilet.'

She got up from the seat with less energy than normal. 'I just wanted to say again, well done for nicking the jewellery robbers and Guy Barton's killer so quickly. It will be a great relief for his wife to know her husband's killer is now behind bars and facing a murder charge.'

'Perhaps not murder, more like manslaughter.'

'Why? I thought Singh shot him?'

'He did but he didn't set out to murder him, in fact they were friends right up until the point Guy insisted on taking a bracelet out of their robbery haul. I don't think I got the chance to mention it last night but Sol Fletcher said it might have been his shout that panicked Singh into firing. When he spotted the gun he shouted in surprise, 'Ajay!' and then Ajay fired.'

She sat back down. 'Christ, we'd be lucky to get him for manslaughter. Accidental discharge or Involuntary Manslaughter would mean he would serve less than ten years. It's not much comfort for Lily Barton.'

'That said, I'm not so sure the CPS agree. Their initial view is, because there are no witnesses to back up Fletcher's statement, they believe he made up the story to make things easier for his mate.'

'I'll go away with that positive thought in my head. We need to talk about this again but not today, Angus. Not until my brain starts to function as it should. I'll catch you later.'

Henderson didn't hear her closing comments as mention of Lily Barton's name reminded him that he hadn't told her about the arrest of her husband's killer. He reached for the phone, intending to call, but replaced it without dialling. Lily didn't deserve to hear news like this over the phone, given her fragile state.

He would tell her in person. He grabbed his jacket and headed out to the car.

In the car park he called 'good morning' to a couple of late stragglers in the murder team making their way to work, leaving them with quizzical faces and checking their watches to make sure they hadn't stopped. He climbed into the car and drove out of the car park. It was a short journey from Malling House to St John's Terrace but enough time for him to get bored with a discussion on Radio 4 about the lasting legacy of a group of long-dead Greek philosophers.

For once, he managed to find a parking spot on St John's Terrace, but at the other end of the street from the Barton house. It was a misty, cold morning and even though it wasn't raining, the air felt damp and seemed to seep through his clothes. St John's Church looked foreboding in the dull, cloudy weather but his view was coloured by his opinion of churches, places he entered most often to attend a funeral.

He knocked on the door of Lily Barton's house and moved back to a lower step in order not to intimidate her. He waited for a minute and when he received no reply, knocked again. He was surprised as he knew from Helen Vincent, the FLO, they didn't go out much and even if Lily was in bed or in the bath, Helen would open the door. He could hear some banging and muffled sounds but couldn't be sure if it was coming from this house or the place next door.

He pulled out his mobile and called Helen's number. He could hear it ringing, as if the phone was close by, in the kitchen or lounge, but it rang out and diverted to voicemail. He didn't leave a message, but instead walked to the end of the terrace where he'd noticed on previous visits a lane at the rear of the houses providing access to the back gardens.

He counted along the doorways until he came to the Barton house. He climbed the small gate guarding the entrance and headed for the back door. After knocking several times, he dialled Helen's number and this time he could hear it ringing louder than before. He peered through the window and could see it vibrating on the kitchen table. His initial reaction was one of annoyance, how could she could leave her phone behind, but he soon realised it indicated something else. Police Officers and in particular, FLOs, were instructed to be in contact at all times, and this convinced him that Helen was still in the house.

He selected a small side window and using a rock from the garden, smashed the glass. He unlatched the window and with the assistance of a wooden bench, climbed in. The kitchen didn't look so different since the last time he'd been in here, making tea after telling the poor woman that her husband had been murdered.

He called out, 'Lily, Helen are you there?'

The muffled thumping he was sure he heard earlier sounded louder now and seemed to be coming from upstairs. He bounded up the stairs and tracked the noise to a closed door. By a process of deduction a bathroom, as all the other doors were bedrooms.

He rapped his knuckles on the door. 'Is there someone in there?'

'It's me, sir. Helen Vincent. I'm stuck inside. Thank

God you're here.'

'How did you get stuck? Is the lock jammed?'

'Lily locked me in.'

'What? Why?'

'I don't know.'

The hallway was dull on account of the murky day outside; he reached over and switched on the light. The bathroom door was made from solid wood and locked using a key. There wasn't a key in the lock and he didn't find one following a cursory search.

'How long have you been in there, Helen?'

'Ten, fifteen minutes.'

'Where's Lily?'

'I don't know.'

'Stand back. I need to kick the door in.'

'I'll jump in the bath,' she called.

He paused a few seconds. 'Are you standing out of the way now?'

'Yes.'

Henderson kicked the door with the heel of his shoe at a point close to the lock. Nothing. He did it again and heard a faint creak. He did it again and again before the door swung open with a loud crack.

Helen, standing in the bath, had the look of pure relief on her face. 'Thank God, sir. Thank you so much,' she said as she climbed out.

'Do you know where Lily is?'

'No, I don't.'

'Your best guess. She didn't lock you in the toilet to go shopping.'

'You don't think...' Her hand covered her mouth.

He nodded. 'Maybe. How did she seem to you this

morning?'

'Better I thought.'

'Maybe she'd made her mind up.'

He pulled out his phone. 'Do you know what car she drives?'

'Yes, a blue VW Tiguan.'

'Do you know its reg?'

'Yes.'

'Was it parked near the house?'

'Yes. I check every morning.'

Henderson opened the bathroom window. 'Can you see if it's there now?'

The window was set high making it a stretch for her to see out. 'The car was parked close to the house but another car is now in its place.'

Henderson called Lewes Control. 'This is DI Angus Henderson, I need you to broadcast the following car license plate on ANPR.' He handed the phone to Helen. She gave the operator the car's registration number. He took the phone back. 'The car is a Blue Volkswagen Tiguan. The owner, Lily Barton, is a suicide risk. She must be taken into custody if spotted.'

Helen remained at the house in case Lily returned, and to arrange a tradesman to repair the broken window and the splintered bathroom door. He drove back to Malling House, his mood as dark and foreboding as the church he left behind in St John's Terrace. He turned into the car park when his mobile rang.

'DI Henderson?'

'Yes it is.'

'Lewes Control here. We have a sighting of the Volkswagen Tiguan that you requested.' The operator repeated the registration number.

'Fantastic.'

'It was spotted by a patrol car in Ardingly village. They were unable to follow as they were in the process of making an arrest but the car turned down College Road.'

'I know it. Thanks.'

Henderson turned the car around and headed out, back to the main road. On the way, he programmed the satnav and when it finally displayed a route to Ardingly, he floored the accelerator. From his knowledge of the area, College Road ran from the village of Ardingly to the town of Haywards Heath with not much else along the way. However, he didn't think Lily would go to the trouble of locking Helen in the bathroom to visit some friends in the town or a secret love-child at Ardingly College.

If planning to commit suicide, he would bet her destination would be a place about half a mile down College Road from the village: Ardingly Reservoir. If he guessed wrong and she was heading off to meet a friend's child at the college or an old boyfriend in Haywards Heath, he would rather walk away with a red face and be accused of wasting time, than to see Lily's lifeless body in the back of a hearse.

If he decided to end it all, a reservoir on a cold November afternoon would feature near the bottom of his list. Around twenty suicides a year took place at Beachy Head near Eastbourne. To him, it seemed more final jumping from a two-hundred-foot cliff down on to rocks than trusting your nerve will hold when you see and feel the grey, cold water of a large body of water.

Along the A275 and then the A272, he behaved like an arrogant executive late for an important meeting, tailgating cars, overtaking when a gap opened up, and receiving in return flashed headlights and blasts from their horns. He didn't think his fast driving would damage the engine of his recently purchased three-year-old Audi, but it was killing his fuel consumption and he was thankful he'd filled the tank only two days before.

At last, the village of Ardingly appeared, and with a sigh of relief, he turned into College Road. Minutes later, he sped down the access road towards the reservoir, ignoring the inconvenience of well-worn speed-bumps but taking care not to mow down a large family of ducks with a death wish, meandering close to the road's edge.

He ignored the car park and drove right up to the shoreline of the reservoir and parked on the slipway. Here, the mist prevalent in Lewes was less in evidence but the air still felt cold and damp. Out in the water, he could see a single rowing boat that looked to be heading towards the middle of the reservoir. He took from the car a pair of binoculars and trained them on the boat. Slowly, he brought them into focus, and there he could see the unmistakable hair, features and face of Lily Barton.

TWENTY-EIGHT

Henderson lobbed the binoculars back into the car and ran towards the Activity Centre at Ardingly Reservoir. The building sat at one end of the long body of cold, dark water, close to the slipway where his car was parked, there to organise and run sailing courses and collect fees from boat owners who stored their craft along shoreline.

Henderson pushed the door open into a warm room, his nostrils immediately assailed by the strong smell of rubber from the wetsuits displayed all around and hot food cooking slowly inside the pie heater in the corner.

'Two in one day, it must be a miracle,' the guy behind the desk said.

'What?' Henderson asked.

'Two customers on a shitty day like this. Someone up there must be smiling on us.'

'I need a boat, a fast boat.'

'Give me a second and I'll need to take a look,' he said turning to his computer. 'Are you booked?'

'Listen friend,' Henderson said slapping his hand down on the counter. 'The woman you hired a rowing boat to a few minutes ago?'

'Yeah, what about it?'

'I think she's here with the intention of committing

suicide.'

'You're pulling my chain, mate. We haven't had a suicide here for, I dunno, since before I started working here.'

At that moment, it dawned on Henderson. The man's nonchalant attitude was due to him not knowing who stood in front of him or why he was there. He pulled out his ID and held it up for him to see.

'Ah right, the cops. What can I do for you, detective?'

'The woman out there in the boat is a suicide risk. I want a fast boat. I need to go out there and bring her in. Now!'

'All right, all right, keep calm or you'll have a coronary.' He jumped off the stool, grabbed a grubby yellow jacket from a peg and walked to the door. 'Follow me.'

They strode past the Activity Centre towards a long line of boats. They passed several before he stopped and pointed at a small boat with an outboard. 'Is this one ok for you?'

'As long as the engine works.'

'It does.'

Henderson jumped in, headed to the stern and started the outboard.

'I see you've been in a boat before.'

'You could say that.'

'Nevertheless, I'm required to come with you because...'

'Save the speech, young man. If you need to get in, get in.'

His companion climbed in and took charge of the rudder while the DI undid the mooring rope. Seconds later, they set off.

'What's your name?' Henderson asked as they sped over the wind-whipped waves. It was cold on the water and he wished he'd brought a warmer jacket.

'Adam. What's yours?'

'Angus.'

'Double A, a good sign.'

'You're superstitious?'

'Aren't all sailors?'

'I suppose they are.'

'So,' Adam said after a few seconds of silence, interrupted only by the high pitched whine of the small outboard, 'you think this woman will try to commit suicide?'

'Yes. She's just lost her husband and she's very distraught.'

'Right, I'm with you now.'

They could see the other boat better now. It wasn't moving, Lily sitting motionless with her back to them. They were still too far away for her to hear them, not that he wanted to shout as it might alarm her. In any case, the noise of the little Yamaha engine would drown out anything he said.

'It's not a very nice way to commit suicide is it, jumping into a lake? I mean it's freezing cold at this time of year and dark.'

'From a selfish point of view, I would rather she didn't as I don't want to go in there to try and save her. I would prefer to talk her round.'

He watched Lily as her figure grew larger in his

vision. He instructed Adam to move closer to Lily's boat but to keep her back facing them, allowing her less time to see their arrival.

'You could shout to her now, we're close enough for her to hear and I can turn the engine down if it helps.'

'Maybe when the boats are closer and we can talk without shouting.'

They were about ten metres away when she looked round but it didn't seem to be at them. She leaned to one side and toppled over the side of the boat.

'Oh shit,' Henderson said. A November dip in Ardingly Reservoir did not appear anywhere on his bucket list.

In seconds, they were close to the spot where she had gone over and before Adam could say anything in protest or support, Henderson removed his jacket and shoes. He hoisted himself up to the side of the boat and toppled backwards into the water.

Whoa! The word 'cold' didn't do it justice. He felt instantly chilled to the bone and any vestiges of his morning hangover disappeared without trace. He envisioned clear drinking water but it was bracken-cloudy, most likely the result of recent heavy rain. Reservoirs he knew, bottomed-out at three or four metres, so if he managed to swim down in error it wouldn't be a lung-bursting trip back up to the top, unlike the ocean. He couldn't see any trace of Lily, and surfaced.

'Head more in the direction of her boat,' Adam shouted. 'I'm sure I saw something in the water on the port side.'

Henderson did as Adam suggested and dived

again. Seconds later, he saw something too. Something blue. Lily had been wearing a blue Puffa jacket. He headed towards it.

Moving closer, he reached out with outstretched fingers and grabbed it. To his relief it felt to him like the material of a jacket and not a fish or a lump of wood. He felt further along and found her arm and when he thought his hand was close to her shoulder, locked his arm under hers and stroked up towards the light.

On reaching the surface, he gasped for air, making him realise he'd been underwater longer than he expected. He looked around for their boat. Adam spotted him and headed their way. Henderson turned to look at Lily. Her face was white and impassive with no flicker of life. He leaned his ear close to her mouth. It was difficult to hear anything for the slap of the water, his own shivering and the noise of the Yamaha, but he couldn't feel the heat of her breath either.

'She's stopped breathing,' he said to Adam when the boat manoeuvred alongside.

'Pass her up.'

With Henderson pushing and Adam pulling her shoulders, Lily was soon on board. Now came the tricky part getting him back on board. Many an amateur sailor had come a cropper doing this manoeuvre, reaching over to help a mate in the water and capsizing the boat. Fortunately, Adam used the experience of numerous sailing courses and children's water parties and pulled him up without drama.

Adam left an exhausted Henderson to catch his breath and started administering Cardio Pulmonary

Resuscitation, or CPR as it was more commonly known, to Lily. With her head tilted to one side, and her arms crossed in front of her, he began pumping her chest.

'Take the helm, Angus, and get us back to the Activity Centre, fast. I called an ambulance.'

Henderson turned the boat and headed back as instructed. He couldn't fault Adam's first-aid technique, but Lily wasn't responding. The throttle on the Yamaha was open to its full extent but to his dismay, the Activity Centre didn't seem to be getting any larger.

'C'mon, c'mon,' Adam said, anguish evident in his voice. He kept going with the chest compressions and on reaching a point when Henderson was about to advise him to stop, Lily uttered a small cough. Seconds later, there came a splutter, then about a half-litre of water came spouting out of her mouth. There followed a fit of coughing and before long, her legs and arms began to move.

She tried to sit up but Adam, looking exhausted, told her to lie still and covered her with his own jacket. He looked over at Henderson and the DI gave him a thumbs up and a beaming smile. Henderson was now wearing his own jacket which he'd left on the boat before diving in. It provided some warmth, but this was almost cancelled out by the chilling breeze which blew straight into his chest, a position he needed to adopt to steer the boat.

When they got closer to the Activity Centre he could see several of Adam's colleagues gathered at the lakeside. Henderson guided the boat into its berth, and many hands reached forward to help them. To Henderson's surprise, when he got out of the boat his legs felt like jelly and it was fortunate help was there, as he doubted he could walk back to the car under his own steam.

The heat in the Activity Centre hit him like a warm-air curtain and with it came the soporific effect of a hot summer sun on a Mediterranean beach and all he wanted to do now was sink into a chair and close his eyes.

'C'mon Angus, no time for sitting around,' Adam said. He led him down a dim corridor and into the men's changing room. Henderson slumped on a bench while Adam switched on a shower.

'Take these wet clothes off and get into the shower. I'll bring in a towel and something for you to change into, ok?'

He nodded. 'Where's Lily?'

'Is that her name? Celia's looking after her. She'll be fine. We're all trained in first-aid and resuscitation.'

Adam left the room and Henderson knew if he laid down on the uncomfortable hard ribs of wood, he would be sleeping like a baby in seconds. A vague alarm went off in his head, warning him that if he was suffering from hypothermia, he shouldn't go to sleep otherwise he might never wake up. Instead, he slowly removed his clothes, not easy as they were sodden and clung to his skin as if glued. He smelled too, an earthy odour of peat and bracken, like he'd been on a two-week camping holiday.

He stood in the shower for what felt like an age,

turning up the heat to a point where he couldn't stand it any hotter until the chill in his bones began to subside. He now felt so much better and proceeded to soap every inch of his body, trying to replace the damp, muddy smell of the reservoir with the whiff of coconuts from the liquid soap dispenser.

Feeling invigorated, he switched off the shower and true to Adam's word, on the bench he found a towel. Beside it, some clothes: a t-shirt, a boiler suit and a plastic bag. He dressed and after squeezing out as much excess water as he could from his wet clothes in the shower, he stuffed them into the bag.

He walked back into the main office area where he found Adam talking to two paramedics, a tall man and a shorter woman.

'Ah, Angus,' Adam said. He turned to the paramedics. 'This is the man I was telling you about.'

'How are you feeling, sir?' the paramedic nearest to him asked.

'Much better thanks, that hot shower did me a lot of good.'

The paramedic approached and looked him up and down as health professionals were prone to do when examining a patient, as if assessing a second-hand car they were about to purchase.

'I would still like you to come with me to the hospital, sir, and have you checked out.'

'I don't think that will be necessary.'

'I'm afraid I must insist.'

Henderson bowed to the inevitable and agreed to go. He turned to Adam and extended his hand.

'Thanks for all your help, Adam,' Henderson said

shaking his hand. 'You really did great out there, even though at first you did think me a complete nutter.'

'Just another exciting day at the Ardingly Activity Centre,' he said grinning.

'I'll bring these clothes back in a few days.'

'No problem, we're not about to run short. There's not much call for sailing courses in winter.'

Henderson waved goodbye to all their helpers and was about to step out of the door when he stopped and searched for something in his bag of wet clothes. He found his car key and lobbed it towards Adam.

'Just in case you need to move it, that is if the key still works.'

'I'll make sure I dry it off first.'

Henderson took a seat in the ambulance feeling like a fraud, as with every minute that passed, his wellbeing improved. The shivers and shakes had all but disappeared and he no longer smelled like a wood-dwelling troll. What else could a hospital do?

A few minutes later, Lily was led out to the ambulance by the female paramedic. She looked worse than he did, but no wonder as she had been in the water longer, much longer than he, and her heart had stopped beating. They helped her into the ambulance and laid her down on the bed and attached an oxygen mask to her face.

He felt a frisson of disappointment as he wanted to talk to her while they journeyed to East Surrey Hospital, the Princess Royal or wherever they were headed. He wanted to ask her why she had decided to end it all, and if she didn't feel any different than she did earlier today, had he wasted his time in rescuing her? In essence, would she try and do the same thing all over again when her health improved?

It didn't fall within the remit of the job to talk Lily down from notions of suicide or rescue her from perilous situations, but as the detective investigating the deaths of her husband and lover, for the moment at least, he felt a sense of responsibility.

Any questions could wait for another time. Looking at her face now, her pale, almost porcelain complexion and listening to her laboured breathing, he doubted she would be out of hospital any day soon.

TWENTY-NINE

'Are you working late tonight, Cindy?' Christine Sutherland asked.

'No, I just want to get this thing finished for Brendan. He needs it for tomorrow's meeting.'

'I thought you completed it days ago.'

'I...I did but he made some last-minute changes, you know what he's like.'

'Tell me about it.'

'Are you off to your Institute shindig?'

'Yep. 'Strategy Formulation for The Modern Business,' the seminar's called but you know I only go for the wine and networking afterwards. Goodnight Cindy.'

'Goodnight Christine.'

Cindy Summer breathed a sigh of relief. Her boss, Christine Sutherland, was a skilled interrogator, looking intently at you in meetings after skim-reading anything you produced. It put her on edge every time. Summer didn't often work late and felt nervous at trying to convince her that her presence tonight had a valid purpose. She could be a controlling bitch, with a handle on what everyone was doing and where they were going.

The key to manipulating her was using the word 'Brendan'. Sutherland hated the company's

Commercial Director, Brendan Flaherty, and the mere mention of his name had her lip curling, ending any further discussion.

She walked over to the drinks machine and pressed the button for a black coffee, even though she didn't want one. Sipping the hot drink slowly, she strolled to the window as if pondering a thorny problem. In reality, there wasn't any need to be this careful as at five o'clock the building emptied and now at two minutes to six, the place looked and sounded deserted.

She looked over at the car park and could see three cars. She knew exactly who they belonged to: her own, the big BMW of the MD and a scruffy Beetle belonging to a hairy oik from IT. She knew the owners of every car in the car park. Cindy made it her business to know.

She turned and walked back to her desk, looking surreptitiously around for any unusual activity. Finding none, she reached into her desk drawer and pulled out a set of keys. She moved to Christine Sutherland's desk and sat down. She selected a small silver key and opened her desk drawers. A week ago she'd done the same, and found letters addressed not to Sutherland, but someone called Melanie Lewis. Assuming this to be a relative or a friend, she had glanced through a couple but became so nervous she stopped.

She felt emboldened now, not because of doing anything different, but she believed the police investigation into Marc Emerson's murder had now ground to a halt. Without a firm suspect, they would push it under the carpet and forget about it, but she wouldn't let them. Marc was special to her, not in a boyfriend-girlfriend way, he was too good-looking for her, but they had been good friends. She owed it to Marc to find out who killed him and she knew he would have done the same for her.

She ignored the letters for the moment and took a closer look at the hanging files, something she didn't do last time. Tucked at the back she pulled out a folder from a file labelled 'Admin' with a 'CV' sticker on the front and laid it out on the desk. It contained a number of neatly formatted CVs. She picked up the one on top and looked through. This was the first time she had seen Sutherland's CV and found it remarkable to see listed all her previous experience, as the woman didn't seem to know much, delegated all the time and never talked about the places where she used to work.

She put the CV back in the file and sifted through the others. Expecting to see older versions of the one she had just looked at, she was surprised to find the next one headed, 'Amanda Sherman'. Why Sutherland had this other woman's CV in her file, she didn't begin to understand but when she examined it in more detail, the information mirrored that of Christine Sutherland, down to dates, places and employers.

She put the papers down on the desk, leaned back in the chair and wrapped her finger round and round the end of her hair, something she did when thinking seriously. In a fair and decent world this would prove that her boss, Christine Sutherland, was a fraud and all Cindy's suspicions had been validated. But the world wasn't fair and decent as maybe it indicated something more boring instead, such as she didn't like her own name or used it as a nom de plume for dating websites.

The truth perhaps lay somewhere in between but it didn't resemble the behaviour of any financial directors she knew, where words like 'conservative' and 'prudent' were more common fare. It smacked of criminal intent or a past or a person Sutherland didn't want catching up with her.

She picked up the letters addressed to Melanie Lewis and read each one carefully. They had been sent from a mother pleading with an errant child to come home and face the music. She didn't go on to say in any detail what the 'music' might be, but mentioned the presence of police around the family home in Lincoln and their desire to speak to her. The letters made little sense when she first read them a week ago, but knowing her boss used Amanda's name on her CV, it was a small leap to assume that Melanie Lewis was also one of her names.

She knew it! The woman was a crook!

She returned to her desk and fished out the business card left by the policewoman who came to Quinlan's offices to speak to Christine Sutherland and Josh Gardner, Sergeant Walters. She dialled the number.

'Detective Sergeant Walters, how can I help?'

'Eh, hello Sergeant Walters, it's Cindy Summer here.'

'Cindy Summer? Sorry? You'll need to jog my memory.'

'I talked to you outside Quinlan's a few weeks back

when you and that big skinny guy came to see Christine Sutherland and Josh Gardner about Marc Emerson's murder.'

'Ah, yes I remember. How can I help you?'

Cindy went on to explain about the file, the CV in Amanda Sherman's name, the mother's letters and mention of the police. She didn't mention Melanie Lewis's name as she didn't want to confuse matters. To her surprise and dismay, Walters didn't jump up and down with excitement.

'Cindy, in my job I've met many people who've changed their names. Some because they're being stalked by a former partner or been the victims of rape and others because they don't like their birth name.'

'I appreciate that but you must admit, it's strange behaviour for a senior finance professional.'

'Sorry, I don't. People from all walks of life do it.'

'What about the letters from her mother telling her to come home because the police have been to their house?'

'Yes, but we don't know what for, do we? It might be for something trivial like an unpaid parking fine or a complaint she's made about someone in her street. Listen Cindy, if you have a problem with your boss, talk it over with Francis Quinlan. It's not a police matter.'

'Don't you see? If she could do something as creepy as this, she could be Marc Emerson's killer.'

'I hope she's not in earshot, Cindy, as she could accuse you of defamation of character. You can't go around accusing someone of a crime without producing any hard evidence, and in my opinion, you don't have any.'

Cindy put down the phone and sulked. It was not the result she expected. She walked over to Sutherland's desk and returned all the papers back to their rightful places and locked the desk. She tidied her own desk, grabbed her jacket and headed downstairs. She'd hoped she wouldn't have to instigate the second phase of her plan, but yet again, lack of action by the police had left her little choice.

**

Christine Sutherland lived in Steyning, one of many small villages to the north of Brighton. Cindy had been there before, but only to take a look. Sutherland didn't own the house, only renting, she said, until she could find a property she wanted to buy. When taken in conjunction with an up-to-date CV, it suggested a woman who didn't intend sticking around.

She found the house without difficulty but drove past and parked further down the road as a precaution. Steyning was a typical Sussex village, with different shapes and sizes of houses on either side of a narrow main road. 'Individual' the house owners would call them, creepy and quirky would be Cindy's view. Sutherland lived in a detached stone-fronted house, extended into the roof to provide extra rooms, and not for the first time she asked herself why a thirty-one-year-old woman chose to live here.

If Cindy earned the big bucks of her FD, she would have a top-floor apartment smack-bang in the centre of Brighton. She would eat out a couple of days a week in many of the fancy restaurants that she couldn't afford even to walk into, attend gallery openings and watch lots of plays and shows at the theatre. No way would she choose to be stuck out in the sticks, living amongst young wannabes with their noisy and unruly broods, untidy gardens and the retired who spent their days gazing out of the window.

She walked up the path, self-conscious at being there but partially hidden by an over-grown cotoneaster plant and darkness not well illuminated by weak street lighting. For burglars, getting into a house was often their biggest anxiety; a neighbour could hear them breaking a window, the house might be alarmed or the kitchen could house a large dog. She had no such worries as Sutherland didn't have an alarm or a dog and the spare key was under a flower pot, its location revealed by Sutherland during an office discussion about being locked out.

She walked into the house, closed the door and stood for a moment, allowing her eyes to become accustomed to the gloom. She had never been in the house before and neither had anyone else from the office except Marc, but she knew what she was looking for. In a study or filing cabinet, she hoped to a find an official document such as a gas bill or a passport, to verify the identity of the woman she knew as Christine Sutherland, and if she was really lucky, something to prove that she was a fraud.

A quick search of the downstairs rooms revealed nothing and up the creaky stairs she went, looking at her watch as she did so. She knew the accountancy institute seminars Sutherland attended ran from 7pm to 8:30pm with a half hour period afterwards to drink wine and network. She wouldn't be back for another couple of hours.

She took her time in the main bedroom but was disappointed to come away with nothing, and she fared no different in the spare room. This left the room at the end of the corridor and given the reasonable size of the other two bedrooms, it was most likely a box room.

To her surprise, it wasn't full of junk but almost empty, except for a chair and a simple wall unit with a few boxes resting on the shelves. Her spirits fell as she expected someone as fastidious as Sutherland to own a filing cabinet or at least a big set of box files. What did she do with important documents like utility bills and tax returns, bin them?

She removed one box and set it down on the floor beside the conveniently sited chair. She sat down and opened the lid. Inside were various folders and when she opened the first one, found it full of newspaper cuttings. The box room was situated at the back of the house and didn't benefit from an intrusive streetlight, so she couldn't make out much. She lifted the folder towards the un-curtained window.

Her heart skipped a beat. The articles concerned a woman called Melanie Lewis. In one, a picture of a woman being led in handcuffs to a white Serco van. She held it up to the light to get a better look at her face. Christ! The caption read, 'Melanie Lewis' but she looked like a younger version of Sutherland; a sister perhaps, or was this Summer's FD a few years back?

She tilted the cutting in the direction of the

moonlight to try and read the date at the top, when she heard a noise behind her. She turned and saw the shape of a hammer coming towards her before the black of the night enveloped her for good.

THIRTY

Henderson left his ward in the East Surrey Hospital at eight in the morning. The doctors had prodded and poked him, run various tests and kept him in for overnight observation, but still couldn't find anything wrong after his unenforced dip in Ardingly Reservoir.

It was more than could be said for Lily Barton. When he went round to see her last night and again this morning, she was unconscious or more likely sedated. He guessed it had something to do with her prolonged time in the water and also her passive approach while in there. When he jumped overboard, he tried not to swallow water, broke the surface to take in air, and when swimming underwater he held his breath, but she did not.

He walked past the main reception area and out of the large doors at the front of the hospital. He stopped walking and looked around for his lift. He felt sympathy for those unfortunates approaching the hospital for treatment or those departing on wheelchairs or crutches to convalesce at home, but not for those having a smoke or taking a sly drink from a hip flask which he suspected didn't contain an energy booster.

He saw Walters's car parked on a double yellow line. He could only see the top of her head, her face lit in an eerie glow as she bent over, looking at something on her phone. He was about to head there when she finally looked up. She drove down, he climbed in and was immediately assailed by a wall of heat.

'My God, it's like a sauna in here.'

'I felt cold waiting for you and don't forget, you've been in hospital with hypothermia. I thought you'd be suffering from the shivers.'

'Nothing wrong with me that a nice glass of Glenmorangie last night couldn't cure,' he said, easing the heating control back to a reasonable 22 degrees.

'Office or home?'

'Home, if you please. I want to change out of these clothes before Rachel drives me back to the reservoir to pick up my car. Then, I can return the stuff I borrowed from the good people at the Activity Centre.'

'No need to go for the car. We picked it up last night. It's outside your house.'

'You did? Great. I hope I didn't put you out.'

'Me? Not one bit.' She paused. 'I asked Phil and Sally to do it.'

'Nevertheless, I'm grateful. Still head for home as I need to change and pick up the car.'

'Did they lend you that gear? If their stuff's as nice as that, maybe I should take a look in the shop.'

'Not these clothes you dope. They're mine. Rachel brought them up to the hospital last night. I meant the things in the plastic bag.'

'Oh, I see. I assumed hospitals were like prisons and they gave you a bag of personal things when you left.'

'What, like a shaving kit, toothbrush and a bus pass? MPs would have apoplexy if the NHS started wasting money on such frippery.'

'Did you see yesterday's *Argus*?'

'Nope. The only newspaper I saw was the Surrey Mirror and now I know enough about business rates in Guildford and bin collections in Reigate to last me a lifetime.'

'You and Lily made it on to the front page.'

'Really? I didn't see any reporters at the scene.'

'A guy called Adam Weir gave a first-hand account of the rescue and took a number of dramatic pictures.'

'What!' Henderson's first reaction was anger at someone intruding into Lily Barton's grief, but he soon calmed as he realised it was Adam at the Activity Centre. Lily would have died without his help.

'He deserves his day in the sun. He helped me loads. How did the whole thing look in print?'

'Dramatic and cold. He got a good one of you in the water, pulling Lily back to the boat. How is she, by the way?'

'Hard to tell. I don't think she's been conscious since she came out of the water but the doctor I spoke to said he expects her to make a full recovery.'

'That's good. Why did she do it? I mean, I might be asking the obvious as she's just lost her husband and her boyfriend, but did she really need to go out there to try and top herself? The woman is smart, good-looking and she's got a good job. She's got a lot going for her.'

'I know, but we're sitting here talking about it calmly and rationally. She's at home without family nearby, trying to come to terms with the deaths of the two men in her life, both of whom, I might add, died in violent circumstances. Maybe it all got too much for her or she couldn't face life without Marc.'

'Could there be more to it?'

'How do you mean?'

'I know we've considered the two murders might be some sort of vendetta against her—'

'Which the FLO dismissed after she talked to Lily about it.'

'I know, but if we frame it from the other side. What if Lily instigated both murders and her suicide is some form of remorse? She might not have carried out the actual killings herself, but got someone else to do them.'

Henderson was about to say something dismissive, something along the line of, how could she suspect such an intelligent and gentle woman; but he stopped. There was no doubt in her presence she had a powerful effect on him, but was it blinding him as to her culpability?

He had researched numerous historical murders and knew it to be a common occurrence. Many a detective had been duped into believing the innocence of the diminutive woman crying over her dead husband, only for forensics or an eye witness to prove that when roused, she could act like a psychotic maniac.

'I must admit, I did consider this idea at the beginning but didn't feel it necessary to follow-up. What made you think of it? Have you uncovered some new evidence?'

'No, there isn't any new evidence but she knew Marc Emerson's movements as well as anyone. She would know he was working late at the Weald warehouse.'

'Yeah, I see where you're coming from, but for her to not only kill her boyfriend, the avowed love of her life, but to do so in such a hideous manner; I think it's too much of a stretch.'

'Ok, but she might have been driven to it. Maybe Marc wanted to finish with her or threatened to tell her husband about the affair or something?'

'It's all so circumstantial; mind you, so are all the other suspects. Why would she kill Guy?'

'Ajay Singh is an old friend of Guy's and she knows him. What if she pushed Guy into getting involved in the robbery knowing it would end in tragedy; or maybe persuaded Singh to do it?'

'If she had some hold over Singh, it's possible, but the impression I have is she didn't like him much and in many ways, I can see why. I don't think the theory's credible.'

'Why not?'

'The more I think about it the more I believe she's not the type, and I know there's no such thing as a typical murderer, but I can't see her in the frame. I just can't see her motivation for doing it or her having the nerve to carry it out.'

On arriving back at his house in College Place, Henderson got out of the car, leaving Walters to drive to the office. The house was empty when Henderson walked in as he'd talked to Rachel last night and he didn't think there would be any need for her to stick around. He went upstairs and changed clothes and sorted out some papers he needed for the day ahead.

He stopped for a moment and looked around at his surroundings: the room where he stood, the rooftops of Brighton through the window, the cruising seagulls enjoying the thermals. A vision of this flashed through his mind when he was in the water and a feeling that he might not see it again. He didn't often dwell on morbid thoughts, but it sure felt good to be back here once again.

He headed downstairs and reached for his jacket when he realised he felt hungry. He'd been served breakfast at the hospital before being discharged but the lukewarm scrambled eggs didn't offer much appeal, and the streaky bacon too streaky for his liking. He left his jacket where it was on the peg and walked into the kitchen. He popped some bread into the toaster and fired up the coffee machine.

With his makeshift snack in his hands, he carried it over to the kitchen table and sat down. *The Argus* lay there, positioned by Rachel before she left for work so he would spot it. The front picture did look a touch dramatic as he could see the edge of Adam's boat and the distinctive shape of two people surrounded by grey water.

He read the article with care, looking for any reference to Marc Emerson. It mentioned that the woman rescued was the wife of Guy Barton, a man found dead a few days ago with gunshot wounds and suspected of carrying out the Lewes jewellery robbery. He could find no mention of him being a suspect in the Marc Emerson murder case. He thought this odd, as newspapers were more often accused of joining the dots where there weren't any, than being circumspect with information already in their possession.

Interviews with neighbours painted the rescued woman as quiet and polite, who didn't converse much over the garden fence. A colleague at the company where she worked, someone who knew Lily better, said it was uncharacteristic for her to do something like this, a woman so self-assured, intelligent and confident, but she had been under a lot of strain those last few weeks. She went on to say all her staff were deeply shocked and hoped she would return to work soon.

Henderson wondered how she could rebuild her life after suffering three major shocks in quick succession; the death of the two people closest to her and her own suicide attempt. He imagined the death of Marc and Guy would be worse than the death of an elderly relative or even a parent, deaths most people in time were able to come to terms with. Both men were young with their lives in front of them. She was a strong lady but with few relatives and friends around her to offer support, it would be a tough task.

Henderson rose and walked into the hall. He didn't know why he was trying to explore and understand the hidden depths of the human spirit. When he joined the police with a degree in Sociology and Psychology, he believed he possessed the tools to do so, but the job exposed him to incredible levels of courage, compassion, bravery, and on the flip side, to the pits of depravity, evil and corruption, unimaginable when starting out. Just when he believed he had an understanding of the subject, someone's unselfish heroism or another's callous disregard for human life would throw all his theories out of the window.

He lifted his jacket from the peg and stepped out of the house into another cold November morning.

THIRTY-ONE

Henderson looked up from the document he held in his hand when someone walked into his office. It was Lily Barton's Family Liaison Officer, Helen Vincent.

'Morning sir.'

'Ah, morning Helen. Thanks for coming in to see me. Take a seat at the meeting table, we'll talk there.' He rose from his chair and walked over to join her. 'Can I get you anything; tea, coffee?'

'No, I'm fine, sir, thanks.' She sat down. 'It's the first time I've been in these offices, they're more swish than our building.'

'You've been in your place a lot longer than us. We only moved here when Sussex House closed in January, but give it a few months and it'll be as tatty as everywhere else.'

'I suppose you're right.'

'Helen, the reason I asked you here this morning is to go over what happened at Lily Barton's house. I need to understand what signals she gave or didn't give prior to her disappearance, and if we failed in our duty of care. I simply want to understand the events leading up to her suicide attempt and see if there are any lessons we can learn. Does that sound ok?'

'Do you think there'll be a disciplinary hearing?'

'I think it's unlikely but questions will be asked,

how a woman on suicide watch came as close as this,' he said holding up his thumb and first finger with a small gap in between, 'to succeeding.'

'I understand.'

Henderson decided to do this for two reasons. First, as Senior Investigating Officer he took responsibility for placing Helen with Lily and wanted to put something about it on file. Second, he needed to be sure that no one could level a charge of incompetence at him or the FLO and denigrate all his team had achieved so far.

'Can I first ask, did you think the terms of reference you received briefed you adequately about the potential suicide risk?'

'I know I was put in there because you believed she might present a suicide risk, but I suppose I assumed before she acted, it would be prefaced by some signal: a bout of depression or excessive brooding. You know, I thought I would see some signs of her going downhill and then I would have spent more time watching her. As it was, she seemed to be coping with it pretty well. She had bouts of tearfulness, for sure, but no deep depression and believe me, I've seen some of that in my time.'

'I'm sure you have. So, she didn't show any outward signs of depression but was there anything else you can think of that might have triggered her actions?'

'Like what?'

'I don't know, maybe a phone call, a programme on television?'

'I don't think so. Hang on though, she had a visit

two days ago from a guy called,' she paused to flick through her notebook, 'Kevin McLaren.'

'I know him.'

'Piecing together what I saw of them and with the story Lily told me afterwards, he tried it on but she wasn't having it.'

'Really?'

'I went to the kitchen when I heard raised voices and it looked at first to me like they were kissing. They both pulled away as soon as they saw me. Lily said she had been fighting him off before I arrived on the scene, and I tend to believe her as she didn't look as if she was enjoying herself.'

'What happened then?'

'She told him to get out.'

'This suggests to me that his advances were unwarranted.'

'It might be, or she got angry at being rumbled and made it look like she was turfing him out to cover the lie.'

Henderson thought about McLaren and what he knew about him. He worked as a self-employed computer programmer and had been a good friend of Marc. He also took a keen, although he would call it unusual, interest in the progress of the investigation.

'I'll bear that in mind, Helen, thanks. Now talk me through the morning of Lily's escape.'

'It started much like every other morning. We sat and had breakfast together. I asked her what she wanted to do and we chatted.'

'What did she say she wanted to do?'

'We'd been shopping in Lewes the previous day

and she said she wanted to chill. She said she was thinking of going back to work and needed to get her head around it.'

'How did she seem?'

'Normal, I would say.'

'Ok, so what then?'

'We tidied up the kitchen and I went upstairs to brush my teeth. When I got there I decided to go to the loo as well so I closed the door. I noticed before I closed the door there wasn't a key in the lock. It had been there all the time I'd stayed in the house but I didn't think too much about it, with only me and Lily around.'

'Makes sense.'

'When I finished, I reached for the door handle and found it locked.'

'And you couldn't call in as your phone was on the kitchen table.'

Her face reddened. 'I've got one of those big Samsung things that doesn't fit into the pocket of a tight pair of jeans. It was my error and I accept I should have had it with me.'

'What did you think at this point? Why did she lock you in?'

'I knew straight away she hadn't make a mistake or it was an accident. I knew she'd locked me in on purpose so she could do something without me being there. I started to panic thinking she might switch on the gas.'

He smiled. 'If she did and lit a match, you wouldn't have had any trouble getting out of the bathroom.'

Helen's story confirmed his previous

understanding of the situation and he believed no fault could be laid at her door, other than to recommend she buy a smaller phone. Helen left his office five minutes later. He entered his report into the file and logged it. He was about to start on something else when DS Edwards came in.

'Good to see you Angus,' she said taking the seat opposite his desk. 'I heard all about your rescue. How are you feeling?'

'I feel fine. In fact, I felt fine yesterday as well, but they insisted in keeping me in for overnight observation, whatever that means.'

'How's Mrs Barton?'

'I've not spoken to her yet as she's been under sedation since her suicide attempt.'

'It can't be easy losing your husband and lover. I don't know if I could cope.'

Maybe she didn't but Henderson did. Edwards could be a tough woman, despite appearances.

'I'll go and see her today or tomorrow, see how she is and try to understand her side of the story.'

'Good idea but make sure there are no reporters or cameramen hanging about; I could do without seeing one of those: 'Brave Copper Meets Reservoir Woman' sorts of stories.'

'Me too.'

'How's the FLO?'

'Shaken by the whole thing I would say.'

'I'm not surprised. Are you recommending her censure?'

He shook his head. 'Lily Barton locked Helen in the bathroom and took the key away. It's a solid wooden door and if I hadn't turned up when I did, she'd still be in there. The only mistake she made was not taking her phone into the bathroom with her. If she'd phoned me, the incident might have played out better and quicker but not by much.'

She shook her head. 'It's a sorry business. I don't see any winners.'

'True.'

'How are the interviews going with the Fenton robbery crew?'

'They're going well. Ajay Singh has been charged with Guy Barton's manslaughter, robbery, being in receipt of stolen goods, gun possession; the works. His comrade, Solomon Fletcher, with robbery but the CPS won't try to pin 'accessory to manslaughter' on him. They intend to prosecute Singh as the sole shooter and if the defence team use Fletcher's shout to try and reduce the murder charge, the CPS will put up stiff resistance.'

'It all sounds good.'

'The Brummie pair will go down for dealing in stolen goods and Gerald Rattigan's minder, Barry Forshaw, for the possession of a gun. I thought his gun looked old and was maybe rented so I flagged it on the system. Birmingham now want to talk to Forshaw about the murder of a drug dealer in Lime Street six years ago.'

'Result!' she said smiling and slapped the desk for emphasis. 'You and the rest of the team have done a brilliant job, make sure you tell them all from me. Have we recovered all the jewellery?'

'I think so. Ajay says everything they took from the

shop was in the two holdalls and if you remember, Guy Barton was killed because he wanted to take away a piece and Ajay wouldn't let him.'

'How could I forget? It seemed such a pointless death when the thieves had all that gear. They wouldn't miss one bracelet. Does the widow know why her husband died?'

'No, and I'm not minded to tell her.'

She thought for a moment. 'It might be a wise move. No point in giving her something else to beat herself up with.'

'Even though we're sure we've got all the stolen jewellery, I don't expect Brian Fenton will agree. He'll probably say half a dozen priceless watches are missing.'

'Bit of a shyster is he?'

'Renowned.'

She shrugged. 'I'm sure we can leave the Robbery Squad to sort him out. Now, this only leaves Marc Emerson. Any new developments?'

He shook his head. 'We've interviewed his friends and family, trawled through his background, talked to people at his former workplace, but no other suspect stands out.'

'Except Guy Barton.'

'Except him and maybe Kevin McLaren. The FLO told me she thinks something might be going on between him and Lily Barton.'

'Not another lover, for Christ sakes?'

'I hope not, more likely she fended off his unwanted advances.'

'What's that woman got, eh? When I met my future

husband, I don't remember beating his competitors off with a stick as she seems to do.'

Henderson shrugged, not wanting to volunteer his theory.

'What do we do about the Marc Emerson case? I mean there's no way the ACC will tell us to wind it down after scoring so many aces, but I'm loathe to spend more money on an investigation that's reached a dead end and making no progress.'

'There's always something else we can do, as you know, but it does feel like we're lacking focus.'

She thought for a moment. 'Here's what we'll do. I want you to concentrate your team on processing the Fenton jewellery gang and the Barton murder evidence. You and a few other officers follow up those last remaining leads on the Marc Emerson case and if nothing surfaces a week from today, we'll put it on the holding file; still open, but no active enquiry.'

'I can't argue with you there,' Henderson said. 'What should we tell the papers?'

'We'll say that following the death of Guy Barton, we're not looking for anyone else in connection with Marc Emerson's murder.'

'It might be a shade economical with the truth, but it's not a word of a lie either.'

THIRTY-TWO

Lily Barton swung her legs out of bed and walked unaided to the toilet. She could tolerate many things about hospital: her restless and noisy fellow patients, the constant scrutiny by nurses and doctors and even the stodgy food, but not pissing into a bed pan. Dignity was well ingrained into her psyche and no way would she compromise.

It was the first time she'd walked there by herself and she felt a sense of achievement, tinged with a feeling of being a fraud. While waking up from sedation, she could hear the mumbling of visitors to Mrs Moore in the next bed, telling the old dear she was a more deserving case than someone who tried to top herself. She'd only do it again, one visitor said, and with a piece of luck, the next time she might succeed. No point in being a drain on the NHS.

She could only agree. If she did decide to kill herself and made another attempt, she would make sure it would succeed with no heroic detective within fifty miles. Such thoughts were now heresy, she didn't have any intention of trying again. She had been in a bad place and a long dip in icy cold water seemed to have knocked that notion right out of her head. The hospital psychologist seemed to agree as they no longer needed someone to accompany her everywhere and nurses stopped looking at her as if she was some kind of exotic species.

To avoid the sniping of the 'more deserving cases' lobby, she could have opted for a private room as her employer provided health insurance. Without close examination of the policy, she doubted it would cover cases of self-harm and even if it did, she would only do so if needing to recover from an operation or requiring peace to sleep, neither of which applied to her.

She took a seat at the side of her bed to await the arrival of a doctor. She'd collared the consultant during his morning rounds and he agreed there was nothing more the hospital could do. Before releasing her, he had to obtain the agreement of the psychologist treating her and arrange for someone from Social Services to call in regularly at her home to check on her progress. She didn't expect such a decision to be taken quickly but she didn't feel like going back to bed. Maybe if she got bored reading her magazine she would take a wander into the day room.

Time passed as she became engrossed in a short story in *Writing* magazine, her mind becoming absorbed in the plot while her business brain whirred into action, wondering why she hadn't heard of this author before. She didn't hear or see his approach but when the sound of shuffling feet made her look up, he was standing there.

She tossed the magazine to one side, leapt up and threw her arms around her visitor, Detective Inspector Henderson. She nuzzled into his neck, kissing him in a bow-wave of emotion and only when they separated did she feel the tears that were tumbling down her face.

'I'm so grateful for what you did,' she said. 'It was stupid of me, devoid of all reason.'

'No need to apologise, Lily. You were under a lot of strain.'

'I know but I'm eternally indebted to your timely intervention.'

'Any time I'm passing.'

She turned and removed a handful of paper hankies from the box beside her bed and dabbed her eyes.

'I brought you these,' he said handing her a couple of magazines and a pack of various pieces of cut fruit.

'Thank you, you're very thoughtful, but I feel such a fraud for taking them. I'm not ill.'

'Well, I'm not taking them back, so please enjoy.'

Henderson reached for a chair and sat facing her.

'How are you feeling?'

'Apart from tearful interludes like this,' she said pointing at her red, streaked face, 'I feel good; better than could be expected.'

'I'm not going to ask you why you did it, but I'd like to hear some reassurance you won't do it again.'

She clasped her hands in her lap. 'What my friends don't know because I've never told them, is my father committed suicide. He worked as a successful banker in the City of London and gave us a nice lifestyle with a fancy house, smart cars and good schools. One Friday evening, my sister and I were earwigging an argument my parents were having in the kitchen and that's when we found out that he'd made an illegal trade that had cost his bank one hundred and thirty million dollars. He'd been sacked and the bank had called in the police as they suspected wrongdoing. Not long after, me, my sister and mum went out for a walk. When we came back, I found him in the garage, a hose from the exhaust pipe stuck through the car window.'

'How old were you then?'

'Thirteen.'

'It must have been awful for you.'

'It was, I assure you, but worse was to come. The big house, the cars, our fee-paying school, the big Christmas presents were all an illusion that collapsed under the weight of my father's casino debts and the legal case the bank instigated to recover its missing money. My mother took to booze with an enthusiasm she once reserved for us and if not for my elder sister, Rebecca, I would never have made it beyond the teenager stage.'

'It's a terrible story.'

'It is,' she sighed. 'On the surface of it, I'm a successful book publisher with cash in the bank and a nice house in Lewes but underneath...I don't know, bad luck seems to follow me around.'

'I always believe in making your own luck and although the events of your childhood can't be changed, I would suggest the more recent events were a result of bad choices not bad luck.'

'I can't argue with you there. If I hadn't procrastinated about leaving Guy and moved in with Marc, things might have turned out better. In answer to your question, would I do it again? All I can tell you is the demons that were dogging my every step since childhood drowned in Ardingly Reservoir in place of me. My sessions with the psychologist here in the hospital made me realise I needed to talk to someone like her now and again. When I get out, I'll do that stereotypical American thing and get myself a therapist.'

'Why did you choose Ardingly?'

'When my father had money, he sent my sister and me to Ardingly College. I loved it there and often sailed in the reservoir. I was heartbroken when the money disappeared and we were forced to leave.'

'Where did you go?'

'We were sent to a state school in Haywards Heath. Much different from the place we were in before and we were bullied because of it and our posh accents.'

'You didn't do too badly, though.'

'No, but you know what the Jesuits say, 'give me a child until he is seven and I'll give you the man.' We both had a good grounding. My sister Rebecca got herself a good job when she left school and not only encouraged me to go to university but helped me financially.'

'What are you going to do now?'

'My sister lives with her husband and two kids in Hertfordshire and she's invited me to stay with them until I decide what I want to do. I'll need to take a decision on the Lewes house. I might sell it and move somewhere else or go back there; I don't know.'

'What about your job?'

'Rebecca lives near a train station with good

connections to London. I'll commute from there in the meantime. I'll go back into the office and behave as if nothing happened; the boss took ten days off; so what? They're a stoic but supportive lot, my staff. In any case, what I do in my day job is jolly. I deal with romance and fantasy books where despite the trials and tribulations of the plot, there's often a happy ending and a fairy-tale wedding.'

'I'm glad you enjoy it. Books like that would get me down.'

'I suppose in your work you see what people are really like. Not suntanned and handsome as they are in books but nasty and money grabbing, if not downright evil.'

'That just about sums it up but even in crime novels–'

'Hello, Lily how are you?'

She looked up. Kevin McLaren stood there, his bulky frame blocking her view of the patients across the room. In his hand he held a large card and a punnet of grapes. Her heart rate increased, but not as a sign of affection.

'What are you doing here? I told you when I saw you last time that I never wanted to see you again.'

'I come in peace. I brought you this,' he said holding up the items in his hand.

'I don't care, I don't want them. Now get the hell out.'

'Lily, I'm sorry for what happened between us. I was out of order. It was a mistake. I want to make it up to you.'

She shook her head in frustration. How many

times did she need to tell him? Women's magazines were full of 'when a woman says no she means no.' Which part of this did he not get? 'Kevin, get out, I don't want anything to do with you.'

'But Lily—'

Henderson stood. He was six foot something but still a few inches smaller than McLaren and not as broad.

'You heard the lady, Kevin, take your gifts and go.'

'No, I won't. Get out of my way.'

'I'm not going to tell you again, leave the hospital now or I'll throw you out.'

'Yeah, you and—'

Henderson moved quickly and grabbed McLaren's arm and twisted it up his back.

'Ah, you bastard that's sore. This is police brutality.'

'It'll be more painful if you don't get the hell out of here now.'

McLaren leaned round to look at her. 'You'll regret this Lily.'

'What, like Marc did?'

'What do you mean?'

'Don't think I don't know you were jealous of him. You looked at him with loathing every time you saw us together.'

'I don't deny it, but it was all for you Lily. I'd do anything for you.'

From the corner of her eye she saw two hospital security guards run in. When they came closer, Henderson released his hold and handed him over to the security guards.

'Did you have anything to do with killing Marc?' Lily asked him.

He was in the grip of the two security guards, but the sneer that crept across his face looked intentional.

'Would you love me if I did?'

THIRTY-THREE

He shifted his feet off the footrest and sat up, the little visitor's chair beside Walters's desk emitting a high-pitched squeak as if Henderson had trodden on a dog's paw. At least it wasn't one of the chairs brought over from Sussex House as they were so rickety, a move like that and an arm or a castor would fall off.

'Did McLaren look angry when he said it?' Walters asked.

'Nope. Cool as you like. I don't think that guy ever gets flustered.'

'Not even when you shoved his arm up his back?'

'He looked pained but didn't lose his rag as many in that position are prone to do.'

'He's a cool character, right enough. Shall we bring him in?'

'I'm not convinced he killed Marc but he might know more than he's telling. Bring him in, but I'll ask Harry to do it because with me, I'd just wind him up and with you and Sally, he'd switch on the charmer.'

'Are you suggesting–'

'Excuse me boss,' Phil Bentley said, standing in front of Henderson. 'There's a bloke called Francis Quinlan on the phone. He wants to speak to you.'

'Ok, Phil. Put him through on Carol's extension.' He looked at Walters. 'I wonder what he's calling about?'

'Maybe it's about that consignment of sausages and steaks he promised to send you.'

'Wouldn't that be nice?' he said reaching for the ringing phone.

'Detective Inspector Henderson here.'

'Good morning Detective Henderson, it's Francis Quinlan from Quinlan Foods. How are you this cold December morning?'

'Not bad. Looking forward to a break at Christmas, if I'm truthful.'

'Ah, me too. It's been bedlam here. I don't care if I never see another turkey stuffing.'

'I'll bet. Now, what can I do for you?'

'One of my staff members, Cindy Summer, is missing.'

'Define missing. For how long; what have you done to try and locate her?'

'Four days but what you must understand, Inspector, Cindy has never, I repeat, never missed a day's work in the six years she's worked for me. She's a diamond, she really is.'

'Cindy Summer, you say?' Henderson said repeating the name for Walters's benefit. She nodded. Good, because the name meant nothing to him.

'Yes, she works in Accounts. I sent someone around to her flat in Hove but her car's not there and her neighbours haven't seen her for days. Even a girl in the office who's her best friend can't raise her on her phone and she's not replying to texts. I'm really worried in light of what happened to Marc.'

Henderson was tempted to say, 'call uniform, they

deal with missing persons,' but he stopped. 'We'll be right over. Gather up as much information about Cindy as you can before we arrive.'

'Thank you Inspector, I really appreciate it.'

Henderson put down the phone and turned to Walters. 'Cindy Summer from Quinlan's has gone missing. I said someone would go over and take a look. You and I can go, everyone else is working on the Barton and Fenton files for the CPS.'

'Ok.'

'Let's go.'

'I remember now, I thought her name rang a bell,' Walters said as they headed downstairs. 'Cindy stopped me and Seb when we went to Quinlan's in early November to talk to Josh Gardner and Christine Sutherland.'

'What did she want?' Henderson asked, opening the door of the building and walking outside.

'She said we should be looking at either Josh or Christine for Marc's killer. Josh worked beside Marc in sales and was jealous of him, she said, and Christine used to go out with Marc and was besotted by him. My notes are all in the file.'

Henderson opened the car door and climbed in. 'Did you follow it up?'

'Yeah, we talked about both of them in the team briefings. She didn't have anything to add but at that stage of the investigation it made me look closer at Sutherland and Gardner.'

He sighed. 'With the conclusion we all know about.'

'Yes indeed. She looks odd too.'

'How so?'

'Small, elfish, pale complexion with straight black hair and wide eyes.'

He smiled as he drove out of the Malling House car park and headed for Brighton. 'I hope Francis Quinlan can come up with a better description than you, or every sighting will identify a cast member of the children's play running at the Theatre Royal this week.'

'I did say she looks odd. There's more.'

'Hit me with it.'

'Remember the day you rescued Lily Barton from Ardingly Reservoir, last Wednesday?'

'How could I forget? I've still got the cough to prove it.'

'That evening, I took a call from Cindy.'

He looked over. 'Really?'

'Keep your eyes on the road, please. Hang on and I'll find my notes.' She opened her notebook and flicked through the pages until she located the page. 'Cindy said she found evidence–'

'She called you last Wednesday?'

'Yep, that's what I said.'

'That's four days ago. Quinlan said Cindy's been missing for four days.'

She thought for a moment. 'Good point, which makes me one of the last, or maybe the last person to speak to her before she disappeared.'

'Might be. Go on with your story.'

'She said she'd found evidence that her boss, Christine Sutherland, is using false names. She discovered two CVs, one in Christine's name and another in some other woman's name, Amanda Sherman.'

'It's odd but not illegal behaviour, in my opinion.'

'I said the same to her, but she said it marked Christine Sutherland out as strange and because she was besotted by Marc Emerson, it follows that she killed him.'

'It's too big a leap for me. We'll take what Quinlan gives us, add it to your phone call with Cindy and see where it takes us. Ok?'

**

Walters fast forwarded the DVD on her computer. At last, she located the time the card reader at Quinlan Fine Foods recorded Cindy Summer leaving the building at the Fairway Business Park. She watched as Cindy walked into the car park and climbed into her Ford Fiesta and drove away.

'We can conclude from this,' Henderson said, sitting in the seat beside her, 'that Cindy didn't get attacked on her way to the car park. Also, nobody followed her out of the building and her car disappeared from view without anyone tailing her.'

'True, but remember what the chairman told us, she rarely works beyond five-thirty. The time-stamp on the camera says six-forty-five. What's she been doing all this time?'

'She called you at six-thirty so I assume between her usual departure time and talking to you, she was rooting through Christine Sutherland's things trying to find evidence of her wrongdoing.'

'I assumed after my conversation with her, she would realise Sutherland's crimes didn't amount to much, and leave it at that.'

'What if she didn't and continued to look but couldn't find what she was looking for. What would she do then?'

'Go home and take stock?'

'We know she didn't do that because Quinlan's people talked to neighbours and they didn't see her return to her house and her car isn't there.'

'Talk it over with friends?'

'She doesn't have many of those and her close friend says she hasn't seen her since Wednesday afternoon.'

'Maybe she found a pub and drowned her sorrows.'

'For four days? I don't think so. Maybe, if she knew that Sutherland was out that evening, she went over to her house to have a nose around.'

'Could be. What do we do now?'

'First, let's get Cindy's Ford Fiesta flagged up on ANPR. Second, let's go take a look at Sutherland's place. We know she's at work and won't be spooked by our presence.'

The traffic was heavier than earlier when they went to Quinlan's, most likely due to parents heading home after picking up their children from playschool or nursery. He suspected the bitter easterly wind would keep most people indoors today and anyone venturing out restricted to those on an essential errand.

'She lives here?' Walters said as they drove into Steyning. 'It's gold-plated suburbia. Having met her twice, I imagined a woman like that would own a big flat along Brighton seafront or a smart apartment like Rachel's old place in Hove.'

'It takes all sorts.'

He parked at the side of the road, close to Sutherland's house in the unoriginally named The Street. He got out of the car and waited for Walters before heading towards the front door. 'May as well ring the doorbell and see if she's got a housemate or an elderly relative staying,' he said. 'I don't want to be walking around the garden and find ten minutes later we're surrounded by an armed response unit shouting for us to lie down.'

He knocked on the door and held a hand up to stop Walters speaking. He was listening for the movement of an occupant or the grunts and whispers of their missing woman. He heard nothing and knocked again. Nothing.

'Let's take a look around the back.'

'Did you notice the guy across the road gawping at us?'

'Is he? It's good to know we have a local nosey parker. Could prove useful.'

'Not if he calls the station.'

'He probably thinks we're from the council and fearful of having his Community Charge increased, he's trying to keep himself hidden.'

The small gate opened without being forced and Henderson, followed by Walters, walked around to the back of the house. It was a long, narrow garden with a rotary dryer, shed and a vegetable plot at the far end. Henderson tried the handle on the back door but it didn't budge. He looked through the window but saw little of interest except the detritus of a rushed breakfast and a householder who didn't believe much in tidying up.

He headed for the shed where Walters was trying to peer inside through the dirty window. The door was locked but one he could open without too much trouble.

A few minutes later, Walters poked her head inside.

'See anything interesting?' she asked

'Nope, a few bits of gardening gear but no boxes or places to hide anything.'

'Nothing much out there either.'

They both headed outside, Walters in the direction of the car and Henderson towards the vegetable plot at the rear of the garden.

'Look at this, Carol. Notice anything?'

She walked up the path towards him. 'Yes, I thought it looked tidy.'

'It's more than that. This ground has recently been dug over.'

'So? Don't serious gardeners dig their plots in the winter? Add some compost and get the ground ready for planting in the spring or something.'

'Very good, Carol, for a flat-dweller. They do, not often in the frost-heavy months like we've had recently, but Christine Sutherland doesn't strike me as a keen gardener. You?'

'No, but as you say, it takes all sorts.'

'Can I help you?'

Henderson looked over in the direction of the voice. A woman with curly grey hair and wearing a thick body warmer glared back at them from across a dividing hedge.

Henderson walked towards her and fished out his ID. 'Police. There's been a number of thefts from garden sheds in the area, we're checking one or two just to be on the safe side.'

'I see. Well ours is fine. My Harry fitted a new lock only two weeks ago.'

'Well done, madam. Can you tell me who lives here?' he said, jerking a thumb towards Christine Sutherland's house. 'It's a very neat garden.'

'A single woman lives there. It's rented, of course. Her name is Christine Sutherland but we don't see her often and if we do, she doesn't talk to the likes of us. A bit stuck-up, if you know what I mean.'

Henderson nodded.

'She must get someone in to do it, the garden I mean, but I don't know when. I never see anyone out there. Mind you, if we drink a glass or two of wine over lunch, me and him will have snooze beside the fire,' she said with a smile.

'Thank you very much for your assistance, madam,' Henderson said, not wishing to hear another anecdote from the annals of the retired in Steyning. 'You've been very helpful.'

'But you didn't check my shed. My husband, Harry, will be most upset.'

'We will do so when we come by next time, don't you worry. Goodbye.'

'You nearly put your foot in it there,' Walters said as they walked back towards the car.

'How?'

'You were so close to being roped in to doing an inspection on that woman's shed and she looks the sort who would call on all her neighbours to join in.'

'Now wouldn't that be a good story to tell in the canteen,' he replied as he unlocked the car. 'Get in.'

He pulled out of the parking space and had only travelled about ten metres when he noticed the road ahead was blocked. The automated arm on a slow-moving refuse lorry reached over and picked up the tall bins lining the pavements as if they weighed nothing, and emptied them into its cavernous belly. It did this every five metres or so along the road. He couldn't hope to overtake, as the road on the other side was full of parked cars, and fascinating as it was to watch this mechanical monster, he didn't have the patience to watch it all the way to the outskirts of the village.

While waiting, he programmed the satnav to take them back to Lewes before executing a U-turn. It felt as if they were driving in the wrong direction but he had little choice until the system re-calculated another route back to Lewes, hopefully before they reached a critical road junction.

'I know this area,' Walters said, 'not far from here we'll see a turn-off for the A283.'

'The road we took coming here?'

'Yep. We'll be joining it further back but it'll still take us back to the Shoreham by-pass.'

'Good. Who needs a satnav?' Henderson said, as the said system sprang into life and indicated the same route as suggested by the sergeant.

They were passing a line of parked cars when

Walters shouted, 'Stop the car! Look over there!'

'What is it?'

'Pull into the side now!'

Henderson slowed and on spotting a gap further ahead, eased the car into the space.

'Back there,' Walters said, 'the maroon Fiesta. I think it's Cindy Summer's car!'

THIRTY-FOUR

'Interview timed at 18:32. Please state your name and occupation for the tape,' Walters said to the woman sitting across from her at the interview table.

'My name is Christine Sutherland. I am the Financial Director of Quinlan Fine Foods in Brighton.'

'Also present is Detective Inspector Angus Henderson,' he said.

'Detective Sergeant Walters,' she said.

'Good,' Henderson said, 'formalities complete. Now, as I said earlier Ms Sutherland, you're here voluntarily and are free to leave at any time, but first I'd like to ask you a few questions. Does that sound ok to you?'

'Fine.'

Christine Sutherland held him confidently in her gaze before looking down at her hands. She was a good-looking woman with shoulder-length dark hair, deep green eyes and prominent cheek bones. Aged thirty-one according to details supplied by her employer, a qualified Management Accountant with a curvy figure that could only be described as voluptuous. Brains as well as looks; a heady combination. Not for the first time did he wonder what power and charisma Marc Emerson had once possessed to attract a bevy of beauties towards him, from a model ex-wife to Lily Barton, and now this enigmatic and attractive woman in front of him.

'Now Ms Sutherland–'

'Call me Christine.'

'Christine, I'm leading the team investigating the murder of Marc Emerson.'

'I thought you already had someone for this. Wasn't the man shot in Brighton, that rat Guy Barton, responsible?'

'Why do you call him a rat? Did you know him?'

'I didn't know him but Marc did and he didn't like him much.'

'You're right. He was one of our leading suspects, but with him dead it might prove difficult to build a case against him. However, there are still a number of loose ends we'd like to clear up.'

'Such as?'

'I'll get to them in time. Tell me about your relationship with Marc.'

'I told her this before,' she said, nodding at Walters.

'I know you did and I've read the interview notes but I want you to tell me again.'

She sighed. 'We were going out, on and off, for about five months.'

'Why on and off?'

'Oh sometimes he would finish with me after an argument, or I would do the same to him.'

'It sounds like you had quite a volatile relationship.'

For a moment she looked flustered. Walters had picked this point up in the first interview. Marc didn't often finish with her, according to other people in the Finance department, it was temperamental Sutherland doing the dirty on him and regretting it the next day. From sitting in the office slowly tearing his cards and notes into shreds and sending them back to him in an envelope, to having a blazing row in the company car park, viewed by all in the offices behind them.

'No, I wouldn't call it volatile. We behaved no different from anyone else I know. We had our ups and downs for sure, but who doesn't?'

'How did you manage your relationship in the office?' Walters asked. 'Did you try to keep it secret?'

'We did at the start but Lewes is a small town and we were soon spotted. It didn't give us much of a problem as Marc was out on the road for long periods on sales calls, and due to the senior position I hold in the company, staff wouldn't dare say anything while I'm around.'

'Was there much?'

'I'm sure there was. Marc is, was, a much sought after catch, especially working in a business dominated predominantly by women. A lot of jealousy and bitching goes on but when he could have his pick of all the women, he chose me.'

'On the night Marc was killed, you were at a hotel in East Grinstead attending a seminar hosted by your accountancy institute.'

'Yes, the Effingham Park Hotel.'

'What was it about?'

'What?'

'The seminar. What was it about?'

'You're interested in accountancy? My, my whatever next? Let me think. The subject was Time Management.'

'Which is what?'

'How to better utilise your time, how to prioritise and delegate; those sorts of things.'

'Do you pay for these seminars?'

'Some of them are free but this one required payment.'

'What's the format for the meeting?'

Henderson knew this as Walters had called Sutherland's accountancy institute and talked to the person responsible for running training seminars, but he wanted to hear it from her.

'We gather in the foyer and have some chit-chat for ten, fifteen minutes, and then go into the meeting room to listen to the speaker. At the end there's questions and after that, drinks and a chance to network. It's the only reason I go, to network and–'

'Did you meet anyone you know there?'

'No. Even though, I've lived in Sussex for less than a year, so I don't know many other accountants.'

'If you went there to network, surely someone could vouch for your presence there?'

'You can see I was there from the payment on my credit card statement. In fact I used my Quinlan credit card to pay for it so Francis Quinlan's secretary should have a copy.'

'How did you feel when Marc died?'

'How the hell do you think?' she said raising her voice for the first time. 'I was devastated. I still love him, if you must know.'

'Who do you think is responsible for his death?'

'Guy Barton, I told you already. He didn't like Marc and Marc didn't like him.'

'I think Guy is more a fist and boots sort of person,' Henderson said. 'Setting someone on fire doesn't look his style.'

'Is this what the police do, is it? Assign 'killing styles' to people. There must be a lot of criminal psychologists working on this case.'

'There aren't any.'

'I don't care if you think it's not his style, I think Barton did it.'

'Christine, when we searched through Marc's things, we found a number of large deposits had been made into his bank account. When finally we managed to trace their source, we found they came from you.'

She shrugged.

'Why did you give Marc Emerson ten thousand pounds, and again, a month later? He obviously didn't want the money as he sent it straight back.'

She sighed. 'When he bought the house in Spences Lane, he wasn't quite ready to move but his hand was forced by his pig of a father-in-law, Jeff Pickering. As a result, he didn't have a lot of savings behind him. He told me he needed more money and I lent it to him. He could be a stubborn brute at times and said he wanted to manage buying the house on his own, so he sent it back.'

'Were you annoyed at his refusal to accept?'

'Why would I be? It's no big deal.'

'Now, as you are no doubt aware, Cindy Summer, a

financial analyst in your department has been missing since last Wednesday. Francis Quinlan is very concerned. Do you know anything about her whereabouts?'

'Me?' she said, the indignation evident in her voice. 'I don't socialise with any of my staff, I make a point of it, and I don't care what they get up to in their spare time. As long as they come in to work every day and do a good job, I'm happy. So no, I don't have a clue what's happened to Cindy but I want her back soon, there's some reports she needs to finish.'

Walters gave him a look that said, ask her about Cindy's car, but he gave her an almost imperceptible shake of the head in return.

'What were you doing on the night she disappeared, last Wednesday?'

She smiled. 'Another institute seminar, and before you ask, this one was about strategy.'

Henderson terminated the interview five minutes later. Walters walked Sutherland back to Reception, before heading back to Henderson's office where she found him sitting behind his desk looking at Christine Sutherland's CV.

'She's a polished interviewee,' she said, 'never gets flustered and answered all our questions.'

'Too good if you ask me. Did you notice the lack of emotion when Marc's name was mentioned and the casual way she dismissed any discussion about the mystery bank deposits?'

'I did. This is the man she hounded with texts and repeatedly appeared on his doorstep, even saying today that she still loved him. Oh, and sorry for not following up the training seminar thing at the time. I didn't realise the attendees aren't required to sign-in and no one takes a note if anyone leaves early.'

'It has the appearance of a valid alibi as she can produce credit card receipts and make it look like she went there, enough to satisfy most enquiries without further scrutiny. But don't apologise for not doing it, she didn't strike any of us at the time as a serious suspect.'

'But she is now.'

'You bet.'

'Why didn't you pick apart her seminar alibi, and mention that we found Cindy's car?'

'Look at her CV,' he said. 'She never stays in one place too long and she's renting the house we looked at in Steyning. I couldn't see any of her personal stuff when I looked through the window. If she ever gets wind of our suspicion that she might have killed Marc Emerson, and we're not there yet, she would immediately scarper, never to be seen or heard of again. I guarantee it.'

'Which means?'

'It means we need to build a rock-solid case and be convinced of her guilt, before we go after her.'

'Sounds good in principle but we've still got nothing concrete to go on; no witnesses, a flaky alibi and no forensics.'

'We do what all good detectives do, now we've got ourselves a new suspect. We comb her background armed with this CV and the alias Cindy Summer told you about. Talk to former employers, family, friends; anyone we can.'

'I'm on it,' Walters said, her enthusiasm restored.

'We need to make it quick. Edwards wants to close the case down by the end of this week and pin it on Guy Barton.'

'Yeah, but we know it's not true.'

'I would prefer to say we think it's not true and we won't know until we've turned over all the stones. There is a possibility Guy Barton is responsible by the simple logic that it can't be anyone else in Marc's circle, once we've eliminated them all.'

'It's not like you to give up without a fight.'

'Who says I'm giving up? Edwards has left me no choice and I don't have the evidence to argue a stronger case. We'll find out everything we can about Christine Sutherland, and if she's no good, then we move on to Kevin McLaren. I've got no intention of letting this one go.'

THIRTY-FIVE

'You should have taken Harry Wallop with you,' Phil Bentley said. 'Norfolk is more his neck of the woods than mine. He would have enjoyed a trip back to his old stomping ground.'

'If I did, we wouldn't get back home tonight,' Walters said, 'as he would be too busy visiting relatives and looking up old girlfriends. Anyway, it's not like you to pass up the chance of a day out of the office.'

'I'm not ungrateful, Sarge, but the list of questions the CPS sent back to me about the Guy Barton murder case will still be there when I get back.'

'Yes, but you'll feel invigorated after an afternoon basking in pure Norfolk air.'

'It's too cold to do any kind of basking but I live in hope.'

Walters had done as much as she could researching Christine Sutherland using social media, police sites and looking at company websites such as Quinlan's and those of her former employers. Now she wanted to meet someone who knew her better than Francis Quinlan seemed to do, and in any case, she fancied getting out of the office for a spell. To that end, they were driving along the A12 towards a village in Norfolk called Newton Flotman to see Sutherland's previous employer at Gresham Fresh Produce.

The name given to Walters by Cindy Summer, Amanda Sherman, didn't raise any flags on the Police National Computer and so she assumed Sutherland was trying out the name to see how it looked and sounded, perhaps with a view to adopting it sometime in the future.

Changing a name was as simple as submitting a form, thousands of women did the same thing every year with a marriage certificate. For everyone else in the UK, it was done by a process known as Deed Poll. In some ways, it made the job of the police harder, although the aliases of habitual criminals were logged on the system. However, another part of her felt, why not? If someone had been lumbered at birth with a bizarre Christian name like Apple or Tinkerbelle or an unusual surname such as Tubby or Bytheway, why shouldn't they do it?

The Norfolk scenery passed by in a blur, a featureless landscape of huge fields dissolving into the distance by a cold, low mist. Little farming activity was going on now, most of the fields had been ploughed in late autumn and left fallow and bare, or strewn with the shredded stalks of harvested corn, slowly composting into the ground.

Gresham Fresh Produce lay down a narrow B-road outside Newton Flotman, a large village about twenty miles south of the only city in the county of Norfolk, Norwich. The road was bordered on both sides by a row of tall straight trees, the only landmark on an otherwise featureless landscape.

They turned into another narrow B-Road and after

half a mile, she saw the sprawling complex of Gresham Fresh Produce. She'd looked the company up on the web and was impressed by some of the pictures at its size, but only by being there could she appreciate the scale. There were three huge barns, a sizeable car park with several lorries parked outside and a three-storey administration block. The complex was surrounded on all sides by fields, giving the impression they were in the middle of nowhere.

They were led without much delay into the office of Managing Director, David Gresham. Aged around mid-fifties, he looked slim and athletic, if the way he bobbed up from his chair to greet them was anything to go by. He had grey slicked hair and a clean-shaven, healthy looking face, reminding her of an American TV evangelist.

'Officers, good to meet you. I'm always happy to help the forces of law and order,' he said as he shook their hands.

'Thank you for seeing us, Mr Gresham.'

'Before we start, can I get you anything? We do the usual teas and coffees but as we are also a major vegetable supplier, I can rustle up some great vegetable drinks. I love the carrot and orange but my p.a. swears by the beetroot and ginger. Are either of you tempted?'

'At the risk of sounding rude, coffee for me,' Walters said.

'I'll try the carrot and orange,' Bentley said. 'I'm trying to add more vegetables to my diet as I play rugby and I've been rubbish these last few weeks.'

'Good man. I can't guarantee it'll make you run

faster but I'm sure you'll enjoy it. Back in a minute.'

'Quite a place this,' Walters said. 'It stinks of money. A big fancy office like this, smart cars outside and did you see their trucks, all less than two years old?'

'Not much to do at lunchtime though.'

'Yeah, and you're closer to nature out here. I bet the bugs are a nightmare in the summer.'

Gresham breezed in a few minutes later and placed the drinks in front of them. 'Sorry for the delay, I got waylaid; you know how it is. Now,' he said, sitting down on the chair behind his desk, 'how can I help you?'

Walters explained about Marc Emerson's murder and how a local person had become a suspect.

'And you're here because?'

'The woman we're interested in, Christine Sutherland, used to worked here.'

'That she did,' he said brushing his hand through his hair, a wistful expression creeping across his face.

'A lovely girl she was. Always pleasant, nothing too much trouble and she improved the quality of the reports I receive a thousand-fold. I tell you this, it might look like a simple business: we bring in vegetables, clean, prepare and package them, but some of our customers are the largest supermarkets in the country. Make a mistake and you're yesterday's toast. When you go into Sainsbury's in Cheltenham and pick up a broccoli or a pack of stir fry vegetables at Tesco in Basingstoke, chances are it came from here.'

He went to quote the millions they made in

turnover, the number of potatoes they sold each year and how the demand for products such as kale and quinoa could rocket when recommended by a popular magazine or celebrity chef.

'In the past, I would never have been able to throw these statistics at you without the great work done by Christine. She revolutionised my management reporting system. Now, I get reports detailing sales for the previous week on a Monday while before then I had to wait two weeks, and my monthly accounting pack comes out on the fourth workday when it used to come out in the middle of the month.'

'It sounds like she made a big difference to your business.'

'Oh, she did, but I don't think she's the woman you're talking about.'

'Why not?'

'Christine Sutherland was murdered two years ago.'

**

Detective Sergeant Sandy Pendle didn't offer them fancy vegetable drinks or smoothies, only the metallic tasting output from an old coffee machine at the end of the corridor. What he did offer was cooperation and Walters would trade that for a healthy vegetable smoothie any day.

If David Gresham and Sandy Pendle were to be placed side by side, a casual onlooker would swear that Sandy was the vegetable farmer and not David. The Norfolk DS had a round ruddy face, untidy fair hair that couldn't be tamed by a mere hairbrush and large, scarred hands that were a stand-in for spades. If he slapped a file on the desk, it would wake up anyone dozing within a three desk-radius.

They were on the third floor of the central police station of Norfolk Police in a town called Wymondham on the outskirts of Norwich. In the same way that the Home Office had combined the serious crime directorates of Surrey and Sussex, it had happened here with Suffolk and Norfolk. Walters had seen the stats and believed that Surrey and Sussex were matched in terms of the quantity and seriousness of the crimes they investigated, but Norfolk looked to her more rural than their neighbour with few large conurbations, while Suffolk had several, and a number of working ports.

'Before I let you see what we 'ave in 'ere,' Pendle said, 'tell me again what you said about the mixed up identities. I'm confused.'

'It hasn't been easy for us either, I assure you. We have a suspect in a murder case who calls herself Christine Sutherland. According to her CV, her last employer was Gresham's in Newton Flotman. When we spoke to the Managing Director at Gresham's, he assured us Christine Sutherland was once an employee there, but the woman he knew is dead; murdered two years ago. He told us a bit about the murder hunt, finding the body and the funeral but he didn't know the status of the investigation.'

'I'm still confused.'

'Sandy,' Walters said, hiding her exasperation from this obdurate man. 'I know this isn't easy so what I suggest we do is this. You tell us about your girl and we'll tell you about ours. Maybe between the three of us we can make some sense.'

A large shovel of a hand reached to open the folder but stopped. 'Appreciate my problem here. We spent months looking for this killer. The last thing we want,' he said nodding towards them, 'is two detectives from down south telling us what idiots we are for missing some bloody obvious clue.'

'Sandy believe me, it won't happen. As far as I know, this is a case of mistaken identity. If we discover it's more than that and our suspect is implicated in this woman's murder, you will be the first to know.'

He looked at her face, searching for the trace of lies or a hint of mistrust. Finding none, he opened the file.

'Christine Sutherland, our Christine Sutherland, left the offices of Gresham Fresh Produce where she worked as Financial Director at seven in the evening on September 4th 2014. She never arrived home. Her husband reported her missing at 9:15pm that evening and when she didn't turn up for work the following morning we started a search. We checked CCTV and spotted her car driving north along the A140 from Newton Flotman and then on the southern ring road.'

'Where does that lead?'

'South eastern parts of the city like Trowse, Thorpe, Whitlingham Country Park and then on to Great Yarmouth.'

'Ok,' she said. She'd heard of Great Yarmouth but none of the others.

'We lost her soon after and never picked up her car

again. Two days later, an early morning runner in Whitlingham Country Park reported seeing a body in some reeds at the side of the broad, I mean the lake. We recovered it and found Christine Sutherland. She'd suffered serious head wounds and while still alive, her assailant had dumped her in the lake. The wounds received had been inflicted by a blunt object. If pushed, the pathologist thought something like a heavy spanner or a hammer.'

'What about suspects?'

'We interviewed her friends, her husband was a suspect for a spell, we talked to runners and fisherman at Whitlingham and we interviewed all her work colleagues. By all accounts she was a hard-working woman who socialised little and spent most of her time looking after her husband and two young kids.' He looked at his watch. 'Shit, there's something I need to do for my boss in ten minutes. I can leave you with the file but I don't want you taking anything away. Ok?'

'No problem, Sandy,' Walters said, pleased at gaining some thinking time.

The file was thick, the result of a large police investigation and she suspected not the only one, but it would do for now. She divided the pile between her and Bentley and, trying to keep it in the same order as the Norfolk detectives, sifted through the contents. The murder had made a splash locally, hitting the front pages of the *Eastern Daily Press* and later in the week, a double-page spread when the body was found.

It made her sad to see pictures of Christine's two young children, one six and the other four. On the anniversary of their mother's death, they would have to endure speculation from some newspapers that seemed to delight in making up motives for unsolved murders: did she come down to Whitlingham to meet a lover, or could she have been involved in a high-level business fraud?

The interviews conducted with work colleagues interested her, having now seen the Gresham operation. The HR department had supplied Norfolk Police with organisation charts and bios of everyone in the dead woman's team, with a helpful one-page print of mini-photographs copied from their personnel files.

She glanced down the list of serious faces to see if she recognised anyone from this morning's visit. Tucked in the middle she spotted a face she did recognise. The name of this woman was Melanie Lewis, but if Walters was not to be misled by the dark hair and the short bob style, so different from the way she looked now, it was the face of the woman she knew now as Christine Sutherland.

THIRTY-SIX

Henderson rose from his chair and walked to the window. His office overlooked the numerous buildings that made up the Malling House complex in Lewes, the hills of the South Downs rising in the distance. It looked a grey, featureless day with thick clouds dulling the light, coupled with a sharp northern wind that encouraged those outside to button up their coats and jackets as soon as they left the sanctuary of the building.

He turned to face DS Walters, seated at the table with an expectant expression on her face, a predator in sight of her prey. 'Let me take this in. Our Christine Sutherland who might be called Melanie Lewis, but we don't know, was once the work colleague of someone called Christine Sutherland, the Financial Director of Gresham Fresh Produce in Norfolk?'

'Yep.'

'The real Christine Sutherland was murdered by person or persons unknown, also for reasons unknown as the Norfolk Police couldn't find anything in her past, present or in any of her relationships that looked dodgy?'

'Yes.'

'And you believe the woman who is the current Financial Director at Quinlan's in Brighton has taken her name?'

'More than the name, boss, she's added all of Christine's experience to her CV. In essence, she's adopted her identity.'

Henderson retook his seat, the day kicking off more complex and confusing than his morning brain could handle. Of course, the couple of glasses of wine and the one, or was it two, bottles of beer last night didn't help.

'I checked the Quinlan FD's CV and the experience and dates match up to the one Gresham gave me for their Christine Sutherland.'

'I'm with you now. What job did Melanie Lewis do at Gresham's?'

'She was a financial analyst in Christine Sutherland's department. She didn't have much in the way of experience and, a key omission, she didn't have any accountancy qualifications.'

'And yet,' he said warming to the story as his brain seemed to have finally woken up, 'according to the CV of the FD at Quinlan's, she's a qualified accountant with a business degree from Exeter University.'

'Precisely, which are the exact qualifications of Christine Sutherland, the murdered woman in Norfolk.'

'We can assume, therefore that the woman at Quinlan's, let's call her Melanie Lewis to save confusion, is guilty of assuming another woman's identity.'

'Right, plus faking her CV and making up her qualifications.'

'I don't want to curb your obvious enthusiasm, DS

Walters, God knows we could use more of it around here, but identity fraud is hardly something to interest a Serious Crime Unit like this one. Yes, it's illegal, but it's way, way down the list of misdemeanours handled by the High Court.'

She sighed. 'I do realise it doesn't sound much but it's enough to haul her in for questioning again, don't you think? Cindy Summer is still missing and now we've got this murder in Norfolk to consider.'

'Hold on, you're getting ahead of yourself. We've no evidence of her involvement in Cindy's disappearance or in the murder in Norfolk. If I remember correctly, Norfolk detectives pulled out all the stops on this one. They interviewed our Melanie Lewis and she gave them a good alibi.'

'No doubt attending another one of those seminars that she can walk out of whenever she wants.'

'You should check.'

'I will.'

Henderson paused, thinking. 'Melanie Lewis feels like a cut-and-run merchant to me. We approach her with identify theft charges and she'll be out on bail before you know it, then poof! She'll be gone never to be seen again.'

'Why would she? She's scored a good job, albeit illegally and no doubt earns good money; much more than me, I might add.'

'Yes, but knowing she gained the job under false pretences means she will have a back door in case things go pear-shaped. If in time a couple of uniforms turn up at Quinlan's offices, she would be down the back stairs and out to her car in a flash. A job she can leave behind, as well as the car, the house, everything.'

'I think what you're saying is we need more?'

He sighed. 'Yes, we do.'

'Don't forget the dug-over vegetable patch. We could get ground-penetrating radar to—'

'Don't go there. To justify radar and the operator and the diggers that go with it, we require more evidence than a nicely dug piece of garden. What if they find vegetable seeds?'

'I guess.'

He went quiet for thirty seconds, doodling on a pad. 'What's the upside if we arrest Melanie Lewis for identity fraud? Providing we catch her before she scarpers, we could charge her and hopefully keep her in custody. When she comes up for a hearing, we would ask the judge not to grant bail as she's a flight risk, and with a bit of luck, she might remain in jail. Now the maximum sentence under the Fraud Act is ten years, but for forging a CV, sentences as high as six months are rare. Chances are, she wouldn't get more than community service.'

'It's not much if she's the killer of Christine Sutherland, Marc Emerson and Cindy Summer.'

'No, but with her in custody, maybe Edwards would authorise the use of ground-penetrating radar or at least a dig in her vegetable plot. I'd get forensics to crawl over her house and if they found any evidence to indicate that Cindy Summer has been there, we would be in a much stronger position.'

'It's throw your cards on the table time, or take a gamble. What's it to be, boss?'

Henderson didn't say much as they drove over to Quinlan Fine Foods. There didn't seem anything to add to the case that hadn't been said, it was now time for action. He wondered if Melanie Lewis was the woman Walters believed her to be, a callous, murdering psychopath. If so, she might have a trick up her sleeve to evade them when cornered.

They drove into the car park at eleven o' clock. Today was Thursday, three weeks before Christmas and while he was sure after his meeting with Francis Quinlan earlier in the week that all the work to stock up supermarkets had been completed, the car park looked to be as busy as before.

In Reception, he asked to see Francis Quinlan as he wanted the approach to Melanie Lewis to be as low-key as possible. If they arrested her in front of her staff, it could cause an altercation and perhaps leave Lewis uncooperative when questioned.

'I'm sorry but Mr Quinlan is not around,' the receptionist said. 'He left about fifteen minutes ago with our Financial Director, Christine Sutherland.'

'Where did they go?'

'I've no idea. I don't keep his diary but his secretary, Juliet Mathews should know. Would you like to speak to her?'

Henderson walked towards the thick carpeted area surrounding Francis Quinlan's office, now becoming familiar after his second visit of the week.

'Good morning, Detective Inspector Henderson, Sergeant Walters,' Quinlan's secretary said. 'I'm surprised to see you back here so soon. Did you come here to see Francis?'

'Yes, we did. I understand he's out.'

'Yes he is. Our Financial Director Christine Sutherland went in to see him about something, and the next minute he put on his jacket and left with her.'

'Did he tell you where they were going?'

'No, and there's nothing in his diary.'

'Have they done this before, nipped out unannounced in the morning for an hour or two?'

'I don't know what you're insinuating, Detective Inspector, but Francis isn't like that. He's been happily married to the same woman for over twenty years.'

'I didn't mean to insinuate anything, merely trying to establish if something like this has happened before.'

'Not to my knowledge and I've worked here longer than Christine. I think it's very peculiar if you ask me.'

'Thank you for your time. One last thing. Which car did they go in; his or hers?'

'To tell you the truth, I don't know.'

'Would you like to take a look?' Henderson said, indicating the windows on the other side of the room, overlooking the car park.

'Give me a moment.'

She came out from behind the desk and weaved her way between desks, heading for the long bank of glass on the far side of the office. Seconds later she walked back, her face resolute.

'I might have guessed, Christine's car is still there but Mr Quinlan's BMW isn't. He hates anyone driving him.'

'Can you give me the car's registration number?'

Out of earshot of anyone in the surrounding office, Henderson pulled out his phone and called Lewes Control. He repeated the registration number of Quinlan's BMW 7 Series and instructed it to be flagged on ANPR but if found, the vehicle was not to be approached.

'I think she's done a runner and took Francis Quinlan as insurance,' Walters said as they walked outside and climbed into Henderson's car.

'Too early to say. I'm thinking it might be something innocent like a meeting his secretary knows nothing about.'

'Like what?'

'I don't know, maybe he's thinking of selling up or buying a rival company and wants to keep it hush-hush.'

'God, you make it sound so plausible, it makes my theory of a hostage situation seem really melodramatic.'

'When have I ever called you melodramatic?'

'This week, last week, the week before that, I could go on.'

'Whichever theory is the right one,' he said, 'I've only asked Lewes Control to locate the car. When they do, it should avoid us becoming involved in a high-speed car chase or bursting in on a top-secret meeting. I'd like to arrest Melanie Lewis with no fuss and no stupid stories in *The Argus*.'

'Let's hope they find it.'

THIRTY-SEVEN

On the way back to Lewes, Henderson received a call. A patrol car driving through the village of Steyning had spotted Quinlan's BMW 7 Series. Henderson instructed the patrol car to wait there in case he needed back-up, and redirected his own car to Steyning.

'Now, Detective Inspector,' Walters said with a smug smile, 'you're good at thinking up legitimate reasons for why things happen the way they do. Why would Francis Quinlan and Melanie Lewis be anywhere near her house in Steyning?'

'The thought of a tryst did cross my mind but Quinlan's loaded and could book into any hotel in Brighton that he wanted. However, his secretary, and I believe many secretaries know their bosses better than they know themselves, did say they weren't having an affair.'

'Ditto a business meeting to discuss something secret, as those same hotels have seminar rooms. I think my hostage theory is back on.'

'You could be right. I've been thinking about what made her run. Do you think someone at Gresham's gave her the nod after you and Bentley went up there?'

'I've been thinking about it too and it's the most likely scenario,' Walters said. 'I got the impression they were a tight bunch up there. Many of them had been working for the company for years and knew each other well. Either that or after the interview with us, she felt the net tightening.'

'In which case, our suspect nipped back to Steyning to grab her things and took Francis as a hostage for what? In the event we turned up? Hold him for ransom, he's a rich guy?'

'I don't know but I think we're about to find out.'

'I'm loathe to call it in without further information but I will. I can't see any other reason for Lewis's behaviour. Call Control and get a few more cars down here in case the situation goes pear-shaped.'

'No problem.'

They arrived in Steyning and parked the car fifty metres from Lewis's house. Henderson spotted the patrol car and approached it.

'Thanks for sticking around fellas,' Henderson said to the officer in the passenger seat.

'No problem, sir. We don't see much action around these parts.'

'You might see some today. I think we could have a hostage situation in Bramble Bank, the dark stone house over there with the red-tiled roof,' he said pointing.

'I see it, sir,' the officer replied.

'Listen up, here's what I want you two to do.'

Henderson approached the house as if he knew someone inside had a sub-machine gun trained on the window; ducking down low and holding his body tight against the walls. He leaned round and peered into the lounge window. Unmoving in a chair sat the bulky frame of Francis Quinlan, a large cut on his head and blood streaking down one side of his face.

As instructed, one officer made his way to the back of the house, while the other waited in the garden and watched the front door in case Melanie Lewis tried to leg-it while the detectives were inside the house. If Lewis saw them and tried to run, all means of escape were blocked.

He turned the handle of the door and walked in. The house felt cold as if the windows had been open perhaps to air the rooms, although in winter only the hardy would think to do so. Henderson entered a short hall with Walters behind him, stairs to the immediate left, straight ahead the kitchen where he could see out to the garden through the window, and to his right, the door leading to the lounge.

He pushed open the lounge door slowly, not wishing to alarm those inside, his mind filled with all the possibilities he might encounter. His caution was unwarranted. The long lounge, with one window overlooking the road and the other the garden, was devoid of anyone, save for the unconscious figure of Francis Quinlan.

Henderson moved to his side and lifted his wrist. He could feel a pulse but the head wound looked severe, fresh blood still dribbling over the dried. Walters checked hiding places behind the settee and bookcase and when Henderson looked at her face, she shook her head. Henderson dropped Quinlan's arm and pointed upstairs.

They moved slowly up the stairs trying to be as quiet as possible, but being an old house, the stairs creaked at every second step. He told Walters to wait on the half-landing and guard the stairs while he pushed open the doors to all the rooms. He didn't find Lewis in the main bedroom, the bathroom, the spare bedroom or a sparsely furnished box room.

'She isn't here,' he said to Walters. 'Tell the officer at the back to check the garden and shed and the officer out front to see if Quinlan's BMW is still there and get him to ask a neighbour if they've seen a taxi call here in the last half hour. I'll deal with the injured man.'

Walking downstairs, Henderson pulled out his phone and called an ambulance. After he made Francis comfortable and did all he could to make sure his airways weren't blocked, he took out his phone again and called the Crime Scene Manager, Pat Davidson. As he waited for Pat to come to the phone, Walters appeared at the patio doors.

'She's not in the garden, the BMW is still outside and nobody saw a taxi. Her car was in the company car park when we went to Quinlan's offices earlier today so if she didn't call a taxi, she must have hightailed it on foot.'

He shook his head. 'She didn't go on foot. Did you see the dust marks in the small bedroom? Boxes were on the shelves of the wall unit and now they're gone, there's no clothes in the wardrobes; she can't be running and carrying all those. No, this is planned. She must have another car.'

'One we can't trace.'

He nodded. The voice of the Crime Scene Manager came on the line. Henderson explained where he was and about the woman they were searching for.

'Pat, what I need you and your team to do is search this place from top to bottom and find out if someone called Cindy Summer has been here. I'll send someone around to her flat and get samples of her prints for comparison.'

'Ok. Sounds straightforward.'

'Next thing, see if you can find something that will tell us something about the car our fleeing suspect drives. I'm thinking about a car registration document or a vehicle tax reminder sent out by the DVLA.'

'You'll want a thorough search of bookcases and any filing?'

'Yes, but also look in places where drug dealers hide their loot, like the inside of the cistern or under floorboards. We're dealing with a devious woman here, Pat, who only had ten or fifteen minutes to take everything she needed and to make sure nothing was left behind for us trace her.'

'Got it. Anything else?'

'Yes. I need some people to dig up a vegetable patch.'

'I know you've lived in a flat for years, Angus, but even you must realise the ground is hard at this time of year. You might be better off getting radar in first.'

'Forget radar. It's after midday now, and from where I'm standing I can see the sun creeping into the back garden. If you don't start the job until late morning or early afternoon, you should find the digging much easier.'

'I can see you're not going to be persuaded out of this one. Leave it with me and I'll rustle up some diggers, but no radar. Anything else?'

'No, and before you ask, I want it all yesterday.'

'No chance. Bye Angus.'

The ambulance drew up outside and moments later, two medics came running in with a stretcher. While they attended to the unconscious man, Henderson pulled Walters aside.

'It seems we were both right,' he said. 'You, because she probably brought Quinlan here to act as a hostage in case we turned up, and me, because she scarpered at the first sign of trouble.'

'How do we track her down? We don't have a clue what she's driving.'

'When we get back to the office, I'll take some of the detectives off the jewellery robbery and Guy Barton's murder and assign them to this. Phone Quinlan Foods and ask Francis's secretary if she knows anything about Sutherland owning another car. You never know, the company might have sold one to her or maybe she brought it with her when she came to Sussex from Norfolk. Also, put a team together to hawk her picture around local garages, see if we can find out where she bought it. I'll get her face into every police station and see if newspapers will run it. If she's out there we'll find her.'

THIRTY-EIGHT

Henderson pushed through double doors and walked past the Friends of The Royal Sussex Hospital newspaper stand. Another day, another hospital. This time he hadn't come to see Lily Barton, she was out and living with her sister in Hertfordshire and doing well, if his last phone call to her was anything to go by.

Francis Quinlan sat up as he approached, on his head a big bandage and on his face a beaming smile. When Henderson reached the bed, Quinlan grasped his hand and held it tight.

'Thank you, thank you Detective Inspector, you saved my life.'

'Do you really think so?'

'I do. According to the doctors if you hadn't turned up for another couple of hours I could have gone into shock and might have bled to death.'

Henderson retrieved his hand and sat down.

'So how are you feeling? You have a mighty big bandage around your head. I can't decide if you're trying to look like a brave central defender or an extra from *The Walking Dead*.'

He laughed. 'It's been a few years since you would catch me on a football field and to tell you the truth, in my time I was more a nifty winger than a central defender.'

'You made the right choice, going into the food

business.'

'I suppose you're right. Football's such a competitive sport; it's hard breaking into the big-time.'

'Do the doctors expect you'll make a full recovery?'

He nodded. 'They think I might lose the plot now and again, but as I did that before nobody will notice any difference.'

Henderson smiled. 'Are you able to tell me what happened?'

'I'm not that far gone, I hope. That bitch Sutherland came into my office and told me we had a problem at Steels Supermarkets. They wanted to see me and her pronto. Normally I wouldn't do calls like this but Brendan Flaherty, my Commercial Director, wasn't around and with no replacement yet for Marc...'

He looked vacant for a moment.

'Where was I? Yes, Steels are based in Worthing, but she said we needed to make a small detour back to her house to pick up something for the meeting. I was standing in the living room in her house in Steyning reading a text on my phone when she spoke to me and I turned. Bam! She hit me on the head with something and I fell to the floor.'

'You were unconscious from this point on?'

'Yes, until I woke up in the ambulance.'

'Do you know why she did it?'

'I don't have a bloody clue. I wish I did. Do you know?'

'Christine Sutherland is not her real name.'

'What? Who is she then?'

'We think her name is Melanie Lewis and she's impersonating a woman called Christine Sutherland.'

'God, you're doing a better job of spinning my head than the sedatives.'

'We'd like to question her about the murder of Christine Sutherland, her former boss at a food company in Norfolk, the death of Marc Emerson and the disappearance of Cindy Summer.'

'Good God!'

'As I said Francis, the only thing we know for sure is she isn't Christine Sutherland, the rest is only supposition until we gather more evidence.'

'Fair enough. Hang on, there's something at the back of my mind but I can't quite reach it.' He paused a moment, thinking. 'Ah yes, I remember now. I called Sutherland into my office a few weeks back. I'm not a skilled finance man, you understand. I've built my company up by cultivating good relationships with buyers and producing the best products I can, so I didn't feel so sure of my ground, if you know what I mean.'

Henderson nodded.

'I was looking through the figures she gave me a few days before and did some plonking on the calculator. To cut a long story short, I said to her the sales and profitability of many of our products are up, so why is the cash position so lousy?'

'What did she say?'

'She said it had something to do with the levels of joint advertising we're doing with a big supermarket and the lawyers we've retained to fight an Industrial Tribunal claim. It sounded good at the time and of course, she's the accountant, but now with a chance to think about it, I'm not so sure.'

'You think maybe there's been some fiddling going on?'

'I wouldn't go as far as to say that, but you see, I watch the cash position like a hawk. In the last company I worked for, before I set up my own, there was a big fiddle going on and this was how they discovered it; the cash flow declined out of line with forecasts. Let's just say my nose was twitching and her answers didn't satisfy me. Now she's shown us her true colours and smacked the boss over the head, I'll get someone in to take a closer look.'

'Good idea.'

'I need to do something. I've lost the best salesman I ever had, my diamond of a financial analyst has disappeared and now my Financial Director turns out to be someone else. What did I do to warrant this? Did I pray to the wrong God?'

**

Henderson drove back from the hospital in pensive mood. Francis Quinlan couldn't have put it better; to lose a top salesman was bad enough but to lose another two employees in quick succession was enough to make anyone feel persecuted.

Instead of driving back to the office, he changed his mind and headed towards Steyning. Pat Davidson told him there had been moans from the digging crew as the temperature was only two above freezing and the ground in the Bramble Bank vegetable garden was as hard as iron. He wasn't going there to hear more of their grumbles, but to prove he wasn't a desk-jockey and could turn up on a cold morning just as well as they could.

The previous day, he went to see DS Edwards to bring her up to date with developments and tell her that Melanie Lewis had moved to the top of their wanted list. He didn't get to say more than a few sentences before she exploded.

'I told you I wanted this case closed down,' she said, before getting out of her chair and pacing around the room. 'The ACC thinks it's being closed down, the Chief Constable does too. I thought we'd agreed after Guy Barton's murder, we are not looking for anyone else. Now you tell me you're back chasing phantoms.'

'It's not phantoms, it's–'

'You interviewed Christine Sutherland, you didn't suspect her then, so why now?'

'If you would just let me get a word in, I'll explain.'

He went on tell her about the identity theft and the murder of Christine Sutherland. She listened but it didn't calm her temper.

'I've heard enough. It seems to me you and your team are trying to do the work of Norfolk Constabulary and chasing some lass from Quinlan's who, I don't know, ran off to Tenerife with some lad she's just met. Then, you've pulled out all the stops to try and track down Quinlan's Finance Director, a woman guilty of nothing more than changing her name.'

'Yes, but don't forget the kidnap and assault of Francis Quinlan.'

'An assault on him which in all likelihood will turn out to be self-defence after he tried to touch her up.'

Henderson was about to say who's talking about fantasy and phantoms now, but he kept quiet.

'Angus, you haven't offered me a shred of evidence that Christine Sutherland, or whatever bloody name she uses, is someone we should be going after.'

'But–'

'No buts. I told you I wanted the Marc Emerson case wrapped up by the end of the week and I meant it. This is Friday, and in my view, the end of the week. At close of business today, I don't want to hear of any sort of activity taking place to find Christine Sutherland or anyone else connected to the Marc Emerson murder enquiry. Do I make myself clear?'

Henderson couldn't park anywhere near Bramble Bank, the space outside the house occupied by Pat Davidson's SOCO van and another van which he assumed had carried the team of diggers. He got out of the car and understood what Pat had said to him on the phone, it did feel colder here than in Brighton.

SOCO teams tried to be tidy but on entering the house, he could see where they had been as carpets were ruffled after being pulled up, empty kit boxes littered the hallway and flat surfaces were coated with fingerprint dust. He walked into the lounge and spotted Pat Davidson standing outside talking to three burly coppers having a smoke and leaning on spades. By the jollity, the relaxed postures and the clean faces it was clear they hadn't started work yet in the vegetable patch.

Pat saw him, stubbed out his cigarette and opened

the patio doors. 'Morning Angus, how are you?'

'Not too bad. I've just been to hospital to see Francis Quinlan, the guy we found lying in here injured.'

'The man responsible for all the blood on the chair, I assume?'

He nodded.

'How is he?'

'Alive and sounding like his old self.'

'Good to hear. I get tired of dealing with dead bodies all the time, it's heartening when somebody can walk away at the end of it.'

'How's it going here?'

'We've done downstairs, now we're doing up,' he said, jerking a thumb towards the ceiling. 'So far, we've found blood on the chair there, which is now accounted for, and blood on the carpet in the box room. Somebody's tried to scrub it but off we've got a decent sample.'

'Good. Did you find any information relating to her car?'

'Afraid not. We've searched through all the books in here and a cupboard in the kitchen full of papers but nothing.'

Henderson gazed through the window; the diggers had finished their smoke and were heading into the sun-kissed area at the end of the garden where the vegetable patch was located. As he watched, he tried to think of all the places where a fugitive might hide a document relating to a 'secret' car.

'What about the shed? Has anyone looked in there?'

'Not yet.'

'I'll do it,' Henderson said.

'It might be dirty.'

'I'll take my chances; as I said on the phone, we need to wrap this up today. Catch you later.'

In the kitchen drawer he found a number of keys all bearing a sticky label indicating what they were used for. It was the sensible thing to do in a rented house. In his house at College Place, he could tell by the shape and size what door a key opened, but this wouldn't be much use to someone staying there for the first time.

He opened the door of the shed and walked in. He didn't believe Melanie Lewis would hide anything of value in here as she wouldn't be able to access it quickly as she made her bid for freedom. Nevertheless, he went through the motions of opening seed boxes, sifting through a small pile of wood, checking inside tins, and looking through equipment and cartons lying on the shelves.

He picked up a wipe-clean annual garden planner and began flicking through the pages. He liked the idea and decided to buy one if he saw something similar in the shops. He turned to put it back on the shelf when he heard someone knocking on the door.

He pushed the door open and saw a member of the digging team standing there, his face harrowed with concern. 'Sir, you need to come and see this.'

He followed the man to the vegetable patch. One of the digging team, down on his knees in the mud, was using a small kitchen brush to sweep dirt away from an object. Henderson stood there mesmerised, like an archaeologist at a dig, wondering if they were about to uncover a valuable artefact from Roman times or a useless piece of rusted junk.

Slowly, the hidden object began to reveal itself. Looking back at him now, he recognised the pale, dead face of Cindy Summer.

THIRTY-NINE

Henderson leaned back in the office chair and put his feet on the desk. On his face, a smile like a well-fed cat. DS Edwards had just left and while he wouldn't say with her tail between her legs, that's how it felt.

The body in the vegetable patch turned out to be, as Henderson first suspected, Cindy Summer. He'd never met the girl before but being slightly odd-looking with long, straight black hair, a thin face and pointed nose, once seen in photographs given to them by Quinlan's, never forgotten.

Over the weekend, the bloodstain discovered on the carpet in the box room had been matched to the dead girl, as did the blood on the claw hammer found under the sink. He didn't need to check if Melanie Lewis's prints were on file, as inside Bramble Bank who else would leave their prints on bathroom taps or on the lamp in the bedroom?

The three diggers and Pat Davidson's SOCO team had proved beyond doubt that Melanie Lewis not only committed identity fraud and kidnapped Francis Quinlan, but she also murdered Cindy Summer. Edwards, to her credit, didn't hesitate in acknowledging this change in events and apologised for her earlier outburst. He'd even received a call from the Assistant Chief Constable, Andy Youngman wishing him luck in finding the missing woman. If only he realised how difficult that task was going to be.

He knew in his own mind that Lewis had been ready for this day and planned it well. Whether she got a kick out of pretending to be someone else, or did it to scam money from companies like Quinlan's, and took pleasure in murdering people who came too close, he didn't know, but she knew a time would come when she would have to disappear.

She made it easy for herself by renting a house, keeping only enough possessions to pick up in one sweep of the wardrobe and by owning a car no one knew anything about. With this level of forward planning, it was inconceivable she didn't have a destination in mind, and his priority now was to find it.

He removed his size nines from the desk, picked up the phone and called the Crime Scene Manager, Pat Davidson. The embargo lifted by Edwards meant they could now examine the Bramble Bank house for as long as they wanted, but Pat and his team had finished on Saturday night as they'd done everything they needed to do.

'Morning, Pat. Angus. Did you have a good weekend?'

'I came into the office on Sunday morning for a couple of hours but didn't leave until four. You know how it is.'

'Sure do.'

'I know what you did because I also saw your car in the Malling House car park.'

'Guilty as charged. Well done for all the work you and your boys did at the house in Steyning. So much for you getting fed up dealing with murders.'

'I spoke too soon.'

'What's your conclusion now after sifting through all her stuff?'

'You say 'all her stuff' but there wasn't much. She either had the removers in before we arrived or didn't own much in the first place.'

'The latter I suspect.'

'Well, other than the blood-stained hammer we didn't find anything else. We found a little hiding place beneath the floorboards in the main bedroom. It looked to be used but it was empty.'

'You didn't find car registration documents or official reminders?'

'No, not even close. If you're lucky, one might drop on her doormat in the next few days.'

He laughed. 'I'm never that lucky. Thanks for all your help Pat.'

He pulled towards him a groaning pile of paperwork, double the size of only a week ago and set to work to try and reduce it. He worked solidly for a couple of hours and at the point where his stomach told him it must be time for lunch, DS Walters walked in. He looked up and looked again, as she resembled a character from Game of Thrones with a face devoid of colour and her nose an odd shade of red.

'It's bloody freezing out there. It's a good job most garage salesmen conduct their meetings indoors and not standing in front of a line of cold metal; a body could seize up in this. Mind you, I'm practically climbing the walls with all the coffee I've drunk to keep warm, just to be polite, of course.'

She took off her coat and sat down. 'Don't you hate modern offices with their concealed heating systems? I used to love it at school in the winter when you came in from the playground and could stick your cold mitts through the bars of the hot radiator.'

'We had them at our school too. How did you get on with the garages?'

She shook her head. 'No sightings of our missing woman. We had a guy at a dealership in Billingshurst who said he remembered selling a car to her but when we asked him to provide a fuller description, he said his buyer was small and fat.'

'It was always going to be a long shot as we don't know how long she's owned the car or if she brought it down with her from Norfolk. Wait a sec...'

'Park it. It's already been done. I called Quinlan's and the HR woman said when Lewis moved to Brighton she owned a car, but sold it when she received a company vehicle. Before you ask, her old car is now up north, the pride and joy of a woman in Manchester.'

'Excellent work, but I fear another dead end.'

'How did you get on with distributing her photograph?'

'A poster with: *Have You Seen This Woman?* is out there on police billboards. I could only get it into a few local papers as according to the Press Office, none of the nationals were interested.'

'Pity. So, what do we do now, sit around and twiddle our thumbs and wait for someone to ID

Melanie Lewis?'

'Can you think of anything else?'

'We're running out of time, boss, if you want the Marc Emerson case done and dusted before the end of the year.'

'I know you shouldn't put a time limit on these things but...hang on. You said Marc Emerson. It's just given me an idea.' He looked at her but it didn't elicit a response.

'I'm guessing from your blank face this isn't something you've done already.'

'If you tell me what it is, I might have a better idea but we've done nothing relating to Marc Emerson in the last few days.'

'I'll tell you while we walk. Come with me.'

Fifteen minutes later both detectives took a seat in the archive room, three boxes of Marc Emerson's personal effects sitting in front of them. For the moment, he ignored the boxes containing equipment such as the laptop, camera, books, and concentrated on the paperwork.

'Tell me again,' Walters said, 'why would Marc Emerson have Melanie Lewis's car registration document?'

'I'm not saying he would have it but don't forget, they were once lovers. They might have gone out in her car for the day and he sent her an email or text talking about it, or we might find an invoice or correspondence with a garage because he took it in for a service.'

'There are long shots and there are long shots, Detective Inspector Henderson, but this one is way out there in the wild blue yonder.'

'More searching and less bleating. Remember, we're looking for something that will tell us something about her car or the address of her bolthole or holiday home. Ok?'

Henderson was gung-ho at adding another thread to the search but as always, his enthusiasm waned when dealing with the personal possessions of a murder victim. All the things they collected: stamps, mugs or coins, all the things they owned: phones, houses and cars, and all the things they strived for in their lives: in their place of work, love life or hobbies, counted for nothing when it ended up in here.

Henderson sifted through papers, letters and unopened mail with a heavy heart. He picked up a small photograph album, a rarity nowadays with the ubiquity of digital cameras and the storing of photographs on computers.

If wading through a dead man's personal effects presented difficulties, looking at their photographs could be far worse. Here was Marc alive and smiling lovingly at the woman who could be responsible for his murder, and she looking back at him with equal passion. Did something happen to make their love turn sour, or is hate a fire burning in Melanie Lewis's heart, like a pilot light, ready to explode into life when something displeased her?

He'd seen pictures of Marc before but never appreciated how handsome he looked. On holiday, with a tan and wearing a t-shirt, shorts, sunglasses and a few days' stubble, he could pass for a male model. The pictures in Tenerife gave way to a British scene, he guessed the New Forest. His heart skipped a beat when he noticed the car he was leaning against wasn't Marc's BMW or her VW Passat.

He held his breath as he turned to the next picture. In this one, Melanie was getting into her car, a dark blue Vauxhall Astra. Marc had taken the shot from the front and there it was, a clear view of the car's registration plate.

FORTY

Henderson guided the car off the M40 motorway and drove towards Oxford Services. He travelled down one long slip road, and then around a roundabout and then around another.

'If I'd remembered these services were such a faff to reach, I might have waited until the next one.'

'You've been driving long enough, you need a break and some food inside you,' Walters beside him said. 'I know I do.'

He smiled as he guided the pool car into a parking space. 'Food and you are close companions.'

'Are you saying I'm fat?'

'Would I be so reckless? No, I'm saying we all have different priorities in life and while I enjoy food, I don't think about it all day. Now, a nice glass of whisky, that would sail my boat.'

'You can keep your whisky,' she said as she got out of the car and stretched. 'I'm looking forward to a burger and chips.'

Walters did indeed help herself to a burger and chips, why not while on expenses, and he opted for something lighter, a chicken salad. He didn't mind a good feed now and again and her burger did smell good, but when faced with another hour or two sitting in a car, the last thing he wanted was a pile of stodge inside him.

They took a table beside the window overlooking the car park and sat down. Henderson liked motorway service stations; the noise, the smells, seeing a good cross-section of the British public moving in and out. There, he would see things he didn't see in the street or at an airport such as a group of disabled kids out for a day at a theme park, a university hockey team en route to Holland to participate in a tournament and tense looking businessmen heading out to difficult meetings.

With his copper hat on, it could be a good place to meet narks and witnesses as watchers found it hard to pick them out in this constantly moving sea of humanity. Criminals liked them too as it was busy with people and cameras so no one could make a move on them, and it was a better place for a meeting with rivals than in the stronghold of someone else's pub.

'My, this is good,' Walters said, tucking into her burger. 'You're missing out.'

'I know but my stomach will be grateful later.'

'How far do we have to go?'

'An hour, maybe two depending on traffic. We first need to get into Gloucester, find the police station and talk to the armed response team. Only then can we drive out to the village where our woman is staying.'

'If she's still there.'

'The locals did a drive-past this morning. The car's still there and you checked with the DVLA, it hasn't been sold.'

'I did, but what if she's dumped it?'

'In someone's driveway? Why would she?'

'If she thought we were after her.'

'As I said before, she didn't deliberately leave a clue in Marc's photo album for us to find so we could participate in some kind of weird cross-country chasing game. I doubt if she even remembers Marc taking the picture.'

'Ok, but what if the memory comes back to her now?'

'Why would it, and why now? If the idea came to her earlier, say around the time Marc was murdered, surely she would have got rid of the car then?'

'Maybe she did and some time tonight we're about to kick the door in on some retired gentleman with a dickey ticker.'

'You do have a vivid imagination, Sergeant, but I don't agree. I'm convinced she's there.'

Walters knew all about the CCTV analysis done by the team and was playing Devil's Advocate, looking for chinks in their armour. When they discovered the make, model and registration number of Lewis's car, Henderson set a team working on analysing CCTV pictures. They knew within a limited time frame when she departed Steyning and sure enough, the car was spotted travelling north on the M23. They tracked her around the M25 and along the M40, following the same route the two detectives were doing now. To dispel any doubt in the minds of the coppers they were about to see, in his briefcase he had a CCTV snapshot of the front of her car. It contained a single occupant, Melanie Lewis.

They couldn't track her final destination as CCTV

cameras didn't cover the rural area where she was heading, but sometime later an on-board ANPR system had pinged inside a patrol car. The officers took no action to pull the car over, as Henderson requested, but instead followed the target to her new home and called Sussex detectives.

'I feel better now,' Walters said, sitting back.

'A clean plate, I'm impressed. I'm not sure I could have finished it.'

She reached for her coffee, no doubt lukewarm like his, but she seemed to enjoy it all the same.

'I hate cold coffee but I need the caffeine kick to be alert on the road. Can't have me being pulled over for inattentive or careless driving.'

The meal complete, they sat around for another five minutes watching their fellow travellers. Following a quick detour to the toilets, they walked back to the car. They departed the service station, Walters now in the driving seat, but didn't re-join the motorway as it wound its way north to Birmingham, and instead took the A40 which by-passed Oxford before heading west towards Cheltenham and Gloucester. The road soon reduced from a dual to a single carriageway and after being stuck behind a succession of slow-moving lorries, Henderson was glad he had bought a newspaper at the service station.

They arrived in Gloucester at two-thirty and by the look of shoppers in heavy jackets and thick coats, it was as every bit as cold as Sussex. They found the headquarters of Gloucester Constabulary, a glass and steel edifice resembling the home of a software gaming company or an international design consultancy, to the south of the city.

They assembled in a meeting room on the second floor, the two detectives from Sussex, two detectives from Gloucester and four members of an Armed Response Unit. The senior of the two Gloucester detectives, DI Mike Abbott, stood at the front addressing the small team. Abbott didn't speak with a broad West Country accent as he expected, but with a course Birmingham burr and Henderson had to concentrate hard to understand everything that he said.

'We have confirmed the woman DI Henderson seeks is still at the house as we've done a number of drive-bys in unmarked vehicles at regular intervals and established her car is still there. We will approach the house as follows.'

He hoped the heavy-set lads in the armed response team could decipher Abbott's thick inflection, because as observers, the Sussex detectives didn't want to get shot or bowled over by a fifteen-stone monster in a Kevlar jacket. Henderson was then invited to tell them more about their target.

He'd already sent a picture of Melanie Lewis to DI Abbott, and her face loomed behind him on the large screen. 'This is Melanie Lewis, wanted for serious assault and kidnap of her boss, identity fraud, one murder we know about and suspected of killing two other people. Don't let the pretty face fool you. She's cunning and smart and will use every trick in her arsenal to escape capture. She is dangerous. She's never used guns to my knowledge, knives and a claw hammer are more her style.'

He looked around at the faces of his small audience, they were listening.

'If we catch her by surprise, and I have no reason to think otherwise, we should be in and out in a matter of minutes. If we don't make contact for a time because the door won't open or she's hiding somewhere, don't take any chances when you finally catch up with her. Put her on the floor and handcuff her at the first opportunity. Is this clear?'

They all nodded.

'Thanks for your time men. Good luck.'

They set out from Gloucester, the ARU in a van, the detectives in a car and a patrol car with two officers inside. It was still light as they left the city, but the local detectives assured the Sussex officers it would be dark when they reached the cottage where Lewis lived, a village to the north-west of Cheltenham called Southam.

'You're not from around here, are you Mike?' Henderson asked DI Abbott.

'It's that obvious, eh? No, I cut my teeth in Aston, in Birmingham. A few years later I got married and had a young kid, so the thrill of tackling some punk with a knife didn't have the same appeal.'

'What's it like in Gloucester? Does it suffer from the same big city problems as everywhere else, or maybe a bit less being in a rich part of the West Country?'

'It's not as relentless as Birmingham for sure but we still get our fair share of sexual assaults, drunken fights, drugs and the occasional murder. What's it like in your neck of the woods?'

Henderson went on to tell him about Sussex with Walters piping up occasionally, but no matter what they talked about during the journey: police, sport, bosses, colleagues, it didn't encourage their driver, DC Phillip Willis, from joining in, who only spoke to confirm directions.

They passed the Ellenborough Park Hotel and turned left towards the target village. In some ways Southam reminded Henderson of Steyning, narrow streets with houses either side but the streets and houses here were more recent, their design and layout more orderly.

They drove past a farmer's field on Southam Lane when the driver slowed, before pulling into the field entrance, secured by a sturdy wooden gate. The ARU van turned in behind them.

DI Abbot turned in his seat to face Henderson. 'She lives in a house about one hundred yards up the road. Are you ready for this?'

FORTY-ONE

They walked along a dark and deserted road, the only sound the clunking boots of the armed response officers and the clank of the scarred and battered door opener as it banged against someone's trouser buckle.

All radios and mobile phones had been silenced and this policy extended to mouthy gobs and noisy spitting or coughing. It didn't present a problem for Henderson, but in a tense situation Walters became nervous and tended to talk too much. If he felt nervous, the last thing he wanted was a wittering colleague in his ear asking a question that had been answered in the briefing. Tonight, he was glad to be in the company of his own thoughts.

They reached the house, one of four small detached properties in a little row. The heavily clad men and the two Gloucester cops moved towards the door. Henderson and Walters walked round the house to the rear as agreed at the briefing. It was a good place to put observers as it made them feel they had a role to play. However, when four beefy men burst into a house, most people gave up on the spot, as the target's whole focus would be on not getting shot, and the prearranged plan of legging it out the back door would soon be forgotten.

Henderson waited until he heard the thump of the

door opener before unlatching the gate to the rear. He counted the thumps and was surprised to find they reached four. Either the big lad wielding it was all padding and no muscle, or Ms Lewis had added a few bolts of her own. His money would be on the latter.

No lights were shining in the kitchen or in any of the upstairs bedrooms, only the lounge which they could see as they approached the house. Nothing illuminated the rear garden. They stood in darkness, in silence, waiting for a sign to indicate the Gloucester men had apprehended their fugitive.

Seconds later, an officer from the ARU walked into the kitchen and switched on the light.

'Right Carol,' Henderson said, 'let's make a move.'

He didn't receive a response and turned round. With the assistance of the recently switch-on kitchen light, he could see the garden better. Melanie Lewis had DS Walters in a tight grip with an arm around her throat and a Glock 9mm pistol pointing at her head.

'Tell those fuckers in my house to get out, go back to their van and head straight back to where they came from.'

'Keep calm, Melanie, we can talk about this.'

'Listen Henderson, I don't want to talk about anything. Now go and tell them what I said or I'll shoot her, you know I will.'

Henderson walked down the path and into the house. He relayed the suspect's message to DI Abbott who took it with a straight face. 'Any chance we can get a shot at her?' he asked.

'It's too risky as she's got my DS in a real close hold. I think you should do as she says.'

Abbott thought for a minute. 'Not much more we can do here. You're right, we should get out. I'll call in air support to track her movements and set up roadblocks.'

'Good idea.'

Abbott turned to face the room where members of the ARU had gathered. 'Right lads, we're finished here, back to the van. Thanks for all your help.'

'What d'ya mean?' the sergeant said coming towards Abbott, trying to intimidate him with his bulk and height. 'That fucker out there's got a gun at a colleague's head. We can't just leave her here to die or be taken hostage.'

'The only other option is a bloodbath and it's not going to happen while I'm in charge. This operation is over.'

There was a tense standoff, Abbott and the sergeant eyeballing one other, neither blinking.

'Fuck it, on your head be it,' the sergeant said. He turned and waved to his men. 'C'mon lads, you heard the inspector. We've been told we're no longer needed, so let's get the hell out.'

The ARU, trooped past, the sergeant at the rear. He pointed a finger at the Gloucester DI. 'If this goes pear-shaped, Abbott, it's your head mate, not mine.'

Henderson walked outside and watched as the armed response officers trooped back to their van and the Gloucester detectives to their car. A small crowd had gathered, people from neighbouring houses, and Henderson called on a couple of waiting uniforms to hold them back.

He turned and walked through the gate into the

back garden, Walters and her assailant were still in the same position. To Walters's credit she looked calm, even though he was sure she must be scared. She realised now wasn't the time for heroics and kept still.

'They've done as you asked,' he said to Lewis. 'All the officers from the house are now back in their vehicles and are heading off.'

'Good, now you walk back and stand where I can see you. If you've laid an ambush, I'll shoot her then you. Understand?'

'Yes.'

'Now go and walk slowly with no sudden movements.'

Henderson did as she asked and glanced around to see they were moving at the same pace. He passed through the open gate and was pleased to see, if anything about this situation could bring pleasure, the only people close to the driveway were a couple of uniformed coppers, a small group of rubberneckers behind them.

He approached the first cop and stood beside him facing Lewis's car, parked at the front of her house, about five metres away. He turned his head and said from the corner of his mouth, 'Are you armed?'

'With this,' he said opening his jacket for him to see.

Henderson looked down. 'It'll do. When she gets into her car give it to me.'

'Who are all these people?' Lewis demanded as she approached.

'They're your neighbours,' Henderson said. 'The

cops in the house have left and the guys here are unarmed, only here to keep these people back.'

'Get the hell out of it, you ghouls,' she said to her neighbours. She waved the gun at them, 'If you don't, you'll get this.'

'Christ, she's got a gun!' Henderson heard someone say, and didn't express surprise when seconds later, the sound of rapidly receding footsteps echoed into the night.

'Let me see your hands!' Lewis said to the little group of Henderson and the two uniforms, before taking a good look to make sure no weapons were in evidence. Satisfied, she scanned the surrounding area, the field opposite her cottage, the gardens of neighbouring houses and up and down the road, looking for snipers. She moved Walters towards her car.

Lewis was being clever, walking sideways and keeping Walters's body in front of her, her back facing the house, all the time watching like an owl looking for danger. The DI knew the walk from the garden to the road had been straightforward, but getting a kidnap victim into a car while making sure no one was trying to make a move on her wouldn't be easy, and Walters knew how to make it difficult.

Henderson nudged the constable beside him. The handle of the pistol felt cold in his hand but it felt good to be armed.

Lewis struggled to get Walters into the passenger seat as she had stiffened like a two-year-old, complaining all the time, 'you're hurting my arm', 'my leg's caught in something'. Lewis leaned in to move something out of the way when a boot flew out and hit her in the stomach, throwing her against the fence. She recovered faster than Henderson expected and got up, her hand still clutching the Glock.

Henderson stepped forward, lifted his weapon and fired. The dart from the Taser struck Melanie Lewis in the neck and 50,000 volts zapped into her muscles, sending them into spasm. She fell to the ground writhing. Walters leapt out of the car and rushed over. She scrambled around, found the gun, and stood, pointing it at the suspect's head.

For a ghastly moment Henderson felt sure she was about to pull the trigger. Time stopped and the hubbub of a Gloucestershire night ceased: no cars on the road, no howl of foxes in the woods nearby, no planes overhead from Bristol airport and no sniffing from PC453 beside him.

Like a cloud moving across the sky on a light zephyr, the anger waned and the steady hand holding the gun lowered. The professional detective had returned.

Henderson ran over.

'Are you all right?'

'I'm fine apart from a bruised neck where she grabbed me.' She looked down at the prostrate figure of Lewis. 'I didn't know my kicks were so lethal, maybe I should take up martial arts.'

FORTY-TWO

Henderson strolled back to his office after a quick lunch, a brisk step for a man who had spent the whole weekend working. In fact, most of the Marc Emerson murder team had been in over the weekend, feeding on information from his extensive interviews with Melanie Lewis.

The interviews he's done with this strange woman proved very interesting. Never had he come across a more engaging suspect, keen to share her triumphs and disasters and exhibiting, in over eight hours of interviews, every human emotion he could think of; all the way from giddy happiness to abject despair. If her brief had not yet considered introducing a plea of insanity, the man was an idiot.

Talk of Marc Emerson brought on her despair as she had hit rock-bottom when he decided to finish with her. Marc refused to participate in her scam to steal money from their employer, despite receiving large sums of money, the mysterious ten-grand deposits the DI had spotted in Marc's bank statements, and threatened to tell Francis Quinlan. She'd set him on fire because no way could she let him spoil her nice little earner and prevent her reaching a lifetime goal of becoming a millionaire before the age of thirty-five. She also said that Marc once told her he wanted to be cremated when he died, therefore by killing him in a fire, she reasoned, gave him exactly what he wanted. When Henderson pointed out that he probably meant when he died of natural causes around the age of eighty-four, she didn't respond.

Lewis killed Cindy Summer because Cindy broke into her house, not because she thought her boss a murderer or a thief, but because she'd used a falsified CV to obtain the top finance job at Quinlan's. The poor girl had been killed by a single blow from the claw hammer found under the sink in the Steyning house, and Lewis had buried her body in her garden that same night. Lewis smiled when talking about the hammer. It made a lovely crunching noise, she said.

On Sunday, they finally discussed Lewis's old boss, Christine Sutherland, and here at some point around midday she attained giddy happiness. She hated Sutherland with a passion as she was all the things she wasn't: happily married, a mother, a qualified accountant and popular with staff, and claimed to have dispatched her with the same hammer used to kill Cindy Summer.

Walters had informed Norfolk Police of their findings and this morning in Reception, a large bunch of flowers awaited the Detective Sergeant. They had been sent by Mr Kenneth Sutherland with a card bearing the message: 'For finally laying my wife's soul to rest.'

If this didn't sum up what he and his team tried to achieve every day of the year, he didn't know what did.

About the Author

Iain Cameron was born in Glasgow and moved to Brighton in the early eighties. He has worked as a management accountant, business consultant and a nursery goods retailer. He is now a full-time writer and lives in a village outside Horsham in West Sussex with his wife, two daughters and a lively Collie dog.

For more information about books and the author:
Visit the website at: www.iain-cameron.com
Follow him on Twitter: @IainsBooks
Follow him on Facebook @IaincameronAuthor

Also by Iain Cameron

Night of Fire is the sixth book in the DI Angus Henderson series. Check out the others.

One Last Lesson

The body of a popular university student is found on a golf course. DI Angus Henderson hasn't a clue as the killer did a thorough job. That is, until he finds out that she was once was a model on an adult web site run by two of her tutors.

Driving into Darkness

A gang of car thieves are smashing down doors and stealing the keys of expensive cars. Their violence is escalating and the DI is fearful they will soon kill someone. They do, but DI Henderson suspects it might be cover for something else.

Fear the Silence

A missing woman is not what DI Henderson needs right now. She is none other than Kelly Langton, once the glamour model 'Kelly,' and now an astute businesswoman. The investigation focuses on her husband, but then another woman goes missing.

Hunting for Crows

A man's body is recovered from the swollen River Arun, drowned in a vain attempt to save his dog. The story interests DI Angus Henderson as the man was once a member of an eighties rock band. When another band member dies, exercising in his home gym, Henderson can't ignore the coincidence.

Red Red Wine

A ruthless gang of wine fakers have already killed one man and will stop at nothing to protect a lucrative trade making them millions. Henderson suspects a London gangster, Daniel Perry, is behind the gang. He knows to tread carefully, but no one warned him to safeguard those closest to him.

For information about characters, Q&A and more:
www.iain-cameron.com

All my books are available from Amazon in Kindle and paperback format.

Printed in Great Britain
by Amazon